MYSTERIES OF LADY THEODORA

AGENTS OF THE HOME OFFICE

RACHEL ANN SMITH

Mysteries of Lady Theo is a work of fiction. While reference might be made to actual historical events or existing locations, the names, characters, places, and incidents are either the product of the author's imagination or are used fictitiously, and any resemblance to actual persons, living or dead, business establishments, events, or locals are entirely coincidental.

First Edition November 2019

Developmental Edits by Gray Plume Editing

Edited by Victory Editing

Proofread by Monique Daoust

Cover design by Impluvium Studios

ISBN: 978-1-951112-03-5

For my children that are forever my inspiration

CHAPTER ONE

HADFIELD HALL 1815

Perched on the side of the four-poster bed, Lady Theodora Neale held the dear hand that had wasted to skin and bone.

Her papa squeezed hers in return, his grasp urgent and fierce despite his frailty. "My dear, please forgive me." His breath was labored, his eyes recessed within dark circles. "Our family has been in service to the Crown for generations, and now it will be your duty to carry on."

A crushing feeling pressed against her ribs at the sound of her papa's struggling breaths. He let go of her to lift a ledger from his bedside table, and she rubbed her wrists.

He handed the volume to her. "You must not share the contents with anyone. Only trust those who bear the same mark as you."

The mark on her ankle burned as if it had recently been placed upon her.

"You must guard it with your life. Our family has been

responsible for this mission for generations, and you must follow the instructions carefully."

A tear rolled down her cheek. "I will, Papa. I will do as you ask."

His last words were an apology of sorts. "I am sorry we have limited funds remaining. I realize I should have been more focused on the estate than our mission. You will be reliant on your cousin's generosity, and I only pray he will take care of you…"

All color suddenly drained from his face.

"Papa?"

On a tortured breath, he whispered, "God be with you, child."

~

HADFIELD HALL, A YEAR LATER

Facing the drafty drawing room window, her back to her aunt, Lady Theodora discreetly pinched the bridge of her nose and closed her eyes. The heartbreaking image of the late Earl of Hadfield on his deathbed refused to dissipate.

The numbness that had seeped into her mind and body that day, leaving her devoid of emotion, was still with her. All her energy was devoted to fulfilling her promise to her papa.

Theo recalled running her hand over the well-worn volume. While there were no visual markings on the cover, the pads of her fingers had rolled over faint ridges and lines of a carefully molded impression. She squeezed her eyelids tighter as she reflected on the image still seared into her memory, the outline of a horse with a falcon perched on its back, circled by laurel leaves, a replica of the mark she bore. The electric jolt of recognition shot through her once more, making her heart beat erratically and her eyes open.

Words contained in the book came to mind:

Only trust those with the Mark.

Train daily.

The sharp sound of a book snapping shut made Theo whip around in the direction of her aunt.

Lady Henrietta Arcot Neale's usually cheerful voice now contained a touch of desperation. "Theo, I do wish you would accompany me to town."

"Beg pardon, Aunt Henri. What was it you said?"

"I was trying to inform you that Landon will insist we return to town with him."

"I'm perfectly happy to remain here. I prefer the fresh country air."

"Well, that might be the case, but we can't hide here any longer." Reaching for her cup of tea, Aunt Henrietta continued, "I haven't been subjected to the *ton* in years. To be honest, I was rather relieved when my papa disowned me."

Theo smiled at the memory of her uncle, George Neale. His marriage to Aunt Henri had upended her ties to her ducal family. A second son who embarked on working as a barrister was not an appropriate husband for the daughter of a duke. But theirs had been a love match, and the Neale family had embraced Henrietta from the moment they met her. Her kindness and intelligence were valued by the Neales rather than considered a nuisance.

The teacup rattled against the small saucer in her aunt's hand. Theo was apparently not the only one unnerved by the *ton*.

But Theo's cousin Landon, the newly minted Earl of

Hadfield, strode into the room, saving her from having to respond.

"Mama." Landon bent to give his mama a kiss on the cheek, then made his way to Theo's side.

Looming next to her, Landon twisted to peer out the window and quietly asked, "Fantasizing about being outdoors? Wishing you were anywhere but here, trapped in a stifling drawing room, listening to my mama?"

"Landon, I was mentioning to Theo that we must venture to town and find you a wife."

Landon stiffened at the word *wife*. "Yes, we *all* should take up residence in town for the Season. Christopher has reassured me all is in order for our stay."

Theo was amazed at the ease with which he bore the brunt of his new responsibilities. Landon had not only inherited the title but also the neglected estate and the burden of caring for Theo. The only item he had not received was the family volume.

At the mention of Landon's younger brother, Theo couldn't prevent her lips curling into a grin. Christopher was of a similar age to herself and had been a boon companion during their childhood. Was he still a carefree fellow? She hadn't seen him but for a brief moment during her papa's funeral a year ago.

Theo straightened her spine, took a deep breath, and prepared to reiterate her arguments for the hundredth time as to why she should remain in the country. "Cousin, I'm perfectly fine remaining here at Hadfield Hall. Papa often ventured to…" Having read the family volume, it was clear her papa had not only left her behind to travel to London but often ventured much further in his investigations. On an outward breath, she finished. "…to town without me."

Landon's hazel eyes were no longer on Aunt Henrietta.

Instead, they bore into Theo. "Don't be ridiculous. I will not leave you here alone with the servants."

Theo donned a mask of cool indifference. The unfeeling woman she had portrayed this past year was in stark contrast to the bubbly little girl he had played with in their childhood. Remaining aloof was the only way she had conceived to keep Landon from finding out the truth about her inheritance. It was imperative he did not find out about the family volume and their familial duties to the Crown.

In the driest tone she could manage, Theo asked, "Why must I accompany you?"

His grin revealed the dimple that rarely graced Landon's features. "You will assist me in becoming better acquainted with my peers."

"Me? I've only been thrown to the wolves once, my debut Season. You were fortunate not to have been there. It was a complete disaster."

Landon's dimple deepened at her response. Damn the man; he had managed to crack her cool exterior. Why was he so determined that she participate in the Season? Was he intent on marrying her off? Landon had mentioned he had set aside a modest dowry for her. It was impressive how he had managed to fatten the estate coffers within such a short period. Her cousin was not averse to hard work and had used his personal funds to invest in some lucrative ventures. They proved successful, resulting in his amassing a small fortune worthy of the Hadfield title.

"Theo, you will accompany us to town come Monday. I'll hear no more excuses as to why you should remain here in the country. Am I clear?"

As if she was swallowing toads, she answered, "Yes, cousin."

Theo fought the urge to fidget as Landon's gaze raked

over her. He eyed her haphazard coiffure. Would he notice her raven-colored hair was now streaked with lighter strands due to the hours spent outdoors practicing?

Her mourning clothes sagged in places where her body had reduced as a result of her training regimen. She ran her hand over the well-worn material. The nervous reaction drew Landon's attention closer to her garments.

Landon sighed. "I will ensure you are both outfitted with new wardrobes."

Aunt Henrietta chimed in, "Landon, you will escort us to the theater—balls and such—will you not? As the patriarch, it is now your duty."

"Mama, I will be busy in town. I still have a law practice to run with Christopher in conjunction with all the estate matters."

Her aunt's nostrils flared. "Christopher is quite capable of running the practice without you. You now have other responsibilities. One of them is to find a wife and produce an heir."

Theo lowered her gaze to the floor in an attempt to avoid her aunt's attention. However, Aunt Henrietta had not forgotten her. "And you, my girl, will accompany me into town. We shall set out after we break our fast on Monday."

Not having grown up with a mama, Theo hungrily sought out Aunt Henrietta's opinion and favor. Her aunt had willingly taken on the parental role and treated Theo as one of her own children. Theo was extremely grateful, for it allowed her to relinquish the management of the household and gained her the freedom to train.

Raising her eyes to meet her aunt's, Theo said, "If that is what you wish, Aunt Henri."

Upon hearing Theo's agreement, her aunt smiled and

clapped her hands together. "Now that is settled, who would like a cup of tea?"

Now was her opportunity to escape. "If you will excuse me, I think I will go outdoors and take advantage of the clean country air while I can."

As Theo made her way to the door, Landon ordered, "Don't stay out too long. You will need to start preparing for your departure. Monday will be here before you know."

Midstride, Theo turned, nodded. *I have three days to plan and prepare.*

THEO STOOD straight with her right foot slightly in front of her left. She raised her arm, holding the blade next to her ear, elbow up, and with a smooth release, she let it go. The blade flew through the air and landed perfectly in the trunk of the tree she used for practice.

Retrieving her knives, she put more distance between herself and the tree. It had taken months to perfect short and medium throws infused with enough power to drive solidly into her target. From farther away, however, she still struggled.

Theo inhaled deeply and raised her arm, preparing to throw the knife again, but her thoughts were muddled and conflicted. She had practiced daily since Papa's death, and now Landon was ordering her to town. *How should I go about contacting Archbroke? How and where to conduct practice sessions? When and how would I find the time?*

Identifying a location where she could train, riding bareback, mounting and dismounting while the horse was in motion would be extremely difficult. Not to mention finding a partner to refine her hand-to-hand combat skills. The servants at Hadfield Hall never blinked an eye at her odd requests, always more than willing to assist, with the utmost discretion regarding her activities around their new lord. With the exception of a few key personnel who would travel with them, Landon had installed a full complement of new household staff, all unfamiliar to her. Theo's muscles tensed, and her pulse raced alongside her mind at the enormity of the task before her.

She could not fail.

Theo released the knife.

It wobbled through the air and landed in the dirt with a thud.

Nowhere close to the intended target.

"Aargh!" Leaves and twigs cracked under her foot. Irritated at her childish response, she let the crisp clean air hit her lungs. *Slow, controlled breaths. Inhale deeply through the nose and release through slightly parted lips.* The directions had been repeated many a time throughout her reading of the volume along with *still your thoughts and focus*. Eyes closed, a whisper of wind brushed against her cheeks, accompanied by the scent of cedar. Muscles relaxed, mind clear, she pictured the blade securely lodged in the tree trunk.

Theo's eyes popped open as her brother's voice filtered through the woods. Stepping closer to a tree, she hugged her body to it. Peeking around the trunk, she searched the forest for any sign of Baldwin.

What was she doing? Baldwin was dead.

Theo shook her head and rubbed her eyes.

Her name being called was louder and clearer now. "Theo! Where are you, girl?" Landon stood with his hands firmly planted on his hips, eyes narrowed, searching the trees.

Theo rested her forehead against the tree. *Landon.* As her pulse and breathing slowed, the idea of Landon catching her practicing had her heart rate increasing once more. If he were to discover her real activities, there would be no hiding the truth from him. She was not a liar. But this was an excellent opportunity to test her skills at evading detection. Landon had the hearing of a bat.

Carefully, Theo retrieved her blades and placed them in a satchel along with the drawing materials used to disguise its purpose. Careful to tread with care, Theo made her way through the trees. The open space between the tree line and the servants' entrance was in Landon's line of sight. She needed a distraction. As she searched the ground for something to use as a decoy, horse hooves thundered down the drive. Landon turned.

With her cousin distracted, Theo raced across the clearing.

Once she reached the servants' entrance, Theo relaxed and smiled. Only after she closed the door to her chamber did she release the giggle that had been building inside her. She had successfully outwitted her astute cousin. With renewed confidence, Theo sauntered over to her hidden valise and emptied the contents, ensuring each item was necessary.

Was she ready? How would Lord Archbroke and Lord Burke, patriarchs of the other families tied to the Crown, take the news of a lady assuming the family's duties rather than the heir? Then again, her papa would not have broken tradition if he hadn't believed she was capable. Why did she continue to doubt herself?

CHAPTER TWO

Irritated his day had been interrupted by a visit from a total stranger, Graham walked briskly down the narrow hall lined with oil paintings of the countryside to the room where outsiders were allowed to wait. Agents nodded as he passed. His ever-present frown prevented them from accosting him. Most only dared address him in his office.

But someone gripped his shoulder, and Graham halted. "Waterford. Remove your hand." Graham peered closely at his most senior agent's features. "Whatever is the matter?"

Lord Waterford didn't meet his gaze but shrugged. "Nothing. Slow down before you bowl someone over."

Graham glanced about and took in Lord Waterford's bloodshot eyes and sunken cheeks. "You need rest and a delicious beefsteak. Join me later."

"Is that an order?"

"No. But perhaps we both could do with a night off."

"Impossible." Lord Waterford shook his head and took his leave.

Graham stood rooted to the spot as Lord Waterford disappeared down the hall. What was impossible? Rolling his shoulders, he continued to the room where the Earl of Hadfield was waiting.

He swung the door open and entered the sparsely furnished room. "Lord Hadfield, to what do I owe the pleasure of your presence today?"

Lord Hadfield turned, and Graham was confronted with an incredulous look. Graham released a sigh. He didn't have the patience to deal with the man's obvious skepticism. It was not uncommon for strangers to expect the Home Secretary to be a gentleman with silver in his hair and a portly physique. He was neither of those things. Although his midsection had increased as of late. He could hear the mental question as clearly as if the man had spoken. Could England's home security be in the hands of a man who didn't sport gray hair?

Strangely, Hadfield stuck out his hand to shake Graham's rather than issuing the customary bow. "Please call me Landon." Hadfield paused before adding, "I apologize, but I'm here to see Lord Archbroke."

He found Landon's request to be addressed by his given name odd, but since the man had only recently inherited the title and become a member of the peerage, perhaps it was not surprising.

"I am indeed Archbroke. Why have you come to see me?"

"I have a letter from my late uncle that is addressed to Lord Archbroke. It was included among his private papers at Hadfield Hall. He left specific instructions for me to personally deliver it to you." Landon withdrew the parchment from his inner breast pocket, and Graham saw the hesitation in the man's movements.

Landon confessed, "I was expecting a much older gentleman, to be honest."

Graham admired the man's honesty but reached out to take the missive that was reluctantly being handed over. "I assure you I am Graham Drummond, the Earl of Archbroke. My thanks to you for seeing the letter was delivered. If you have no further business, I must take my leave as I have many matters to attend to." Graham carefully placed the parchment in his own breast pocket. His gaze never leaving Landon's.

Graham would love the opportunity to play cards with the man; he would win a fortune. Landon's thoughts were as easy to read as a book. Old Lord Hadfield had apparently not informed his heir of the missive's contents, which Graham found odd since he had been told Landon had acted as his uncle's lawyer and representative for years. Plus there was the issue of the Hadfield inheritance.

While the man had failed to restrain his features, he did refrain from uttering his thoughts. Landon was the first to break his gaze, and with a shake of his head, he made his way out of the room.

With the door closed, Graham looked down at the parchment he pulled from his pocket. He was intimately aware of old Hadfield's ties to the Crown. Landon was a male descendant and should have identified himself with the mark. Upon receiving the book, the instructions were clear. Perplexed at Landon's behavior, Graham went to stand by the windows, seeking better lighting. Breaking the seal on the parchment, he read:

Archbroke,
If you are reading this letter, I have left this earth to join my beloved wife and son.
A bond that has no equal has tied our families for generations. I have broken tradition. I have entrusted the Hadfield volume to the last descendant of my direct bloodline.
I ask of you to provide support and protection to its owner, for God knows she will need it.
Hadfield

Archbroke read the missive twice. "She! What on earth! How could he do this?"

Pacing, Graham racked his brain. Had he ever been introduced to Hadfield's daughter? No images came to mind. He would have to seek her out but, most importantly, figure out a way to get his hands on the book. It could not remain in the hands of a lady. Was she a wallflower? Or worse, a flittering ninny with nothing but the weather to discuss? Muttering obscenities as he left the room, he nearly ran into one of his senior agents.

Hastily Graham said, "Move, man. I'm late for a meeting."

Midstride, he changed directions. He would have to postpone meeting with his assistant. Stomping through the halls, he exited through the front door. Sunlight blinded him. *Blazes!* What time was it? He had entered his offices barely before dawn and had intended to whittle down the mountain of paperwork on his desk.

His coachman stood to attention. "Lord Archbroke, where—"

"Go back to whatever it was you were doing." Graham gave the man a once-over. "Are you reading?"

"Yes, my lord." The man raised the book for Graham to read its title.

"Headlong Hall?" Graham's brows furrowed. "Is that the fellow who concocted the ridiculous word…"

Standing straighter and puffing out his chest, the coachman recited, "*Osteosarchaematosplanchnochondroneuro-muelous.*"

"Hrmph. What was the author's name?"

"My lord, that would be Thomas Love Peacock."

Graham tugged on his snug-fitting waistcoat. "Well, continue on. I won't be needing you this afternoon. I'll walk today."

The look his driver gave him suggested he should walk more often. With a shake of his head, he pressed forward with no set destination.

Where could the chit be this time of day? He stopped as his lungs were on fire, and his heart raced. Taking in his surroundings, he was a few blocks away from Bond Street, not far from where he started.

Who in his network would be able to provide him with a detailed description of the girl? Breathing in deeply, he tried to calm his mind and body. Rutherford. The jeweler had a propensity to remember all his customers and their offspring. Graham set off with a spring in his step. After a block or two, his lungs opened up and no longer burned. Striding up to Rutherford's shop, he pushed open the door, and the bell tinkled, announcing his arrival.

"Lord Archbroke!" Rutherford's head swiveled back to the patron in front of him. "We will have to look at these fine earrings another time, sir." After replacing the jewels behind the counter, Rutherford shooed the man out the door. Graham stepped to the side as the harried gentleman passed him.

"My lord, please do come in." The jeweler walked back to the counter. "How may I be of assistance?"

The bell jingled again. Blast the man. Rutherford had

forgotten to lock the door behind his last patron. A woman with striking green eyes entered, garbed in an oversized mourning dress that was likely to have been black once but now appeared gray. What caught Graham's notice was she walked without sound. No swish of skirts. No tapping of heels. Shrinking back into the shadows, his gaze followed her as she approached the jeweler.

The wise old man ignored Graham and plastered a wide smile on his face. "Miss, how may I assist you today?"

"Mr. Rutherford, my friend, the Countess of Devonton, recommended your fine establishment to me."

Her voice was even, with no hint of which shire she might have descended from. Interesting. The hairs on his arms stood at alert. Graham shifted his weight to the balls of his feet. His body was willing him to move closer to the stranger. Rolling back onto his heels, he planted his feet.

The woman scanned the store before returning her attention back to Rutherford. Had she heard his movements? He had been spending too many hours behind a desk.

"Ah. Lady Devonton's family have been patrons of mine for generations. What is it you seek?"

"I'd like to purchase a pocket watch for my cousin, Lord Hadfield."

Graham took a slight step backward. Hadfield was her cousin. Could this beauty be Lady Theodora? Rutherford's gaze fell to the spot where he stood. The fool would give him away if he continued to stare. Too late.

The raven-haired angel narrowed her gaze. "You there. Come out from the shadows." She tapped the tip of her parasol on the floor, punctuating her demand.

Stepping forward, Graham waited for her next move.

Without hesitation, she moved to stand before him. "What were you doing standing in the dark?"

Good gracious, the woman was stunning. Her eyes twinkled like two flawless emeralds. Cheeks the color of summer peaches. And those lips, they were perfect for kissing.

She waved a hand before his face. "Are you daft?"

A choking sound came from Rutherford. "Miss! You are speaking to Lord…"

"Rutherford, I'll return later when you are not busy." He wasn't ready to meet the lady if she was indeed Lady Theodora. Graham shook his head. He had stood there like the dullard she had called him instead of formulating a plan. What was wrong with him?

He took a step forward to leave. The magnetic pull of the woman had him walking closer to her than necessary, brushing her slight shoulder as he passed. A jolt of energy shot through him. Graham glanced back at the woman once more. If this dark-haired spitfire was indeed Lady Theodora, convincing her to relinquish her family's volume would be a challenge.

Graham loved a challenge.

CHAPTER THREE

Theo paced, wringing her hands and wearing a path along the new plush rug in the refurbished London town house. Anxiety clawed at her as she awaited her best friend's arrival. She hadn't seen Lucy in over a year and had missed her wedding to Lord Devonton. Theo had sent her best wishes—not the same as being there for such an important life event. Besides, Theo was uncertain she could hide the truth about her inheritance from Lucy.

They had never kept secrets from each other, not even when Lucy worked for the Home Office as a decoder during the war. For days, Theo had agonized over whether to share the specifics of her lifelong mission. As inquisitive as Lucy was, she would puzzle it all out sooner or later. Theo could only hope that if she asked Lucy not to pry, Lucy would respect her wishes. With a deep sigh, she relied on Papa's last words for guidance: *Only trust those who bear the same mark as you.*

Theo tore her gaze from the floor as the butler appeared at the door. "Lady Devonton has arrived."

"Thank you, Morris. Please show her in and have

Maggie bring some tea." Theo released a deep breath; she had much to say and apologize for.

Lucy breezed past Morris and rushed to embrace Theo in a tight hug.

"Theo!" Lucy's eyebrows scrunched together and formed a severe downward slope. She stepped back, continuing to hold Theo's hands in a tight grip. "There is absolutely nothing to you! You must start eating, or you will blow away. Seriously, are those relatives of yours mistreating you? You must come and stay with Blake and me."

"Aunt Henri and Landon are wonderful. They treat me with care and consideration. I wouldn't have you think otherwise. I haven't had much of an appetite."

Theo managed to pry one of her hands out of Lucy's death grip and motioned to the settee, accidentally bumping Lucy's protruding stomach. "Good gracious. You did not inform me you were enceinte! Please, let's sit." Glancing again at Lucy's form, Theo admired the cleverly designed dress that disguised Lucy's condition.

Apparently, she was not the only one keeping secrets.

Still gripping Theo's hand tightly, Lucy slowly lowered herself to the settee. Theo stared in awe. Lucy was going to have a child. A family of her own. Only a year ago, she had sent correspondence of her plan to set up her own household, but that had been before she met Lord Devonton. Lucy had been adamant no gentleman would allow her to continue her activities for the Home Office once married.

Having inherited the family obligation to the Crown, Theo now fully understood Lucy's logic. Even if she were to find a gentleman to love, how would she keep the secret of her duty from him? What marriage could survive such lies? No. Marriage and a family were now not a possibility.

A new kind of grief stabbed Theo's chest, and she pulled away from her friend. Lucy reluctantly let go.

Concern shone in Lucy's eyes as Theo moved farther back, placing herself out of Lucy's reach. Theo couldn't continue to meet Lucy's searching gaze, and her eyes began to fill with tears. "I want to apologize for not attending your wedding. I'm sorry. I have been an awful friend, especially since Matthew is still away on the Continent."

"I do miss my brother." Lucy's warm hand clasped hers once more. "But do not be silly. I understand. You were going through a tough time with your papa's passing and having to become reacquainted with family. I know in my heart if you could have, you would have made the trip to town. But that is all in the past."

If only she could share with Lucy the full truth of what she had been doing this past year. Of all the people in her life, Lucy would understand and support her endeavors; after all, Lucy herself sometimes engaged in scandalous missions. Like the one that led to her becoming Lady Devonton.

Lucy shifted, and Theo sensed she was about to be pulled into another hug. She again increased the distance between them, pretending to readjust her skirts.

Lucy pointedly looked at Theo's gown. "I see we need to go to the modiste as soon as possible."

The statement held an underlying threat. When Theo met Lucy's gaze, there was no doubt in Theo's mind. Her best friend had issued a challenge. One she wasn't sure she was ready for. Lucy was an excellent chess player, always two steps ahead of others, and there was a spark of mischief in her eyes. What was the woman up to?

Aunt Henrietta suddenly appeared like a fairy godmother. "Theo, I didn't realize we had company."

Theo rose to greet her aunt. After a quick embrace, she said, "Aunt Henri, allow me to introduce to you my best friend, Lucy, Lady Devonton. Lucy, this is my aunt, Lady Henrietta Arcot Neale."

Lucy had never been good at hiding her thoughts. Theo could read her like a book, and she didn't miss the look of shock on Lucy's face upon meeting Aunt Henri. Her friend must have pictured an old matron the likes of the marriage-minded, fire-breathing dragons of the *ton*. But Aunt Henrietta was a sweet, round-faced woman who radiated warmth and love, whom Theo now saw was garbed in the fashion of long ago.

"Lucy, it is nice of you to come and visit. I want to thank you for your kind invitation to your wedding and express my sincere apologies that we were unable to attend." Aunt Henrietta was rambling, but she did that with strangers.

Lucy began to reply, "Lady Henrietta—"

Aunt Henrietta raised a hand halting Lucy's response. "My girl, I haven't abided by formalities since the day I married my George. Please call me Aunt Henri or Aunt Henrietta, since you are like family to Theo."

With a wide smile, Lucy said, "If that is what you wish. Aunt Henri." Lucy paused for a moment, which was unusual for her. It was as if she were letting the name sit on her tongue a second to see if the familiar address suited. But the pause was no longer than a heartbeat and Lucy continued, "What do you say we go visit the modiste? I could send a note around to Mrs. Lennox. While she is not French, she does design fashionable dresses to suit her clients' figures rather than re-creating those horrid fashion-plate dresses. She charges fairly and assists in supporting her parents, siblings, and extended family. I fully endorse her with my patronage and recommend her to everyone possible."

"That would be lovely. What do you think, Theo?" Aunt Henrietta smiled, but Theo heard the strain in her voice.

Theo's thoughts on the matter were the kind one did not share aloud in company. Trying not to cringe, Theo banished the image from her mind of standing about being measured and pinned for hours. What she should be doing was figuring out a way to get outdoors so she could practice throwing knives.

Snapping out of her reverie, Theo retorted, "I think she will have her hands full with the two of us, Aunt Henri. If Lucy recommends her, then I'll put my full trust in her to outfit us both."

CHAPTER FOUR

Aunt Henrietta peered out the carriage windows and frowned. "Lucy, are you sure the driver knows where he is going?"

"Aunt Henri, of course he knows!" Lucy giggled. Once Lucy had regained her composure, she confessed, "I might have failed to mention Mrs. Lennox's shop is not on Bond Street, but I promise you she will create the most wonderful gowns."

Seeing her aunt's frown, Theo refrained from giggling herself.

Aunt Henrietta replied, "I'm not worried a wit about me. I want to make Landon proud." Aunt Henrietta gave Lucy a wicked grin before continuing, "If I had my way, I'd wear my own clothing and to hell with what the *ton* thinks or says. But it is my dearest wish for both Theo and Landon to find someone to love this Season. I will endure the fittings and set a good example for Theo here."

As her aunt patted her leg, Theo finally joined in the conversation. "I'll endure as many fittings as you can, dear Aunt Henri."

The carriage rolled to a stop, and the women alighted from the carriage with Evan, Lucy's footman, assisting them down to the street. As the women entered the small shop, a bell over the door tinkled.

A young female voice came from the back. "I'll be right wit' you."

Theo smiled at Lucy. "Definitely not French."

Lucy laughed. "But wait until you see her creations." She shrugged and ushered Aunt Henrietta to a comfortable-looking chair. Theo's aunt hesitated for a split second, then settled into the seat, adjusting and readjusting her skirts.

Meanwhile, Theo walked around the small shop, touching various bolts of silk, velvet, and even twill and cotton in dark colors. It was odd for cloth such as twill to be displayed. She wasn't aware of any ladies of the *ton* who would make a gown out of the material.

Theo glanced up from the fabric and spied her friend entering the back room. Without making a noise, she followed behind, and as she drew closer, she overheard Lucy saying, "Ah… Emma, this will be perfect."

Lucy held what looked to be a maid's dress. Maybe Lucy was purchasing it for one of her kitchen maids or chambermaids, although most households only supplied the footmen with uniforms. Knowing Lucy, her establishment would be far from what anyone would describe as typical. *But why would Lucy procure such a garment?*

After Lucy folded the dress carefully, she put it aside and picked up an emerald-green silk concoction with a sheer overlay in front which left nothing to the imagination. The gown was cut to reveal a woman's bare back, with the skirt designed to sit slightly above her bottom. Theo couldn't imagine Lucy wearing something so daring.

Surely Blake would not allow his wife to leave the house in such an ensemble.

Theo hadn't seen much of Lucy in the past two years, nor had she been privy to Lucy's dealings with the Home Office. Since the dress was obviously not for a society event, Theo reasoned it must somehow be connected to Lucy's secretive activities. Perhaps Mrs. Lennox assisted Lucy with her wardrobe, supplying disguises, which would also explain the maid's dress.

As Theo turned to leave, Lucy said, "I believe this is an exact replica of the gown Blake illustrated. Not only will he be astonished but also delighted that you were able to create it. I cannot thank you enough." Theo held in a giggle; perhaps Mrs. Lennox had created the dress for Blake's enjoyment.

By the time Mrs. Lennox and Lucy reappeared in the main room of the shop, Theo was sitting patiently next to Aunt Henrietta.

"Aunt Henri, Theo, let me introduce Mrs. Lennox to you both." Lucy pushed the woman forward, and she curtsied.

Aunt Henri shot up out of her comfortable chair. "What on earth are you doing?" Aunt Henri reached out to clasp the modiste's hands. "Get up, get up. I hate formalities! Now, dear, what is your name?"

Mrs. Lennox rose and grinned. "Emma, m'lady."

"Emma, my dear, I'm not your lady and you shall call me Aunt Henri like the other girls." Aunt Henri resumed her seat and proceeded to inform Emma, "Theo and I will need to be outfitted with full wardrobes, my dear, gowns for every occasion. We will need at least one of each for next week. Do you have anyone to assist you in getting the dresses done in time?"

Theo stared at her aunt in shock. Sweet Aunt Henri

had turned into Wellington, issuing clear and concise orders. The woman possessed hidden strengths, Theo would not underestimate Aunt Henri again.

Emma said, "I've three little sisters and two cousins who'll help me."

"Perfect. I'm sure Landon will pay you extra to meet this rather unorthodox timeline. Now, what designs do you have in mind for Theo? I'd prefer her gowns to be completed prior to my own."

Emma nodded in agreement and said, "I'll jus' git me notebook to show ya then."

Theo raised an eyebrow in Lucy's direction. "Will you be ordering more gowns?"

Lucy groaned, "No. Emma made all my gowns to accommodate my increasing size. I come in, and she adds another panel or two, adding color or different material or lace, and voilà, it's like a new gown. Then it will fit for a week or so before she has to perform magic again."

Theo's chest expanded, and a bubble of laughter escaped through her lips.

Lucy stared at Theo. "What was that sound?" Lucy reached out and grasped her by the shoulders and gave Theo a slight shake. "Make it again."

At the absurdity of Lucy's actions, Theo released a giggle which sounded rusty to her own ears. But the sight of her friend crossing her eyes and sticking out her tongue, as she had when they were children, made Theo bend over and clasp her stomach, gasping for air as she laughed. Straightening to inhale a deep breath, Theo was wrapped up once more in Lucy's embrace.

Lucy bounced on her toes. "I'm so glad you came to town. Oh, how I've missed you!"

Theo tried to extricate herself, but the sprite of a

woman was stronger than she looked. "I've missed you too."

Theo squeezed her eyes shut as Lucy released her. She wanted to tell Lucy everything, but that would put her best friend in danger. Ironic. It was only a few years ago Lucy had declared it impossible to have a husband and a family due to her responsibilities to the Home Office, and now she had both.

But it would not be the same for Theo, for her obligations to the Crown were only to be shared with those who bore the mark.

Theo plastered a false smile upon her face and twirled away from Lucy's all too intelligent and piercing gaze.

"Well, shall we pick out fabric?" Theo fingered the twill and eyed Lucy.

Emma gasped. "Oh, that is not for you, m'lady." Rushing to remove the bolt of material, Emma hauled it to the back and out of sight.

Theo kept her eyes on Lucy. The telltale stiffening of Lucy's back meant not all was as it appeared in Emma's shop. Baldwin's altered shirts and breeches were worn through. Could Emma be the answer to the predicament of obtaining new training garments?

Theo took the opportunity to hone her skill at remaining still and taking shallow breaths as Emma measured, pinned, poked, and wrapped her in various materials. Her mind, though, raced with plans to arrange time away to practice.

Theo read Lucy's lips. "She looks lifeless. You can't tell if she is alive or not."

"What was that, dear?" Aunt Henri asked.

Lucy turned so Theo could no longer read her lips, but Theo's hearing was impeccable.

"Theo's been standing there for three hours without

the slightest movement. I've never known her to be so…" Lucy dropped her chin to her chest. "I don't know exactly how to explain… but there is certainly something different about her."

Emma's sketch pad snapped closed. "All done for today."

Theo stepped down from the platform while Aunt Henri shot up to her feet and held out a hand to assist Lucy as she rocked back to gain momentum to rise.

Debating whether to ask Emma about the other gowns she had seen in the back, Theo twisted at the waist to face Emma. "I was wondering if you wouldn't mind…" Theo's nerves stopped her from continuing.

Emma didn't even blink. Instead, she cocked her head. "I can whip up all sorts of garments. If you need somethin', just tell me what you be needin'."

Theo smiled and nodded. Emma had understood her unspoken request. Relieved, she gave Emma a brief hug and left the shop.

Theo had a foot raised and inside the carriage when she paused. "I forgot my reticule in the shop. I'll return in a moment."

Aunt Henrietta gave her a curious stare while Lucy shrugged her shoulders and adjusted her skirts. Theo rushed back into the shop. Emma glanced up from the bolt of material she was arranging.

Before she lost her confidence, Theo said, "Emma, I need a pair of breeches, a lawn shirt, and a greatcoat. If you could help me obtain a cap to cover my hair, I'd greatly appreciate it."

Emma winked. "I'll 'ave 'em ready wit' your order."

Theo was so giddy with excitement that she nearly forgot to retrieve her reticule left on the bench.

CHAPTER FIVE

The rustling of newspaper, smoke from cheroots, and the smell of sandalwood made Graham's shoulders relax as he strode into his club. The tension in his neck and back caused by the constant strain of his role and sitting at a desk for hours was slowly melting away. He needed a brandy. Walking over to his favorite chair, he caught sight of Blake Gower, the Earl of Devonton, the husband of his best decoder. Swiveling on his heel, he changed directions and approached what he now saw was a rather disheveled Lord Devonton. The man's hair was disturbed, his cravat hung loosely around his neck, and his waistcoat was unbuttoned.

Graham chuckled at the placid, ultraconservative Foreign Office agent's appearance. He couldn't forgo an opportunity to tease the bedraggled man. "Devonton. I say, marriage appears to agree with you. And one must commend your valet's handiwork."

Without an invite, Graham slid into the chair next to Devonton. With his legs crossed at the ankles, Graham relaxed and rested his interlaced fingers upon his chest.

Blake ran his hand over his face once more. "Archbroke."

From the corner of his eye, Graham noted the stony stare Blake hurled his way. The corners of Graham's lips twitched, almost forming a grin. His friendship with Devonton was relatively new and still somewhat tenuous. While Devonton had not prevented Lucy from working for Graham and the Home Office, after their recent marriage, Graham was still suspicious of the man's motivations for marrying one of his most valued agents.

Graham turned to face Devonton. "How is Lucy feeling these days?"

Devonton's shoulders slumped forward. "Better." Shifting forward, Devonton rested his elbows on his knees that were spread wide and rolled his glass between his palms. "She's not tossing up her accounts anymore, which is a relief."

An image of his resilient agent ill sent a shiver down Graham's back. It was no secret that Devonton cared for his wife deeply. If loving a woman could cause such havoc on a man's nerves, then love was an emotion Graham would have to live without. Or perhaps Devonton's ragged state was due to the abstinence from the activities that led up to her condition. Graham eyed the drink in Blake's hand.

Blake held up his glass. "I'm drinking brandy tonight. Care to join me?"

At Graham's nod, Blake motioned for a waiter to bring another glass.

"After the week I have had, I will drink anything." Graham remained astonished at the actions of old Hadfield. Especially if the woman he had run into at Rutherford's was indeed Lady Theodora.

Graham was honor bound to protect the chit. No, not

chit. Beauty. Frowning, he continued to mull over the possible reason for what had possessed old Hadfield to bestow such a hefty duty on his daughter. The woman at the jeweler had not been some flighty young girl. Definitely not a wallflower. But how would the brazen woman do on missions? They often required stealth, extreme self-control, and keen intelligence. What of the ability to defend oneself from knife attacks or even the occasional flying fist? He nearly groaned out loud at his last thought.

"You know, you left the office hours ago. Aren't you supposed to don your mask of a dandy and shed that rather serious look?"

Graham ignored the barb. "What is on the social calendar tonight?"

Devonton's eyes widened and raised the hand that housed his glass to his chest. "You're asking me?"

Not known for his social skills, Devonton was still an enigma among the *ton*. Devonton had been commissioned by the Foreign Office to spend his time on the Continent during the war and had only returned to England after the Corsican had been exiled. At the first hint of interest from Devonton in Lucy, Graham had investigated Devonton's background and reviewed his service records. Graham was extremely protective of his agents, particularly Lucy since she was the sole female in the group. He was pleased to find that Devonton was acquainted with and respected by several gentlemen among Graham's set with whom Devonton had attended Oxford.

Graham raised an eyebrow and prompted the man to reply.

"I'm a married man. I go wherever my dear wife instructs me to go."

Graham considered Devonton's statement. He lifted his glass of brandy to his mouth and sipped, preventing a cutting reply from slipping through his lips. He needed answers, not the man's ire.

Devonton exhaled a long-suffering sigh. "Lucy is expecting me at the Fairmont ball later this evening."

Graham shifted marginally to lean forward, giving the perception that he was listening very carefully.

"She is attending with her best friend, Lady Theodora, who has recently come into town along with her Aunt Henrietta. I believe her cousin, Lord Hadfield, will arrive to escort his family home, and I'm to retrieve Lucy. I've yet to meet any of them. I'm curious to meet Lady Theo since Lucy holds her in such esteem."

At the mention of Landon and Lady Theodora, Graham straightened in his chair and planted his feet firmly on the floor. Lucy was an excellent judge of character. The angel at Rutherford's had mentioned she was a friend of Lucy's. His curiosity was piqued. It would be unusual for Lucy to associate with anyone insipid or vacuous. The overcrowded annual Fairmont ball would be an excellent setting to assess the woman. An ominous chill ran down the back of his neck. Lady Theodora had in her possession a volume that contained decades of secrets, information, and all contacts related to the protection of the Crown.

Graham lifted his glass and waved it toward Devonton. "Perhaps I should join you this eve."

Devonton finished his drink and lifted the empty glass, waiting for the waiter to refill it. "I'll have my hands full this season with Harrington and Hereford away."

At the mention of Lucy's brother, Lord Harrington, an agent for Graham who had ignored his direct order to remain in London, and the Foreign Office agent, Lord Hereford, Graham scanned the room. "How so, Devonton? I was of the belief Lucy preferred to remain home with a book than to embark upon the endless social route."

"Lucy has informed me that now that she has experienced marital bliss, she wants the same for her two dear friends, Lady Grace and Lady Theo. My wife has proclaimed it her mission to see at least one, if not both, find suitable husbands by the end of the Season."

Graham couldn't help but shake his head. "I assume she has formulated a strategy to accomplish such a task."

"Indeed, she has, and you know how effective she is."

Graham grinned. "Indeed, I do."

"I'm happy to say my role will remain fairly uninvolved. I'm to dance with the ladies occasionally and scare off any suitors Lucy deems unsuitable. I do believe Lucy has decided to match them with one of the eight gentlemen Matthew had endorsed last season."

Remembering that he, himself, was on the list, Graham mentally noted to be prepared and on guard to ensure he wasn't ensnared in Lucy's plan. "I would wager Lady Grace's heart has already been claimed by another."

Graham glanced at his pocket watch. They would have barely enough time to eat before having to leave. He mentally cringed at the thought of donning his dandy persona. But Graham had only himself to blame for conceiving such an idiotic but effective tactic in warding off matrons and debutantes looking to trap him into marriage. For over a decade he had honed and elaborated his alter ego, but these days it was harder and harder to transition into the role. Archbroke the dandy would be free to roam the ball and observe without hindrance. Graham's heartbeat quickened for his disguise may also facilitate an opportunity to sequester the mysterious Lady Theo, allowing him to confirm her true identity.

Landon sauntered into the club. Graham rose to meet the man who had undeniably ruined his week.

Standing, Landon matched him in height. "Archbroke."

"Hadfield, may I introduce you to Blake Gower, the Earl of Devonton."

Devonton rose as Graham continued with the introductions. "Devonton, this is Landon Neale, the new Earl of Hadfield."

Devonton was several inches taller, but Landon did not appear to be intimidated.

Landon stuck out his hand. "Lord Devonton, a pleasure, but please call me Landon." With ease, Blake shook the man's hand. As their hands fell back to their sides, Landon said, "I received a note informing me that we are to escort our ladies home from Fairmont's later tonight."

"Yes. I'm hoping by the time we arrive at the ball, Lucy will be tired, and we can leave without too much delay."

Landon smiled and relaxed his stance. From the man's body language, Graham assessed that Devonton and Landon would swiftly become fast friends.

Landon chuckled. "I've yet to see your wife tire. In the past week, Theo has returned many a day in clear exhaustion after venturing out with Lady Devonton. Your wife is truly amazing."

Blake's chest puffed out, and with eyes filled with love and devotion said, "There aren't many who can keep up with Lucy. Once she has decided upon something, I doubt anyone could stop her. I had high hopes her condition would slow her down and we'd not have to attend balls and such."

With evident consternation flashing across Landon's features, he added, "According to Theo's calendar, she is to attend an event every evening for the next fortnight. I miss the days…"

"What?" Blake's cheeks filled with color. "Every night. Absolutely, not! I will not allow my wife to be traipsing about Mayfair evening after evening. Lucy and I will be having a discussion this evening. She needs her rest. This is—"

Cutting Blake off before he could rant more, Graham looked at Hadfield and asked, "Is it not your wish to marry off Lady Theodora?"

"No. Theo should enjoy the Season. With her brother's and then her papa's subsequent deaths, she has been in mourning for the past two. I think it would be best for her constitution to have a bit of fun before having to marry. I was raised to believe that one should marry for love."

There was steel in Landon's tone; however, Graham couldn't prevent himself chuckling as he said, "Love! You cannot be serious. The only love match I have been witness to in a decade is…" Sliding a smug grin in Devonton's direction, he went on, "Devonton and Lucy. And honestly, it is rather annoying to be in the same room with them together."

Blake cut Graham a harsh look and growled, "Archbroke, you don't know what you speak of."

Trying to bait Blake, Graham asked, "Do you deny your marriage is a love match?"

Before Blake could confirm or deny, Landon spoke up. "How much time before we have to leave for the blasted ball? I need a drink."

Graham took pity on the two of them and motioned for a server. "Bring us a bottle of your best brandy and a round of beefsteaks."

They sat and ate, savoring their drinks, none of them too eager to leave. Graham was only half listening to

Hadfield's opinions on the latest investments and his efforts to restore the Hadfield coffers. Had old Hadfield run the estate into near bankruptcy? What other irresponsible actions had the old man taken? Old Hadfield must have had a sound reason for breaking a decades-old tradition. Graham began to wonder if the old man hadn't trusted his heir.

CHAPTER SIX

Lord Markinson's familiar smile allowed Theo to relax, and she ventured a grin of her own. He had been one of her brother's closest friends despite his tendency for rakish behavior.

His large palm dwarfed hers just as it had when they were younger, learning the steps. "I was curious as to how long you would remain in hiding."

They danced the quadrille and were momentarily separated. The blur of three dark figures entering through a side door caught Theo's attention. She recognized Landon, but he was flanked by two strangers.

She craned her neck to observe the trio. The tallest was intently searching the room, surveying the refreshment table and the walls lined with ladies chatting in small groups rather than the main dance floor. Who was he looking for?

The handsome stranger to Landon's left leaned to his side and spoke to the tall one, nodding in the direction of Lord Waterford, who was dancing with Lucy. Straightening to his full height, the man's eyes shot daggers at Lord

Waterford. He must be Lord Devonton. Lucy had described her husband as a giant. Theo couldn't help but smile. She could practically see waves of heat and steam radiating from Lord Devonton as he eyed his pregnant wife in another man's arms.

"I see your cousin has arrived." Lord Markinson released her from the turn.

Theo snuck another glance at the trio. Lord Devonton was likely several inches taller than most. He was only slightly taller than Landon and the lighter-haired gentleman that her eyes kept wandering to. There was a familiarity about him.

"Do you know the others he arrived with? I don't recall having been introduced to them before."

"Lord Devonton and…" Lord Markinson did a double take. "Lord Archbroke."

Lord Archbroke. It couldn't be. The man's clothing was garish, cravat tied with rolls and curves that reminded her of a turkey neck. What color was his waistcoat? Rose-pink. Theo's gaze followed the trio as they made their way to the refreshments table.

Lord Devonton's coat stretched taut, his muscles flexed, as Lucy slipped but fell into the competent arms of Lord Waterford. Lord Archbroke placed a hand to halt Lord Devonton's advance. At something Archbroke said, Lord Devonton's eyes softened, reflecting concern and… love.

Theo followed the line of Lord Devonton's gaze to Lucy, who returned her husband's stare with a wink. What would it feel like to be loved so passionately and with such fierceness?

Inexplicably, Theo's gaze fell back to Lord Archbroke. The gentleman was of similar height to Landon, but he exuded strength and authority in stark contrast to his appearance. He was a dandy. From her papa's notes, she was expecting a mature, intelligent, reserved gentleman. Not a peacock.

"Is anything the matter, Lady Theodora?"

"No. Why do you ask?"

"You seem rather unsettled by the appearance of your cousin and his friends."

"His…"

"I'm not one to brag, but this *is* the first time my dance partner wasn't wholly focused on my devilishly handsome face."

"I'm sorry…" Even as she spoke the apology, Theo's gaze was pulled again to Lord Archbroke. The tingling on the back of her neck was a warning. The man's posture appeared relaxed and idle, but the intensity of his gaze reflected an underlying layer of intelligence and raw power. Absurd. But her instincts were warning her to be on guard. His silly lopsided smile masked fine features that otherwise might have been described as handsome.

What was it about this man that had her nerves on high alert? Now that he was closer, she could see his eyes. She had seen those peculiar cool blue eyes before. As their gazes collided— Oh no. Lord Archbroke was the man at the jeweler's shop. The disheveled lord she had accosted. Theo shuddered as if chilled by the night air.

Lord Markinson ran a hand down her arm. "Are you cold?"

Theo blinked and looked up at her partner as the other couples made their way off the dance floor. "Not at all. It's rather warm with the crush of couples. But I'm a tad parched."

He winged out his arm. "Would you care for some punch?"

"That would be lovely." Theo followed his lead without thought of their destination.

When he stopped but did not leave, Theo turned in confusion. The slight movement under her hand reminded her that she still had not released him.

As her hand slid from his arm, he winked at her. "I'll return with refreshments."

An eerie feeling someone was watching her caused her skin to prickle. Theo subconsciously raised her hand over her coiffure and down her rose-colored gown, but her gaze caught Lord Archbroke's eyes trailing her hand. His visual assessment brought about a sensation that quickened her pulse. She had never been affected by another with such intensity before. It was those blue eyes. How could she have mistaken the man for a dullard?

Theo started at her aunt's voice. "Lord Markinson is a rather handsome gentleman—although, my dear, how are your toes?"

How was it that Aunt Henri was by her side?

"Is anything the matter?" Aunt Henri asked again.

What was her aunt's first question? "My toes?"

"You made the most unusual faces. I assumed it was due to his lordship stepping on your toes."

"Oh, no. Lord Markinson is a lovely dancer, Aunt Henri. I'm not used to wearing these horrid slippers, and they're pinching."

"You certainly cannot wear your boots to a ball." Aunt Henrietta frowned down at her own feet. Theo was sure her aunt was suffering the same discomfort as neither of them was accustomed to being on their feet for long periods.

The shuffling of boots behind her alerted her to men approaching.

Aunt Henrietta clapped her hands with glee. "Thank goodness you have arrived!"

Landon stepped around Theo and leaned down to give his mama a kiss on the cheek.

Theo loved how affectionate her family members were with one another. Since taking up residence at Hadfield Hall, she had been showered with kisses and hugs that she eagerly returned, having not received them before.

"Mama." He bussed Theo on the cheek before asking, "How are you enjoying the evening?"

Theo cataloged her various impressions of the night. They ranged from total boredom to highly intrigued upon the arrival of Lord Archbroke. Ultimately, she gave Landon a weak smile and said, "I'm ready to leave if you are."

Disappointment flashed across Landon's features. Theo's attention was immediately drawn to the sight of Lucy storming toward them with her husband close on her heels.

Once Lucy was within speaking distance, she declared to the group, "I'm so sorry, but I cannot stay longer. My stodgy old husband…" She waved her hand toward Lord Devonton.

Lucy's eyes widened. "Oh, Theo!"

Lucy drew in a deep calming breath and pierced Lord Devonton with a look that was a mixture of aggravation and affection. She placed a hand on her husband's arm to steady her. "It is my pleasure to introduce you to my husband, Blake Gower, the Earl of Devonton." Lucy continued to mumble, but Lord Devonton's chuckle made it hard to hear her clearly. Lucy wouldn't have referred to her husband as Mr. Worrywart, would she? Previously Lucy had only sung Lord Devonton's praises. How calming, how intelligent, how understanding, how handsome… she had gone on and on about the man she had married.

Smiling and evidently unperturbed by his wife's behavior, he gracefully took Theo's outreached hand. "It is a pleasure to finally meet you, Lady Theodora."

Lord Devonton released her hand and straightened. The man's height was intimidating.

Theo raised her chin to ensure her voice projected. "Please call me Theo. I've heard so much about you, Lord Devonton, that I feel as if I already know you."

Theo peeked around Lord Devonton. Where was Lord Archbroke?

Frown lines appeared as Lord Devonton replied, "A pleasure, Theo, and you must address me as Blake. I'm sorry we can't stay longer, but I think Lucy should be resting and not…"

Lucy's husband's reassuring manner made it an easy transition for Theo to think of him as simply Blake rather than Lord Devonton.

The poor man winced as Lucy elbowed Blake in the ribs. "Oh look. Archbroke is coming this way. Blake, I must speak with him, and I will not leave until I do so."

All eyes turned to watch Archbroke approach. The man's steps were minced. He stopped a half dozen times to address a matron or gentleman, all of whom wore a look of disinterest, but none gave him the cut direct. He straightened his waistcoat—at this distance and lighting, Theo realized it wasn't rose-pink but a horrid shade of orange that she had never seen before.

"He informed me that color is referred to as gamboge," Landon whispered in her ear.

"Gamboge?"

Landon nodded.

As soon as Lord Archbroke was within reach, Lucy placed a hand on his upper arm. Theo was struck with an urge to slap Lucy's hand away. What was it about this peculiar man that provoked such odd reactions?

"Archbroke. Don't you look fine this evening." Lucy turned her mischievous eyes to Theo.

Fine? Was Lucy blind? Archbroke's attire was atrocious. His cravat was the same red as a wattle. It was no wonder the image of a turkey had come to mind upon first sight of him. From a distance, one couldn't tell the color of his jacket, but up close, Theo saw it was a dark forest green, cut slightly too snug for his form. The appalling color scheme of his evening wear was only heightened all the more by the elegance of Blake and Landon's ensembles.

Lucy giggled. "Theo, it would be my pleasure to introduce to you Graham Drummond, the Earl of Archbroke. He is a very close friend of Matthew's, and I believe he also knew both your papa and brother quite well." Lucy gave Theo a very pointed look and raised an eyebrow at her.

Blinking, Theo reached out her hand. "Lord Archbroke, it's a pleasure to meet a friend of the family."

No one in their little group noticed Graham's slight hesitation. Lucy confirmed his suspicions that the raven-haired beauty from Rutherford's was indeed none other than Lady Theodora, herself. He didn't possess Devonton's ability to recall every detail of a person's image, but Lady Theodora had garnered his full attention at the jeweler's, and her features had haunted him ever since. He had gone against protocol when he stared at her as she ran her delicate hand over her exquisite hair, down her swan-like neck, and against her soft silk gown, allowing her to detect his presence.

Graham reached out to take Theo's hand and brushed

a light kiss across her gloved hand. "Lady Theodora, the pleasure is all mine." His blood warmed despite the material preventing his lips from experiencing the intimate touch of skin.

Her cousin was emanating a level of heat that could roast a man alive. Meeting Landon's glare directly, Graham straightened but did not release the lady's hand. What had caused Landon's ire? Was it due to the ridiculously high tone he adopted when in society, or was it because he presumed to kiss his cousin's hand? He would have to deal with Landon at a later time. Graham prioritized he needed to whisk Theo away and have a private word with her. The strains of a waltz gave the perfect opportunity to draw the woman away from the group.

"Lady Theodora, may I have this dance?" A turn on the dance floor would afford them a level of privacy, enough for him to assess the beauty before him. She certainly wasn't a wallflower, and those deep emerald eyes held intelligence and something he was struggling to name.

Rather than releasing Theo immediately as he should, Graham drew her closer and gently placed a hand on her lower back. His palm met with well-defined muscles. She had been training. Intrigued to find out more of the woman who had taken on the Hadfield duties, Graham deftly guided her through the throng and onto the dance floor. How long would she remain silent?

Unperturbed by her lack of effort to engage in conversation, Graham was uncharacteristically at ease with the woman in his arms, and dancing with her was more pleasure than obligation. She wasn't a missish innocent. She looked to be at least of age with Lucy, who was three and twenty. He hadn't bothered to take note of the debutantes or the available misses. He was far too busy to properly court a woman.

A quarter of the way through the dance, Theo raised her chin and took in his features. "Lord Archbroke, I was expecting you to be a man of many more years than…" Her eyes roamed over him, and every inch of his skin seemed to come alive. "Than what, forty?"

Forty, bloody hell! Did he look that old?

He lightened his hold at her waist. His fingertips had inadvertently dug into her side on hearing her estimation. "Lady Theodora, I am nine and twenty. Good God, do I really look forty?"

He must be spending too much time buried at the Home Office or his own office at home. Perhaps he was a little soft around the middle, not as muscular or defined as his agents, and he definitely had more than a few wrinkles on his forehead. It was no doubt from dealing with all the infuriating agents at the Home Office who constantly tested his authority. Despite rumors of him being too young to be an effective leader, he had also heard it said by many of his agents that he was by far the most intelligent and honorable man they'd the pleasure to work for. And they did so with pride, for Graham was a genius and ran the Home Office far better than the prior two generations.

Graham caught a mischievous sparkle in Theo's eyes. Hmm… was the minx teasing him? Interesting.

"With your voice not yet fully developed, how could I have been mistaken?" Had he spoken in his regular tone or the one he adopted as a dandy? He would have to be more careful.

Theo continued, "Nine and twenty, my lord. You are but four years my senior. My sources gave me the impression that I was to seek out a great mastermind. Could that be you?"

The woman before him was no ninny. Her clever questions and wit proved as much. He squeezed her hand to reassure himself she was indeed real. The subtle change in his grip heightened her breathing, drawing his attention to the rise and fall of her bosom.

Theo's cheeks were aflush with color. "Is it you I seek?"

Raising his eyes back to meet hers, he blinked. Never had a woman distracted him from a task. He needed her to reveal herself.

Graham lowered his voice. "There is only one way to find out, *Lady* Theo. Meet me in the garden just before the supper dance."

For the first time all evening, a flicker of doubt flashed through Theo's eyes. Would she be up for the assignation? He wanted to uncover the mysterious Lady Theodora. How much had she learned from the volume?

He waited as Theo weighed the risks of meeting him in the garden. Her gaze darted around him only to return to his with a spark of a challenge. He admired her brilliant green eyes framed by artfully shaped brows, her cute, pert nose that sat above lips which were full and bowed. It was a moment before he registered she was speaking again. "Perhaps this evening is not the best time for us to become better acquainted, my lord."

Resuming his role of a jovial dandy, Graham said loudly for others nearby to hear, "Oh Theo, please call me Graham or Archbroke." Then to unnerve the woman, Graham leaned in closer and in his deep natural tone whispered in her ear, "I disagree. I believe tonight is as good as any other time."

Theo shivered. Graham suppressed the caveman response to haul her over his shoulder and make her quiver more. The last strains of the waltz indicated the dance was about to end. She was taking too long to make a decision. If she was to inherit the duties of the volume, she needed to be decisive. In a tone that had his agents hopping to do his bidding, Graham said, "You will only receive this one opportunity to prove you are worthy of my assistance."

He guided a silent Theo over to her aunt and cousin. Releasing Theo from his embrace was harder than Graham anticipated. For some odd reason, he wanted her to remain close to his side. Never had he experienced such possessiveness.

To Graham's surprise, Lucy and Blake were still in attendance and were making their way off the dance floor and toward him.

Lucy waited until she had his full attention. "Archbroke, you will not leave until I've had a word with you."

Graham had worked with Lucy for many years, and he treated her more like a sister than an agent under his supervision. It brought him great pleasure to tease her in public, for most of the time their other interactions were of a serious nature. Adopting the obnoxious voice that made even him cringe at times, he said, "Lucy! I believe breeding has brought out your most endearing qualities."

Lucy tugged on his arm and pulled him aside. "Archbroke, I'm in no mood tonight. I've had enough harassment from my beloved husband. I am fully aware that I have another human growing within me. I do not need to be reminded every five seconds." Lucy cut him a look that said she was not in the mood for any more nonsense. "I want Lord Hadfield's file."

Graham cleared his throat. "Lord Hadfield has recently acquired the title. There is nothing of import in his file."

"Don't be obtuse, Archbroke. I want the old earl's file, and I want it tomorrow."

"Lucy, you know you are breaking all the rules by mentioning such things here. You should be reprimanded."

Ignoring Graham's comment, Lucy continued, "I'll be

by to pay you a visit in the afternoon." Lucy turned and placed a hand on her husband's lower back as he faced away from them to provide privacy.

"Damn women agents."

Blake peered over his shoulder and said, "The office I work for—"

"Don't even start, Devonton. Rein in your woman."

Initially, Graham had been reluctant to work with Lucy directly. However, he was unable to find a male counterpart who was able to decipher codes as swiftly or effectively as Lucy. Over the course of the war, she had garnered his trust and admiration. Graham stared down at Lucy, who was impatiently tapping one foot. The woman was extremely stubborn and was sure to persist until he relented. "Very well. I'll see you after luncheon."

Graham was rewarded with a brilliant smile. He had to admit Lucy was easy on the eyes when she wasn't scowling at him.

Lucy rubbed her slightly extended belly and peeked up at Devonton, "Blake, I will find you as soon as I return."

Blake caught hold of his wife's elbow and bent low for her to speak into his ear. Graham had impeccable hearing.

"I need to speak to Arabelle. I promise to leave after I've received her update."

Last Season's diamond? Hmm. Lord Hereford's sister. What information had the Foreign Office agent sent to her that Lucy, an agent of his office, would need to obtain?

Lucy left her husband's side and was making her way out of the ballroom. Once he was sure Lucy was out of earshot, he asked Devonton, "Do you know what she is up to?"

"My wife?"

"Yes. I can tell that Lucy is up to no good."

The man's lips twitched. "She is certainly up to something."

Making the excuse of checking on his wife, Blake left Graham to ponder what scheme Lucy had concocted or had involved herself in.

GRAHAM MADE an appearance in the card and billiards rooms but hadn't yet engaged in either entertainment. He was ever mindful of Theo's whereabouts and with whom she interacted. There was no shortage of gentlemen seeking her attention, and she was often partnered with one lord or another for a dance. She should be laughing and enjoying the attention, but instead, he found her smile was strained and her body taut and alert. He caught her often scanning her surroundings, not in an obvious manner but precisely as he himself had been taught.

His gut clenched. She was marked. But where on that exquisite body of hers would it reside? Images of him finding it on the underside of her breast, on the inside of her thigh, or perhaps on the round of her bottom flashed through his mind.

His own mark was on his left upper arm between his shoulder and elbow. It had prevented him from removing his shirt while being intimate with a woman, for no one but those marked themselves were allowed to lay eyes upon it.

Standing apart from the crowd and leaning on a column, Theo stifled a yawn. She apparently found the handsome young Markinson a bore. Markinson, two years Graham's junior, still bore the trappings of youth in his face. Graham's features reflected years of stress and worry which, according to Theo, made him appear well beyond his nine and twenty years.

Perhaps it was time he engaged in more physical activity. Dance more at these engagements, hone his fencing skills at Angelo's or enter the ring at Gentleman Jackson's instead of standing and watching the fights. His personal training had suffered the past three years since he had taken over as head of the Home Office. It should have kept him in relatively good shape. However, he was consistently stuck behind a desk.

Training. When to find the time. It would be challenging for a woman to have access to the facilities needed for training here in town. Perhaps he could conceive a plan that would allow him to spend more time with Theo, to evaluate her capabilities. What other possible reason could there be for him to want to spend time with this alluring woman? His interest in knowing how she would feel under him would have to remain a curiosity. Those were thoughts of the "do not consider" variety, and he tucked them away under lock and key. Compartmentalizing thoughts, and particularly feelings, was like breathing to him.

Glancing at his pocket watch, it was approaching midnight, and therefore the supper dance would be commencing soon. He left the ballroom and entered the gardens through the service entrance. Would Theo do the same, or would she enter the gardens via the terrace doors off the main ballroom? Graham was waiting in the shadows and nearly fell into the bushes when Theo whispered right behind him, "You are late."

CHAPTER SEVEN

A bubble of laughter threatened to escape her lips but caught in Theo's throat as Archbroke growled. "How in the hell did you sneak up on me?"

"I think you have forgotten some of your training. Are you truly Lord Archbroke?"

"Only one way for you to know for sure."

The instructions provided that the mark would be revealed in order of rank, starting with the most junior. That meant she would have to reveal her mark before Archbroke. Yet the man had hinted he might reveal his mark first. She must not show her confusion or hesitate with this man.

"Lady Theo, would you care to honor tradition and go first?"

Tradition! Damn tradition, she was the first female in her entire family to have ever received the book. Females in her family only received the mark to identify their family link to the Crown, and those within the network would offer them protection if necessary. She could only hypothesize as to why her papa chose to break tradition and give her the book instead of Landon. While Landon did not bare the mark, her papa could have easily rectified that. She dearly wished her papa had explained his reasoning.

"I've only recently realized that my family doesn't stand firm on tradition."

Theo was expecting some type of disparaging comment, but Archbroke surprised her with his matter-of-fact response. "It would appear that way. However, my family does. Now we haven't much time. Do you need assistance?"

Theo rolled her eyes up to the heavens. Clouds shifted, revealing a three-quarter moon. Balancing on one leg, she removed her foot from her slipper. Theo reached under her skirt and rolled down her stocking just past the mark. Raising her foot and ankle forward, Theo made sure her skirt covered the rest of her leg as Archbroke knelt and tucked her foot into his palm. Leisurely he assessed the mark that resided upon her ankle.

Archbroke's voice deepened to a velvety baritone. "Lovely."

Her muscles relaxed as the pad of Archbroke's thumb stroked up and down the sole of her aching foot. A moan nearly escaped her. After having her toes pinched all night in slippers that were far from practical, his touch was heavenly. Theo wiggled her toes as they began to tingle. His fingers wrapped around her ankle, and he traced the outline of the circle of laurel leaves, bringing her attention to the purpose of their clandestine meeting.

Why was Archbroke drawing out the moment? He should have released her as soon as he had confirmed the mark's existence. But Theo was loath to remove her foot from his hand.

As her muscles continued to relax, Theo's body swayed, causing her to place her hands on his shoulders.

Rather broad shoulders, Theo admitted to herself. Once she had regained her balance, Archbroke began to roll up her stocking under her skirt with one hand. Instinctively, her calf tensed as his hand gently glided up over her knee and slowly up to midthigh. She shivered as his roughened palms roamed in search of her garter. Her thighs were no longer soft and lush. Hours of training had transformed them into lean, toned muscles, allowing her to run and jump distances she had never imagined possible. Would Lord Archbroke find her body enticing or manly?

Once his fingers found what they sought, he efficiently moved her garter into place to hold her stocking. Blue eyes peered up at her. Theo shifted her hand, her thumb caressing his neck along his collar. Lord Archbroke's sharp intake halted her movements. Would he continue his exploration of her? Her mind was flooded with memories of the time she had accidentally come across Baldwin with one of the upstairs maids and later that evening as she had listened to the maid tell another how Baldwin's fingers had pleasured her. As Lord Archbroke's hands moved up her leg, Theo had an insane thought of his hands continuing higher and touching her in the intimate way the maid had described.

But with swift mechanical movements, Archbroke removed his hand and placed her foot back into her slipper. Head bowed, Lord Archbroke rose to his full height, which allowed Theo to search his features. No trace of a smile. Small frown lines etched across his forehead. Had she misread the flash of hunger in his cerulean eyes? Theo hoped the color that flooded her cheeks would be hidden in the shadows despite them being mere inches from another. Could he have guessed the lewd images that she had summoned?

Archbroke's blank gaze flittered to the left, but when it

settled back upon her, the spark had returned. "Forgive me. We will have to continue this another time."

Unsettled, Theo raised her chin. Lord Archbroke's words were in direct conflict with what she suspected was desire. She yearned to get closer to him. Theo opened her mouth to argue with him, but the crunch of leaves beneath boots stopped her. Before she could utter a single word, his lips were upon hers.

Theo gasped and he deepened the kiss. She had no experience with kissing, but at the delicious taste of Archbroke, she recklessly mimicked his actions. She ran her tongue along his lower lip. Archbroke released a half sigh, half groan, music to Theo's ears. The bushes rustled, and they jumped apart.

Theo looked up at Archbroke. His pupils were dilated. Was it due to the dark or the result of the kiss? She had never evoked such a response in a gentleman before.

He gently pushed her toward the service entrance. "Go. I promise to arrange everything. You will receive what you came here for."

Her feet were moving toward the house, but her thoughts remained on his parting words.

LANDON PUSHED BACK A PRICKLY BUSH. "Theo!... Theo, are you out here?"

Was the man trying to compromise his cousin? He should be more discreet in his search for Theo.

Landon's hand brushed up against Graham's arm. "Hadfield. What are you doing out in the gardens?"

"Have you seen Theo?"

"No. Why would your cousin be out here?"

Hidden in the shadows, Landon's eyes narrowed as he

searched Graham's features. Long gone was the dandy, replaced by the imposing head of the Home Office. "Archbroke, you have too many personalities for my comfort. I'm not sure with whom I'm dealing. The dandy who arrived at the ball, the gentleman I spoke with this morning, or the acquaintance who relaxed with me at Brooks's. No matter which is your true self, stay away from Theo. You are shrouded in complications."

"Hadfield, I cannot comply with your wishes."

Voices floated from the other side of the hedge. Graham put his finger to his lips. Landon bristled at his action, but thankfully, he remained quiet.

Graham leaned in closer to listen to the conversation.

"Arabelle said she would meet me just beyond the hedge. Please, Blake, stay here. Keep a lookout and make sure no one is about."

"Wife, I am not letting you out of my sight, and I too want to hear Arabelle's report."

Ahh. It was Devonton and his wife. Graham silently moved over the pebbled path to gain a better position to listen to the couple. Thank goodness Landon had not followed. Lucy and Blake were too skilled to not detect him. It was not an easy task to remain undetected.

The swish of silk skirts indicated that a lady was approaching. "Lucy? Lucy where are—"

"Arabelle, over here."

"Oh, thank goodness I found you. I'll admit it is exhilarating to assist you, but I feel like I'm on pins and needles all the time."

Blake interjected, "Arabelle, did you obtain the necessary introductions last week?"

"Yes, Lord Devonton. I was able to befriend Lord Addington's sister, Cecilia. She is a sweet girl. I'm sure she is unaware of her brother's activities, just as I was ignorant of my brother's."

Instead of Devonton's voice, it was Lucy who responded. "Your brother would not ask this of you if he hadn't felt it necessary, Arabelle. You know what you are to do next, correct?"

What had Lucy got Hereford's little sister mixed up in? What was Lucy working on? Was it for the Foreign Office? She was his agent, not theirs, and despite marrying an agent of the Foreign Office, her loyalty should remain with him. The minx was keeping information from him.

Lucy's voice brought his attention back to the conversation. "Send us a note if you need anything, anything at all. If you obtain the information we seek, we will need to arrange a meeting. Do not share anything with anyone but us. You must be very careful and not let Cecilia suspect a thing."

Lady Arabelle nervously replied, "I must return to the ball."

"We will be right behind you to make sure no gentleman accosts you on your return." Had Devonton intentionally raised his voice for Graham to hear? Surely Landon had not given away their presence.

As the couple made to leave, Graham stepped out of the bushes, but before he moved too far out of reach, Landon placed a firm hand on his shoulder. "We still have to come to an understanding."

Shrugging off Landon's hand, Graham replied, "I'll be at my offices tomorrow. Please come by at your convenience, and I'll be happy to discuss the issue with you. I'll ensure you are granted entry."

Graham left to follow the couple, but they were already gone. He would have to summon Lucy to his office in the morning. He couldn't afford to wait til the afternoon for answers, especially since the woman could be extraordinarily stubborn when she wanted to be. If her activities were linked to her brother, it was doubtful she would be forthcoming with answers. Graham missed Matthew, for he was one of his most reliable agents. Had she received word about her brother's whereabouts on the Continent?

CHAPTER EIGHT

Graham swung his legs to the side of the bed and padded over to the mirror. He groaned at his reflection before beginning his morning ablutions.

"Mills, I intend to visit my fencing club today. I will need my equipment readied."

His valet, who had served him from his earliest memory, inquired, "My lord, will you be visiting this afternoon perhaps?"

In the mirror's reflection, Mills's usual deadpan face was scrunched, and his lips were moving, yet Graham could not hear a word. "Will there be a problem?"

Graham continued to watch as Mills busied himself laying out Graham's ensemble for the day. After a moment or two, the valet shook his head and replied, "No, my lord."

Turning to dress, Graham released a deep sigh. Mills was a horrible liar. "What is the issue?"

While Graham donned his breeches, shirt, and waistcoat, he waited for an answer. When none was forthcoming, he prompted, "Mills."

Mills relented and said, "My lord, you have not donned your fencing gear in… over five years. I would hazard to guess your uniform is…" He was clearly trying to find the right words so as not to offend his master. He smiled as he said, "…outdated."

Graham took pity on his valet and asked, "Are you saying my gear will no longer fit me?"

"My lord, I have your current measurements. It will only take me a day to procure a more appropriate uniform for you."

Graham tied his cravat, ready to be done with the conversation. "Very well. I will postpone my visit until tomorrow."

Mills released a breath of relief and rushed to say, "Thank you, my lord." He left the room as if the devil were on his coattails.

Alone, Graham stood in front of a full-length mirror. The corners of his lips turned down. Placing a forefinger on each temple and his thumb on the tops of his cheekbone, he stretched the skin upward. He really should smile more. Releasing his features, he shook his head and rolled his eyes heavenward.

Returning his gaze to the mirror, Graham ran his hand over the stretched material of his waistcoat, giving his midsection a solid pat only to have his hand sink into flesh instead of meeting hard muscle. Urgh. He had the form of a middle-aged man, not someone in his prime.

Bowing his head in disgrace, he made his way to the corner of his dressing room where he pulled up a floorboard to retrieve the family volume. As he flipped through the pages he had memorized as a young man, he wondered how similar the Hadfield volume would be to his own. He resolved to find out, but the only way to view the book would be with Theo's permission. Would she share her volume? If she did, would she demand to view his?

Graham disliked sharing. Always had. His sisters attributed it to him being the baby, but the reality was that he was never made to share. He always got his way. It was inconceivable to share something this valuable. Unless… he had ultimate trust in the individual.

The roughened edges cut into Graham's finger. The words on the pages reminded him of why he worked intently day in and day out. His role at the Home Office allowed him great access to resources and information to continue his family's duties to the Crown. Apparently, he had let the daily activities and missions of the Home Office consume him. Ashamed that he had neglected his true duties and responsibilities, he vowed to resume a more regimented practice schedule. He returned the book, placing it under the floorboard. He squared his shoulders and stood taller, fully resolved to begin his new scheme immediately.

Graham made his way down to the breakfast room only to be greeted with a scene he was unprepared for.

"Uncle Gam, Uncle Gam!" yelled Clare. His four-year-old niece jumped and reached out her arms, waiting for him to pick her up.

Graham leaned down as if to give the girl a hug, but at the last moment, he lifted her and threw her in the air. Clare squealed with delight. After the third toss, she yelled, "Down, Uncle Gam, down!"

Graham's eldest sister shook her head before she admonished, "Really, Graham, she just ate. Please put her down gently."

"Flora, why are you and your brood here this early?"

Flora's features fell. "Have you forgotten? You agreed

to watch over the children while Beckham and I journey to Paris for a fortnight."

He was mortified at his forgetfulness. Beckham, Flora's husband, a future duke and a diplomat, reminded Graham of his own papa, wholly consumed by duty and responsibilities. Graham was fully aware that while there was a playful side to his own personality, it had never presented itself and was always overshadowed by his intellect. Humor and fun were certainly never encouraged by his papa, as they were deemed a waste of time and effort.

"While I have some business to attend to this morning, I will be available to attend to the children later in the day."

Flora's maternal nature saw that she nursed her children and was loath to leave them without family nearby. "I'm not leaving them in your sole care. Good gracious, I'm not that silly. Nanny Jane and their governess, Miss Holden, will be here. Mama will arrive next week. She is currently attending a house party in the country, but I should think you can manage this week."

The tension in Graham's shoulders eased at the declaration that his sister had seen to it that he had the necessary help.

Graham rolled his eyes. "Flora, I'm more than happy to have the children here. I won't be gone long." Standing behind his sister, out of sight, he stuck out his tongue and crossed his eyes for the children to see.

Clare hid her giggle behind a napkin, while his six-year-old nephew, Maxwell, choked down a mouthful. "He said just a few, Mama. We will be fine. I can take care of us both. You have nothing to worry about."

Graham looked at Maxwell. He was a very serious young boy who reminded Graham of himself at his age.

Graham decided his nephew was in need of some fun, and he would dearly like to hear the boy laugh with joy like his little sister.

Perhaps he would take the children on an adventure after his meetings. Graham went to the sideboard to fill his plate. As he sat down with a plate piled high, he remembered his image in the mirror and sectioned off a third of the food before eating.

Nanny Jane came to escort the children up to his old schoolroom.

Graham looked up from his plate and said, "Thank you for trusting me with the children."

With what looked to be guilt, Flora replied, "The children adore you. However, you do tend to be preoccupied with work, and I hate to remind you, but… they were originally to stay with Abigail, but her children have the measles."

Graham was not surprised that the children were initially to stay with his other sister and her four children, but he was taken aback at the pang of guilt that shot through his chest at having forgotten about their stay.

Graham was never one to pay much attention to the details of his sisters' comings and goings. His papa had Graham accompany him to all his meetings, and Graham sat eagerly listening to the various arguments in the wings while the House of Lords was in session. Graham had taken a keen interest in all his papa's dealings, and it was around the age of thirteen that his papa had handed over the estate accounts.

Initially, upon receiving the new responsibilities, Graham had viewed them a challenge rather than a chore, but as his duties grew, his opinion of balancing the books changed. By the age of sixteen, he was assisting his papa in the debates at the House of Lords. Again, in the beginning, Graham enjoyed drafting propositions. Artfully developing speeches was stimulating. But his papa's delivery was lacking, and the Lords often overlooked the ingeniousness of the statements contained within.

It wasn't until Graham turned twenty that his papa began to take him to the Home Office. The culmination of his previous experiences were to ready him for the enormous responsibility of overseeing the government department, one he relished. Within a year, it was apparent to all who ran the office. Officially, Graham had not assumed the role until his papa's death three years ago.

Graham gave Flora a smile. "Nevertheless, I'm going to take this opportunity to get to know my nephew and niece."

"Thank you, Graham. I'll write to the children. Beckham and I are not to be gone for long, and Mama will arrive soon." Flora bussed him on the cheek and left Graham sitting alone at the table.

With the room quiet, he reflected on how isolated he was. Banishing any hint of ennui, Graham rose from the table. As he turned to leave, he caught sight of his image in the mirror. Had he selected the laurel green waistcoat or his valet? How was it that the mere sight of the color green had images of Lady Theodora flooding his mind? Unsettled, Graham left for the Home Office.

A STEADY CLICK-CLACK echoed in the hall. There was no doubt Lucy was about to enter, but what Graham questioned was why she was interested in Hadfield's file. The woman was far too intelligent for her own good, and Blake was far too lenient with her.

Lucy entered and walked directly to sit in one of the wingback chairs facing Graham's desk. "Archbroke, what on earth happened last night?"

"You are late." Graham made a show of looking at his pocket watch, "It is ten past the hour."

Relaxing back into the seat, Lucy rubbed her stomach. "You try to walk around with an extra fifteen pounds around your middle."

Graham's gaze faltered at her statement. Her gaze flickered to her husband, who stood guard by the door, and back to his midsection. Yes, the woman was far too perceptive, but way too kind to make a comment.

Breaking the sudden tense silence, Lucy forged on. "What did you say or do to upset Theo last night? Landon is certain her refusal to attend the theater tonight is your doing."

"I have absolutely no idea what you are ranting about. I thought you were here to request personnel files."

"Theo has decided not to attend any of the social engagements we have scheduled for the remainder of the week. How on earth is she going to meet her future husband if she continues… oh my goodness… I sound like Matthew!"

"Yes, I was about to say those words sound awfully similar to those your brother spouted last Season. I wouldn't worry about Lady Theo. There were plenty of eligible bachelors vying for her interest last night." Theo was alluring. Her wit and intelligence had piqued his interest. If she were to continue her family's service to the Crown, she would need those qualities and more. It shouldn't have rankled him that she had paid attention to others. He had observed her last night to assess her abilities and not because he couldn't keep his eyes off the woman.

The corner of Lucy's lips tipped up. "Archbroke,

perhaps you could champion her. Anyone worth his salt would know that if you endorse Theo, they would be a fool not to be interested."

"Champion Lady Theo?" Graham wanted no part in Lucy's scheme.

"Yes. If you were to dance with her, say a kind word or two here at the office or your club, I'm sure it would induce a few good men to seek out her company or perhaps try to court her."

"I have it on excellent authority that Hadfield is quite happy for Lady Theo to remain unwed this Season." Why did that fact please him?

"Wed? I mentioned courtship. Who said anything about getting married? Theo has been sequestered in the country too long. I think it is time for her to seek out new experiences… like receiving her first kiss."

Had Theo granted him her first kiss? He had acted upon impulse, convincing himself no one would think twice of a couple kissing in the gardens. Graham had been overjoyed when Theo responded, tentatively at first and then quite willingly. His taste buds tingled at the memory, a mix of citrus and honey.

Graham mumbled. "I'll be damned if she is to be kissed by another."

Lucy swung her feet, gaining momentum to stand. She leaned forward with her hands on the desk, her face mere inches away from his nose.

Lucy's eyebrows mirrored the letter *V*, and her cheeks were awash with color. "Oh, so you did kiss her last night! You rogue! How dare you take advantage of my best friend!"

Graham's eyes bore into Lucy's. He would not be bested by a woman who barely came up to his chin. Had he actually admitted to kissing Theo, or had the woman deciphered his features as easily as the complex codes he had assigned to her? He needed to be more careful when dealing with Lucy.

"It is complicated."

Lucy's triumphant smile was a prelude to what was sure to be a long list of demands. Without any preamble, she began. "You will seek out Hadfield's permission to court Theo in full view of the *ton.* There is to be no scandal."

"Court, Theo? For what purpose, exactly?"

Lucy hesitated, and he could see the worry in her eyes.

"I've known Theo practically all my life. She is troubled by some matter, and I believe it has to do with her papa's death. We have never kept secrets from one another; she is hiding *something.* Since her papa's passing, she has become secretive and far more reserved. Landon has informed me that for the past year she has been withdrawn and doesn't spend any time playing the pianoforte or fishing, her two utmost favorite activities. I've noticed that she is preoccupied with thoughts that, for some reason, she will not share with me. I must find out what is causing Theo to behave so out of character. If she is in some sort of trouble, I must help her. No. *We* must help her."

Graham knew precisely what was occupying Theo's thoughts and time. The manual Theo inherited made its recipient feel as though they must learn everything overnight. He knew from his own experience that being exposed to the whole book all at once without someone's guidance was overwhelming. The only way to succeed was to master each lesson before moving on to the next. Last night Theo's instincts proved her worthy of the volume.

Resolved to assist Theo in her training, he would have

to teach her how to walk the fine line between deception and truth when dealing with those closest to her. There were some in his employ that appeared to be able to deceive without care; however, he despised lying and deception. His solution had been to isolate himself from those who cared about him. It was the same technique Theo had adopted.

Perhaps it was time to employ a new strategy.

Agreeing with Lucy immediately would only raise her suspicions. "I'm sure that as soon as she settles into town hours and its activities, the Theo you are accustomed to will return. There is no need for the appearance of a courtship."

"Theo hated her first Season. She would do anything to escape town and return to the country. You must assist me in convincing her to stay and find out what is causing her to behave so strangely." Lucy might be a brilliant strategist but not better than he.

"Fine. I will agree to seek out Hadfield today, and *if* Theo accepts my courtship, I will do my best to help her in any way I can. But in doing this, you must cease making inquiries. Are we clear?"

There was no *if* in Graham's mind. Theo would immediately see the advantage of the appearance of a courtship, wouldn't she? He would present her with the facts. That would surely convince Theo to accept his guidance and assistance to train in town. But if she was anything like Lucy, it might not be an easy task. He would have to rely on his instincts. He had to admit that when it came to the female race, his perceptions were not always on point.

"You must make her accept the courtship. She is my dearest friend, and you are the only one with the wits and resources to figure out her troubles. There is no one better to help Theo."

"Do you trust me? If so, tell me we are in agreement, and you will no longer involve yourself."

Lucy conceded, "I will give you two weeks. Don't disappoint me, Archbroke."

"Two weeks! How do you suppose I'll be able to succeed where you have failed?"

Lucy smirked as she turned to leave. "You are the genius, not I." She rounded the table and placed a chaste kiss on Graham's cheek.

With her hand on Blake's arm, Lucy turned and smiled. "I expect a full report in a fortnight." And with a giggle, she left his office, escorted by her husband.

Graham mumbled, "I'm sure she's been waiting all these years to say those words back to me."

As Graham leaned back in his chair, he began to devise a plan. He concluded that this project would require more than a well-planned strategy. What he needed was to obtain more knowledge and skill in dealing with females. He reached for parchment and quill and quickly drafted a note to the one woman he knew would have the experience to aid him, Madame Sinclair. She had worked with him over the years, assisting in obtaining critical information, as men were rather boastful in the boudoir.

At a scratch at his door, Graham commanded, "Enter."

Lord Waterford, one of Graham's most reliable and accomplished agents, entered. "Hadfield is in the library, my lord."

Graham pressed his seal to the parchment. He gave the missive to Waterford. "Have this delivered to Madame S immediately."

Raising an eyebrow, Waterford took the document and placed it in his breast pocket. "Certainly. Am I to await a reply?"

Graham nodded in the affirmative and strode through the door to meet Landon. He was not particularly looking forward to the discussion with the man but wanted to have it done with.

~

GRAHAM FOUND Landon lounging in one of the chairs near the window bay. He looked somewhat relaxed and oddly comfortable, as if he had frequented the office often.

Without removing his gaze from the windows, Landon said in a deadly tone, "I should call you out."

Graham did need to improve his stealth if Landon had detected him with such ease. He would have been murdered if he had been on a mission. Cursing himself for his laziness, he proceeded to approach Landon.

"Why would you call me out?"

"For…"

Deciding it was best to get the deed over and done with, he asked, "Hadfield, will you grant me the honor to court Lady Theo?"

"No."

Graham had not expected such a quick negative response.

"As I informed you last evening, I intend to spend a great deal of time with Theo."

"You are to stay away from Theo, Archbroke, or you and I shall meet at dawn."

"Neither of those alternatives works for me." Graham desperately searched his mind to recall everything noted in Landon's file. He held out what he considered an olive branch. "What if I could assist you in your efforts for universal suffrage?"

"There is nothing worth trading Theo's happiness for."

"Have you asked Theo what her wishes are with respect to spending time with me?"

"No. However, I'm certain it is in her best interest not to associate with you. Not only is the position you hold here hazardous, but I sense you are a danger to her. I will not have her endure more pain or heartache. She has suffered enough these past years."

Such strong convictions and intuition. It was a great shame that old Hadfield had not followed tradition and left the book to Landon. A man like that would be a great asset to the Crown.

"What, may I ask, are your specific concerns regarding my character? I can assure you I'm a gentleman and well-respected."

Quick as a whip, Landon replied, "You failed to mention honorable, trustworthy…"

Before Landon could disparage him further, Graham uttered, "I can assure you there are hundreds of men who rely upon me daily to ensure the safety and well-being of those they care for. I take on that responsibility very seriously, and I would take the same care with Lady Theo."

Graham sensed he had made a small crack in Landon's wall and, taking full advantage, pressed on. "I promise you Lady Theo would be my number one priority over all other matters."

Landon searched his features, perhaps for a sign of lying. Since it was the truth, Graham was positive Landon would only see clarity and determination.

Landon growled, "Make sure she is."

Success! But it was a tall order he had set for himself.

Why promise such a thing—to place someone above all else? Graham had a department to run, agents to deploy, the mystery of Devonton's abduction last year to solve, and now his own niece and nephew to watch over.

What was I thinking?

Obviously, his priorities were in a muddle, pushed aside by the image of lush lips paired with emerald-green eyes that fairly danced with intelligence and daring.

CHAPTER NINE

Theo leaned against her door. Sneaking in and out of the town house without using the servants' entrance, which was always bustling with activity, was proving far more challenging than she had initially expected. She began to strip off the greatcoat that hid her male attire. Someone was approaching. Frustrated, she mumbled, "I need to find a maid to assist me. Where are those new gowns?"

Through her door, Landon said, "Theo. I need to speak with you."

"Landon, you are supposed to have a footman deliver a message summoning me to find you in some room or other, not seek me out yourself."

"I'll wait for you in my study."

"Good gracious, what could be that important? Lucy will be here shortly, and we are to pay a visit to the modiste."

"Lady Devonton can wait in the drawing room."

As his footsteps faded, Theo hastily hid her breeches and lawn shirt and donned one of her more practical day dresses that allowed the luxury of forgoing stays. Not wanting Lucy to wait too long, Theo walked briskly into Landon's study.

Landon peered up over his spectacles, but his quill continued to move as he completed his notes. Theo began mentally listing all she was going to order from Emma. She needed clothing more appropriate for her training. Longer breeches would be preferable to knee-high ones and lawn shirts more fitted to her body. Standing before Landon, she began tapping her fingers against her leg. She would need to speak to Emma about the design of the garments.

Landon removed his eyeglasses. "Theo, I have given Archbroke my permission to court you."

"Beg your pardon?" She must have misheard him. Lord Archbroke was going to court her?

"Archbroke asked, and I said yes. Do you have any objections to him courting you?"

Theo's brain screamed; this was his plan to arrange everything! It was only a courtship and not a betrothal, nothing to be concerned about. The idea of spending more time in Lord Archbroke's company set her heart aflutter. Theo's lips curved into a smile. It was a rather smart move on his part. She glanced at Landon, who was patiently waiting for her response. He looked like a man undecided, which was not a common occurrence for Landon.

"I'm certainly flattered by his interest, seeing as we were only introduced last evening."

"If you would prefer to have more time… to meet other gentlemen, I will inform Archbroke that…"

Theo placed her hands behind her and rolled to the tips of her toes and bounced. "No, no. I look forward to getting better acquainted with Lord Archbroke. Lucy holds him in high esteem, and I trust her judgment." Theo rolled back onto her heels and waited.

The thud of Landon's left index finger hitting his desk echoed through the room. Theo met hazel eyes that were alert and searching.

Finally, Landon ceased his tapping and released a sigh. "Then I will invite Archbroke to accompany us to the theater later this evening."

"Actually, I sent a note round to Lucy this morning informing her that Aunt Henri and I would not be attending."

"I'm sure Lucy will understand if you change your mind. Mama can stay at home if she wishes. I've convinced my younger brother to join us this evening."

"Christopher?" Why was Christopher taking her aunt's place? Was Landon suspicious of Lord Archbroke's apparent interest?

"Yes. He can't hide from the *ton* forever."

"Well, Aunt Henri will be delighted at the news." At least one of them was excused from the horrid playacting.

THEO EYED Lucy's handsome footman as he assisted her into the coach.

As soon as the door closed, Theo asked, "Does Evan go everywhere with you?"

Lucy shifted so Theo could sit next to her on the forward-facing seat. "Oh yes. Blake would never let me out of the house without either Evan or John accompanying me. Has Hadfield not assigned you your own footmen?"

"Landon is still getting accustomed to the title himself. I'm not sure he is even aware I'm still without a lady's maid."

Lucy whipped about to face her. "What? How on earth do you dress?"

"So far, Aunt Henri and I have made do with assisting each other. Aunt Henri doesn't want to burden Landon with the additional expense."

Resettling back into her corner, Lucy said, "I'll have Blake talk to Landon."

"Really? Would Blake do that? Did Blake hire the servants that aid you?"

"Oh, no! Evan and John have been in my employ for years, and Carrington, well, you know she has been with me since we were young. The three of them came with me when I married Blake."

Theo's brows furrowed. "I believe I would prefer to be the one to decide upon who will assist me." With the restrictions of the mark, finding a maid would be a challenge. A maid could assist only once Theo had covered the mark. It would be an unusual request but an absolute. But how to begin her search?

"I shall speak to Evan and John and see if they are aware of anyone who might be available to become your footman. Carrington might also assist in identifying someone suited to be your maid. Once we have identified them, I'll have Blake approach Landon. Does that sound like a satisfactory plan to you?"

"That would be grand." Theo threw her arms around her and gave her a hug as in their youth. It was a relief to share some of the burden.

The coach rolled to a stop. As they alit, Lucy instructed Evan, "While we visit Emma, contact Archbroke and ask that he arrange for two footmen and a lady's maid for Theo."

Theo must have heard wrong. She thought Lucy had said she would speak with Lord Devonton, not Lord Archbroke. However, considering Lord Archbroke's position, he would have a larger pool of resources to fill the positions. She trusted Lucy. Lucy trusted Lord Archbroke. Theo would have to have faith in Lord Archbroke and his capabilities. Certainly they would be required to rely upon each other, but the man caused Theo's brain and body to react in a way they never had before.

Rushing into the store, Theo found Emma in the back room.

"Emma, I need to place another order. I require..." Theo stopped speaking when Emma put a finger to her mouth. Emma turned to look over her shoulder and shook her head. Lucy was peeking into the backroom.

Emma made a vague response. "Lady Theo, it's me pleasure, and me cousins and sisters consider it an honor."

"Do you think any of them would want to be my lady's maid?" Perhaps, her request would prevent Lucy from suspecting anything further.

Wide-eyed, Emma nodded. "Me li'l sis, Bessie, will be squealing like a pig as soon as I tell her." A frown marred Emma's features. "Guessin' now I'll have to call her Wallace if she is to be a lady's maid." Lowering her voice to a whisper, she continued, "It's a great honor to be in the service of one who bears the mark."

"You know of the mark?"

"Aye. Me whole family has been servin' in one way or another, m'lady."

Flouncing into the back room, Lucy asked, "What are the two of you doing back here? Are you conspiring against me?"

Theo laughed. "Why on earth would we be doing that?"

"Theo, you were always the best at pranks. So much so both our brothers dared not pull one over on us, for they knew the retribution it would cause." Lucy turned to Emma, and conspiratorially said, "She looks innocent, but in that head of hers is a mastermind."

"Mastermind? Not me. You are, by far, the better strategist. Is there a soul who can beat you at chess?"

Lucy linked her arm and drew her back to the front room. "Surprisingly, only one."

"Who?"

"Archbroke."

Lucy's answer should not have surprised Theo. Both her papa and brother had made entries in the volume referencing Lord Archbroke's genius.

Lucy fingered various materials. "What did you think of him?"

Theo asked, "Of whom?"

Staring at her, Lucy replied, "Archbroke, silly. He seemed rather taken with you last evening."

Reviewing the events of the night, Theo couldn't recall any interaction with Lord Archbroke that would have led Lucy to believe such a thing. "Why would you say such nonsense?"

Without hesitation, Lucy answered, "Archbroke asked you to dance. He never dances. Plus he kept a keen eye on you for the rest of the evening."

"He was a fine enough dancer."

Lucy turned and stared. "Fine? Pray tell, why are your cheeks so rosy?"

Theo raised her palm to her cheek. The heat was undeniable. Would she have to be on guard with everyone going forward? The idea did not sit well with her. Why had her body heated at the mere mention of Lord Archbroke?

Emma interjected, saving her from answering Lucy's prying questions. "Lady Devonton, 'ow long before you're off to 'alford Castle?"

Lucy proceeded to pick out and hand Emma the material that would be added to her current gowns to allow for more breathing room. "I hope to stay through the Season. Although Blake is eager to return as soon as possible, he wishes to oversee the changes to the nursery and ensure that the other renovations are completed before the little tyke arrives."

At Lucy's inflection, Theo eyed her best friend. Pregnancy agreed with Lucy. She was like a walking beacon of happiness. Having known her since childhood, Theo attributed Lucy's radiance to Blake and their growing child.

Would she ever be lucky enough to find a husband whom she could love and trust? Her inheritance would require someone understanding, yet if she were to continue the legacy, she would need to produce an heir. Among her confused thoughts, an image of Lord Archbroke filled Theo's mind. Wavy honey-blond hair, Roman nose paired with ice-cool blue eyes. Eyes that held warmth nevertheless and whose color flustered Theo to no end. The appearance of a courtship would mean she would be spending time with Lord Archbroke. A lot more time. Her nerves soared with excitement at the mere idea of being in his company. She needed to remember that he had most likely contrived the courtship to allow him to assess her ability to perform her duties to the Crown, not—as Lucy had hinted—that he might be interested in her as a woman.

Distracted, Theo rubbed a velvet in the same shade as Lord Archbroke's eyes.

"That would be an excellent color on you, Theo."

Eyes on me? Focus. The woman said color. Not the man or his eyes.

"Emma, don't you think Theo would look splendid in that blue velvet?"

"Yes, Lady Devonton, a very complimentary color for Lady Theo. I'll 'ave a dress made up immediately."

After spending another hour selecting material, lace, and buttons, Theo was anxious to talk to Emma about placing the order for the items she needed. However, it seemed that Lucy was intent on not allowing them a moment of privacy.

Resigned she would not be able to talk with Emma about her second wardrobe, Theo asked, "Would you be able to send word to Bessie requesting her to attend me today?"

Emma's eye's widened, "Aye, m'lady. I'll tell me da and mum, and Bessie will be ready."

As THE COACH approached the Hadfield town house, Lucy stated, "Theo, I'll not accompany you in. I must locate my husband. I hope to have your retinue assembled and escorted here later this afternoon. I'll ensure Wallace arrives early enough to make sure you are ready for the theater tonight."

"You are truly the best friend anyone could ever ask for. I'll never be able to repay you, and I'm in your debt."

Lucy grabbed Theo by the shoulders. "You are like my sister, and I'd do anything for you." Forcing Theo to look her in the eye, Lucy blurted, "If you are in any kind of trouble, you know you can trust me, and I'll help you any way I can."

Meekly casting her gaze down, Theo replied, "I know."

"Theo, you are keeping secrets from me, and I desperately want to help, but you first have to tell me—"

Theo shook her head. "I can't, but I do appreciate your concern."

"I'm worried about you. When or if you are able, I hope you will confide in me."

"I love you like a sister. There is nothing for you to worry about." Theo gave Lucy a quick embrace and threw open the coach door before jumping out, only slowing her pace when she was out of shouting distance, for Lucy was one not to let matters lie. It would only be a matter of time before Lucy pried the secret from her. But Lucy was not marked.

CHAPTER TEN

Blake and Graham relaxed in the billiard room at Brooks's. A small impish hooded figure entered the room. Lucy. She closed and locked the door behind her. Before she even lifted her hood, Graham muttered, "Good Lord, woman. Is there no place you dare not enter?"

He turned to Blake. "I can't believe you allow her to venture in here."

With one eyebrow raised, Blake replied, "Allow?"

Ignoring Graham, Lucy approached her husband as he stepped back from the table. Blake smiled down at his wife as she placed her hands on his chest and raised her face for a kiss. Blake bent and kissed her as if Graham were not present.

"Good God, man. The woman is already pregnant."

Not breaking the kiss, Blake held up a hand to silence Graham. Finally, Lucy came up for air and spoke. "My love, I was hoping you could inform Hadfield of the need to have two extra footmen on staff and…"

They were a curious couple. Among close friends and

family, they were free with their speech and blatantly flaunted their physical attraction to each other. To love and be loved by another with such abandon was something Graham secretly wished for.

Blake cut off his wife's speech and kissed her with urgency combined with tenderness. It was as if Blake's sole intent was to completely wipe all thoughts from his wife's mind. To accomplish that with Lucy would be a monumental task, but Blake was clearly up to the challenge.

Graham's thoughts shifted once more to Theo's soft lips, her slight waist beneath his hands. Clearing both his mind and throat, he croaked, "Would either of you care to show some self-control?"

"Sweetheart, Archbroke and I have already discussed the matter with Hadfield. John is on his way as we speak to introduce the new staff to Morris." Blake's voice was a tad rough. Lucy was not the only one affected by the kiss.

Still looking slightly dazed, Lucy said, "But I haven't even informed you of Wallace or..."

With a cheeky grin, Blake gazed into his wife's eyes. How was it that he was able to communicate with her with a mere look? Curious and a tad envious, Graham continued to observe the couple.

"Well, I guess I'll return home then." Lucy lowered her hood once more and headed for the door.

"Before you leave, Lucy, I will remind you of your promise to me not to interfere," Graham said.

"I'll postpone any inquires for two weeks and not a day more, as agreed."

Blake eyed his wife. "What the devil are the two of you speaking of? What inquiries?"

"Lucy is worried about Theo. She asked for my assistance in determining the cause of what Lucy has termed Theo's odd behavior."

Lucy raised her hood and looked up at Blake. Concern clearly reflected in her features. "I confronted Theo today, and while she did not share her troubles, she acknowledged she was keeping secrets from me. Secrets! We have never held secrets from one another, yet she claimed she could not discuss this matter with *me*!"

Blake slid a glance Graham's way. "Place some trust in Archbroke for the next fortnight." The glare Graham received was a clear message that he was not to fail in determining the source of Theo's troubles.

It did not go unnoticed by Graham that while Blake was undeniably giving him an order, he had simultaneously allayed further arguments with Lucy by placing his hand on her lower back and rubbing in small circles. Comforted by the gesture, Lucy nodded her consent.

Blake accompanied Lucy to the door. "Archbroke, we will have to continue our game another time. We will see you later this evening."

The love and devotion Blake showed Lucy was so rarely seen amongst his peers. Was he capable of such intense emotions? The couple's marriage appeared to be founded upon trust, not mere convenience or pure physical attraction. Blake clearly valued Lucy's opinions and intellect. A partnership. What should Graham seek out? A partner or a wife deemed suitable by the *ton*?

Graham glanced at his pocket watch. A quarter past two. Blast! The children. How had the hours slipped by? Ices would surely have Max and Clare forgiving him for neglecting them. He would invite the children to dine with him before he headed out for the theater. It was unconventional. It would be nice not to eat in solitude. Perhaps he would make it a regular occurrence while they resided with him.

CHAPTER ELEVEN

Theo scanned the crowd. The lower seats were filling quickly with ladies in brightly colored gowns, some that were suspiciously low-cut. At the last moment, Lucy had decided their group should watch the performance from Graham's box. It was situated next to the royal box and was significantly larger than both Hadfield's and Devonton's. The possibility of being this close in proximity to the prince regent himself made Theo nervous. Which was ridiculous since the man wasn't even present this evening. Theo's shoulders sagged as the weight of her responsibilities fell upon her.

"Theo, you look divine tonight." Graham's baritone voice startled her.

Her nose tickled. Did she detect the scent of lemons? It wasn't tart or acidic, but sweet. Odd. The smell reminded her of Gunter's ices. She stared at his lips. Would they taste of lemon?

His lips were moving. "Enjoy the performance, and we will discuss how to proceed on the morrow."

Theo rapidly blinked. "Proceed?"

At her question the corner of his mouth turned upward. "With our courtship." The lopsided grin belied his dry tone.

She narrowed her eyes. The arrogance of the man. He spoke to her as if she were a child. What a prat!

Starting at the very top of his head, Theo slowly lowered her gaze inch by inch. She stalled at his lips and again at the sight of his lavender cravat adorned with white miniature daisies. She continued her perusal. Graham appeared unfazed, while her pulse quickened and her stays restricted her breathing.

Graham chuckled. "*You are* in agreement a courtship would allow us to get better acquainted, are you not?"

Theo responded with, "Indeed it would. However, I've yet to confirm it is you whom I seek."

She would not trust him or accept this faux courtship until he revealed his mark to her. She raked her gaze over him one more time. Where would his mark reside? On his chest? Her palm itched to explore. Instead of reaching for him, she ran her hand down her skirt and her gaze met Graham's. His blue eyes twinkled with mischief.

He brought his gloved hand out from behind his back and gestured to their seats. "I will provide you all the reassurance you need, Theo. Patience."

Again that tone. She didn't care for it. Not one bit.

The lights dimmed, and each member of their party moved to take their seats. Flanked by Graham on one side and Landon on the other, the icy greeting Landon gave Graham did not escape Theo's notice.

Why had Landon given Graham permission to court her if he indeed did not like the man?

The curtains were raised and the lights shone bright on the stage. Theo caught Graham looking at her. Interestingly, his gaze was fixed on the spot along her neck he had nibbled previously.

Theo shifted to adjust her skirts and whispered, "Meet me in my chambers later tonight. I'll leave the window slightly ajar for you."

Graham cleared his throat. "As you wish."

Theo returned her attention to the play but was conscious that Graham's gaze remained on her. Her skin tingled from the intense heat radiating off him. She shifted restlessly. Graham discreetly placed his hand on the underside of her skirts. His movements were slow and intentional. Graham's palm began to graze along her thigh. She fought the urge to fidget. Was he testing her ability to remain calm? His hand hovered over the blade strapped to her thigh. She slowed her breathing as instructed in the manual. The handle of her dagger dug into her as he patted it twice before he removed his hand.

Graham leaned closer and whispered, "Perfect. Well placed."

She should be outraged, but Graham's praise had instilled a deep-seated sense of pride and confidence Theo hadn't experienced since the death of her brother.

She caught Lucy watching them closely, brows creased. It was when the curtains closed that Theo realized she had not conversed with either Graham or Landon throughout the play.

Landon rose and guided Theo to the foyer to await their carriage.

Graham pulled Theo aside, gently maneuvering her away from her cousin. "I will see you soon."

There was a roughness to his voice. Was he eager to be alone with her? The gleam in his eyes cast a spell of excitement over Theo.

"I will be by shortly; however, we must settle the matter posthaste as I have another appointment this evening."

In utter disbelief, Theo nodded. A vexing image of Graham visiting his mistress floated before her. She was a ninny for thinking he might have any romantic or lustful intensions toward her. Why had she asked him to come to her bedroom? He wasn't eager for her company. It was another woman's chambers he sought out.

She reminded herself that theirs was to be a false courtship, arranged out of duty and responsibility. It would do her good not to entertain any romantic ideas even if she had spent the past hour dreaming of Graham touching and kissing her as he had at the Fairmont ball.

Drat. She was a fool. Reflecting upon the events of the evening prior, her first kiss was probably the result of Graham's quick actions to avoid detection and not out of desire for her.

~

GRAHAM PRESSED himself against the stonework of Hadfield house. His agent's report had made mention that Theo had appeared extremely nervous upon her descent. The narrow ledge was indeed a tricky feat. Balancing on his tiptoes, he pried open Theo's window. He would have to instruct her to widen her stance and distribute her weight the next time she exited her third-story room to decrease the chance of her breaking her pretty little neck.

He slipped through the window and scanned the room. A fire illuminated an empty bed, the counterpane neatly folded, ready for Theo to retire. The sitting area housed a cozy settee, perfect for reading.

"Theo?" he whispered. "Are you here?"

As he turned to close the window, the point of a blade

pressed into his side just below his rib cage. His dormant training resurfaced. He twisted his assailant's hand into a position that would break the wrist should he desire it. The blade clattered to the floor.

"Ow...," Theo squeaked.

"Obviously, we will need to practice your hand-to-hand combat skills."

He did not release her but instead pulled her closer and began to rub the wrist on which he had inflicted pain. Her muscles relaxed, and she leaned into the caress.

Then she stiffened and pulled away. "Archbroke, please reveal your mark. Then you may leave and attend to whatever or whoever awaits you."

Graham started at the edge in her voice.

Not wanting to release her just yet, he closed the gap between their bodies and tilted his head toward those lips beckoning to him.

Theo swiveled and twisted her hands, reversing their positions, and Graham found his arm held tightly behind his back. Her grip was stronger than he had imagined her capable of. Still, she was no match for him.

Graham rolled his shoulder forward and down, pulling Theo off balance. With her grip loosened, he pulled his elbow closer to his side and swiftly turned, bringing his nose within inches of hers. Her breathing had quickened, and she stared at him wide-eyed. Graham edged out of reach.

Did he want to continue this game of cat and mouse? No.

She had learned much from the volume, but she still had much to learn. Theo would be a quick study. His blood pressure had soared at her touch, bringing to life muscles that had laid dormant. Yes. He would enjoy assessing and assisting her to develop the necessary skills required for missions.

Theo moved forward, ready to attack again.

He held out a hand. "Stop."

Graham removed his coat and waistcoat.

It wasn't until he pulled out his shirttails that she seemed to find her voice. "What are you doing?"

Not answering, Graham proceeded to remove his shirt. Glad the room remained dimly lit, he used his shirt to cover his midsection while he turned to show her his upper arm. She closely examined his mark. Had she doubted his identity? Or was she merely curious as to its placement?

Her hand balled into a fist at her side. His skin tingled with the desire to feel the tips of her fingers trace the mark that was identical to hers. His breath hitched. He craved her physically. He uncurled her hand and placed it on his triceps. Her tender touch was like heaven. The pads of her fingers pressed gently against the mark. His arm twitched, and the minx smiled up at him. Even in the dimly lit room, her eyes sparkled with mischief.

She took a step closer as the tip of her tongue darted out to moisten her lips. Her hand began to trail down his forearm, and she leaned in to peer at the outline of his inked skin. Theo's lips were a hairbreadth away. What was the vixen up to? There was only so much restraint he could muster. His other arm tensed, squeezing his shirt closer against soft rolls instead of pressing into his once lean and muscled stomach. He withdrew from her. Not meeting Theo's perplexed expression, he dressed.

"Did I do something wrong?" Theo asked.

In a harsh tone born out of embarrassment and frustration, Graham replied, "No. I will call on you tomorrow."

Graham climbed out of her window and disappeared

from Theo's sight. Landing perfectly on a tree branch below, he swung down to fall to the ground, landing on his feet. He might be carrying extra pounds, but he remained nimble as a cat.

Theo was peeking out, a puzzled frown on her face. There was no trellis or tree branch high enough to allow him to gain access to her window. He whispered, "From the rooftop."

Theo's gaze went immediately to the roofline, and her eyes widened.

Proud to have impressed her with his prowess, he made his way to his coach. He might be rusty, but he hadn't entirely lost his skills! Now on to his next task.

To seek advice from a woman who had never failed him.

CHAPTER TWELVE

Graham had not ventured to Madame Sinclair's establishment in years. Assessing the well-kept town house that bordered Grosvenor Square, it hadn't changed. But had its mistress? He took two steps at a time.

"Paget, is your mistress in?"

The butler patiently waited for Graham to provide a code word. That word would dictate where he was to be escorted.

Graham cleared his throat and croaked, "Rahab," which gave him full access to roam as he wished, unescorted.

Nodding, Paget opened the door and allowed Graham to proceed. Graham walked through the empty foyer past a room arranged with card tables, each currently occupied by men with luscious courtesans adorning their laps.

The sight of the beautiful and willing women reminded him that he had been celibate for months. Balancing his duties for the Crown and as Home Secretary had left little time for his former mistress. When she sought more from their relationship, he had ended it without hesitation.

A lovely, curvaceous woman approached dressed in emerald-green, her gown the same shade as Lady Theo's eyes.

The young woman dropped into a deep curtsy, obviously for the sole purpose of allowing Graham to view her ample bosom. "My lord."

Placing a finger under her chin, Graham raised her face to him and with gentle pressure upward indicated he wished her to stand.

"You are extremely tempting. However, not this evening. Please inform your mistress I will meet her in the library."

With a pout, she turned to do Graham's bidding.

He had been a lad of twelve the first time his papa led him to the library and instructed him to remain in the room until his return. Graham had occupied himself with the books on the shelf, whose subjects ranged from Greek mythology to the ever-popular Minerva romance novels. Among the volumes, he had found various titillating instructional manuals written in foreign languages with detailed pictorials. He had accompanied his papa on many occasions before the day came that his papa informed him he was to meet Madame Sinclair in a chamber. Graham had turned sixteen a fortnight prior. He was taken aback to find not a woman of middling years but in fact a fresh-faced beauty in her midtwenties.

What had his papa intoned when Graham had inquired as to why he was meeting with Madame Sinclair?

Because a gentleman always treats his wife with respect. He does not burden her with his baser needs.

Graham groaned. His dear papa's life lessons had not quite weathered the test of time.

He settled in front of the fire, and a memory of Madame Sinclair, dressed only in a red silk robe, flashed before him. She had immediately taken in that he had removed his coat, waistcoat, cravat, and shoes.

"I see you have made yourself comfortable."

"I have, indeed. I would like to clarify the purpose of my visit this evening."

Madame Sinclair let out a sultry laugh.

Raising one of the instructional volumes Graham had found in the library, he said, "I'd like to discuss the merits and downfalls of the various scenarios within this volume with you. I do not wish to perform any at this point in time."

It had been the beginning and the foundation of their relationship. Twice a month Graham would visit, and they would review and discuss various books found in the library including volumes on Roman history and the serialized romances. Each enjoyed the visits and lively discussions, and throughout the year, slowly, Madame Sinclair had breached Graham's personal boundaries.

It began with simple caresses and progressed as he endeavored to learn every aspect he possibly could. Madame Sinclair was more than willing to indulge Graham in his various requests since she was privy to a side of him that no other was allowed to see. A side of him no one suspected existed. He enjoyed her company and exploration for three years.

When it became apparent that her feelings for him went further than they should, Madame Sinclair was the one who firmly reestablished the boundaries of their relationship. Although they ended their intimate relationship, they continued to correspond, and Madame Sinclair proved to be one of Graham's most valuable informants.

Madame Sinclair entered the library, and Graham rose. "You were always fond of this room."

In her eyes he saw that her love for him still burned brightly. A heaviness settled in his chest, for he could not return the sentiment. Instead, he attempted to smile as he replied, "I spent a great many hours in here."

"You did, indeed. Although the hours you spent here were not wasted."

With a genuine smile, he reached out to embrace her. As he moved his hand down her back and over her form, it registered in his mind that her body had matured and was now softer and more luscious. Instead of stirring his body as it might have once, Graham stepped back only to see her eyes flutter shut. He didn't want to cause her pain, yet her features told him that was exactly what he was doing.

"In your note, you mentioned you needed my assistance with a personal matter…" She arched an eyebrow as she raked her gaze over his body. "I'm not willing at this time to renegotiate the terms of our relationship. Perhaps it's only a temporary condition…"

"Josie." He had not spoken her given name in years. Had she shared her real name with another? Did she have a lover? The loneliness in her gaze told him she had not.

Graham reached out for her hand and led her to a chair. As she arranged her blue silk robe, he meandered over to the fireplace, placing distance between them. He did not want to hurt the woman who had passionately schooled him in the art of lovemaking.

Without preamble, he blurted, "I need your help in dealing with a female."

"My dear, I can reassure you that you have all the skills necessary to deal with any woman."

"It has been years since I've conversed with a woman at length." Graham frowned as he admitted, "In fact, you are the only woman with whom I've ever truly discussed matters… on any subject, really."

Deciding to get to the matter at hand, he continued, "I need to gain the trust of a gently bred woman. She is currently extremely remote, if not chilling, and I believe rather overwhelmed with a task her deceased papa has asked of her."

Pacing, he ran a hand through his hair multiple times.

"Archbroke, will you cease moving about and speak plainly?"

How was he to explain to Josie his dilemma without hurting her feelings? "I'm at a loss as to how to convince the lady she should let her guard down around me while simultaneously instilling the importance of keeping all others at bay."

Her heart was in her gaze as she spoke. "You are the most intelligent man in England. You have an innate ability to assess a situation or individual and deem what is needed to accomplish your goals. What is it about this particular woman that has you behaving with such uncertainty?"

He ran his hand through his hair once more, as if it would delay considering the effect Theo had on his mind or body—let alone his soul.

Josie's voice cracked. "Offer her everything of yourself. Acknowledge she is her own person, listen to her wishes, grant her freedom of choice, and most importantly, be true to your heart."

Graham was still trying to decipher the meaning of her words when the door softly clicked shut. He wanted to track Josie down, make her explain, but he knew instinctively she needed time alone.

What had she meant by *most importantly, be true to your heart*?

He had lusted after women. He had admired them for

their intellect. But his heart, always protected and untouched, had nothing to do with it.

CHAPTER THIRTEEN

Graham strode into the breakfast room where Max sat ramrod, straight in his chair. Quite elegantly, the boy placed a bite on his fork and delivered it into his small mouth.

"Max, why don't we go riding this morning?"

The child was a model of perfect dining etiquette. He was six! He should be playing with his food or at least rebelling at what was served.

With a regal turn of his head, he said, "Uncle Graham, I have studies to attend to this morning, and I don't wish to leave Clare behind."

Evidently, the boy needed to learn how to behave like a six-year-old. Graham himself had been mature and had taken his responsibilities as the heir very seriously. His papa, however, was not as serious in nature and often had him gallivanting about town.

Graham stuffed another sausage in his mouth and talked around it. "I had no intention of leaving Clare behind. She will ride with me."

"You really shouldn't speak with food in your mouth,

Uncle Graham, you could…"

Pretending to choke, Graham started to cough and pound on his chest. Max bounded out of his chair to smack his uncle on the back with his small but solid fist. Snaking his other arm out, Graham reached around and grabbed the boy and began to tickle him until he finally let out a squeal of laughter.

"Uncle Gam, I want to play too!" Clare yelled as she entered the dining room. She jumped into the fray, and Graham quickly had her giggling with laughter too.

Morris had quietly moved the furniture out of the way to allow the three of them to roll about without injury.

How long had it been since Graham had genuinely laughed?

His sisters had left many years prior when they married, and three years ago his mama had moved to the dower house to grieve in solitude, leaving Graham and the servants to reside alone in this large town house or his sprawling country residence in Devon.

Both children clutched their sides and released wails of laughter. Satisfied they had had enough, Graham put them on their feet and returned to his breakfast.

Nervously Max looked over at Graham and confessed, "Uncle Graham, I've only been seated on a horse once before, and… that ended in disaster. Mama hasn't allowed me to ride again."

Not able to ride? Why had Beckham not ensured his son was proficient in what his own papa referred to as the gentlemanly pursuits? What other activities has Max been missing? A crazy image of Graham being the one to escort Max to Madame Sinclair's establishment when the time came brought a smirk to his face.

"Well, your mama is not about. I shall ride with you until you feel comfortable to ride alone."

Max, full of excitement, nodded eagerly but then slid a glance at his sister.

"How about I arrange for Clare to ride in the landau with Nanny Jane?"

Clare sat up straight in her chair, indignant. "Uncle Gam, I don't want to ride in the lanoo with Nanny Jane. I want to ride properly too."

"Hmm." The stubborn set of Clare's chin had Graham biting back a smile. "How about you ride in the landau while I ride with Max? Then we will have a footman take Nanny Jane home, and you, my dear, will ride with me upon my Arabian."

With strawberry jam covering one cheek and her wide grin, Clare jumped down from the chair and climbed into Graham's lap. She wrapped her chubby arms around his neck to give him a hug. Graham's heart did a flip. Apparently, it was not immune to at least one girl. Clare had his heart. Images of his own future children flashed before his eyes.

Children with dark hair and green eyes.

"We could walk faster than this," Theo complained.

Chuckling, Landon flicked the reins, prompting the horses to once again move forward. His focus remained on the traffic in front of them. "Mama was informed by Lady Jersey that it is critical I escort you to the park and parade you about. All the eligible bachelors require an opportunity to take in your visage."

"Since you have already given Archbroke your permission to court me, I find this an utter waste of our time."

"Well, Archbroke failed to appear this morning to request the outing, so I'm doing my duty."

Theo mumbled, "He is probably still abed with his mistress."

Landon didn't even hesitate. "He doesn't have one and hasn't for months."

Theo wasn't sure what shocked her more, Landon's willingness to discuss mistresses with her or the fact that Graham didn't have one.

As if thinking of him conjured the man himself, Theo saw Graham approaching. He was mounted with a little girl in front of him and a small boy on a pony riding alongside.

He tilted his head in their direction. "Hadfield, Lady—"

Graham was cut off by the girl's squirming. She seemed eager to get a better view of Theo. Once Graham had tightened his grip on her, he resumed. "Lady Theo. May I introduce my niece, Miss Clare Beckham, and my nephew, Master Maxwell Beckham, although my sister insists we all call him Max."

Trying to whisper but failing miserably, little Clare said, "Uncle Gam, Lady Tee-o is very pretty."

Leaning forward, Graham feigned a whisper. "Clare, you are absolutely correct. Lady Theo is beautiful. No other woman compares." Graham winked at Theo, prompting a glare from Landon. Theo could feel her cheeks burn.

Max's mount was becoming restless at the sedate pace. Graham easily reached for the reins and instructed the boy to rub the pony's neck and tell it to be at ease. Graham certainly had his hands full.

Landon suggested, "Perhaps we should take a different route. Archbroke, would you care to lead us?"

Returning the reins to his nephew, Graham nodded his agreement and moved off to the right to a path that would take them to a more secluded part of the park. They approached a wide clearing with enough room for the children to play and run about.

Graham dismounted and caught Clare as she jumped into his arms. The sight reminded Theo of all the times she had done the same, jumping fearlessly into Baldwin's arms, never once fearing he would drop her. She longed to be able to trust another like that.

Holding Clare with one arm, Graham turned to Max. Instead of catching the boy, Graham instructed him how to safely dismount and fall to the ground. A lump formed in Theo's throat, and her breathing stilled as Max did as instructed, landing solidly on two feet. Graham ruffled the boy's hair and praised him.

Ready to stretch her legs, Theo took Landon's hand as she hopped down from the landau to the ground.

Graham and the children approached. Landon went down on one knee to be at the boy's eye level and said, "You are a fine horseman, Max."

Max beamed and looked up at Archbroke. "Can Lord Hadfield and Lady Theo join us for the afternoon?"

"You had best ask Lord Hadfield if they have any prior engagements arranged."

Clare wiggled and slid down Graham's side, and as soon as her feet touched the ground, she went to her brother and whispered in his ear. Theo had a sneaking suspicion that, while the girl was barely out of her leading strings, she was extremely intelligent.

Pulling out a ribbon and ball from his coat pocket, Graham handed over the items to the children. Conspiratorially, the children grinned as Max took Landon's hand and pulled him forward, saying, "Lord Hadfield, perhaps you could throw the ball with me since my sister is atrocious at it."

Then Clare grabbed his other hand and pleaded, "No, play with me."

The children led Landon away leaving Graham alone with Theo, which she suspected was Clare's plan all along.

"What do you think of us practicing here?" Graham asked as he placed Theo's hand on his arm. She stiffened at the intimate gesture. He might not have a mistress, but he had certainly made it clear to Theo that he had some sort of engagement last night. She would wager that he had been with another woman.

"The chance of us being seen is too high."

Raising an eyebrow, Graham suggested, "Perhaps at night then."

"The park is littered with vagabonds at night, it would certainly not suit."

"Do you have any suggestions?"

"I'm not as well acquainted with the town as you… Should I leave *all* the arrangements to you?" Theo's words dripped with sarcasm.

Graham's back straightened as if preparing for battle. "We will meet here two nights hence an hour before midnight."

Gone was the sweet smile she had plastered on her face for the *ton* to see. She stopped, making Graham come to a halt. Making sure she had his full attention before speaking, she said, "That will not be necessary. Lucy has invited me to attend a defense lesson at her home tomorrow. She is a firm believer women should be able to defend themselves from any lascivious attacks from overzealous men."

Graham patted her hand that was still on his forearm. "I wonder if Lucy would allow me to help instruct?"

"Since she has forbidden Devonton to be in attendance, I seriously doubt she would make an exception for you."

Graham's demeanor exuded superiority. What caused him to be so sure of himself?

As he led her back to Landon and the children, he asked, "Do you have any plans for later this afternoon?"

"I am to accompany Aunt Henri for tea with Lady Barstow. She has been extremely kind in accepting Aunt Henri back into the mix, and I find her son rather charming."

An odd look crossed Graham's features. If she didn't know better, she would suspect him of jealousy. Lord Barstow was a fine-looking gentleman, in his prime, fit, and no creases upon his forehead. Could Graham be jealous of Barstow?

"Claim you are exhausted and beg off. We are to begin training this afternoon."

Theo did not care for Graham's tone and never took kindly to orders from anyone. In a voice full of cheer, hoping it would irritate Graham, she replied, "I'm not feeling at all tired, my lord."

Obviously irritated, Graham tried rephrasing his request, "I'm taking you fencing this afternoon."

While it still sounded like an order to Theo, the opportunity to fence was one she wouldn't forgo. "Perhaps I could do with a rest before we attend the Hereford soirée."

Graham was unable to suppress his groan. "Who decided to accept that invitation?"

Theo frowned at the sharpness of his question and fired back, "Devonton."

"Hereford's decision to tour the Continent while his sister was still unmarried with no other male relative to oversee her is plain irresponsible."

"Devonton and Lucy feel it is their responsibility to ensure Arabelle's Season is a success. We will support them also."

Graham stiffened. "We?"

"Yes, we… since we are courting." Should she be making such demands, given their courtship was for appearances only? There was a slight shift in Graham's posture.

Staring into Theo's eyes, he said, "Yes, we are indeed courting."

She was unsure how to interpret Graham's demeanor or tone. There was an underlying gravity. Was he insinuating his intentions were in fact true? Theo's eyes naturally landed on his lips, her breath becoming more shallow. Did she want their courtship to be in fact real and not a farce?

Trees meant to provide patrons relief from the sun provided them a curtain of privacy out of Landon's view. Graham bent his head and tenderly kissed her. His warm hands rested upon her waist as his lips lightly caressed hers. Instinctively, her tongue peeked out and touched his lips. He tasted like warm bread and honey. He tugged her forward and deepened the kiss. Theo immediately opened for him, her hands pressed up against his chest. She should try to push him away, but instead she curled her fists and pulled him closer. Lost in the kiss, Theo didn't notice little Clare until she was wedged between the two of them.

A very serious Clare admonished, "No kissing, Uncle Gam. You have to marry her first!"

Theo swallowed a laugh and picked Clare up. Clare immediately wrapped her legs around Theo's waist, and she wound her arms around Theo's neck. Pulling Theo's head closer, Clare whispered, "Lady Tee-o, you must not kiss Uncle Gam even if he is handsome."

Theo hugged Clare and pulled back to wink at the child before saying, "You are right, Clare. No kissing your handsome Uncle Graham."

CHAPTER FOURTEEN

Eager to fence again, Theo paced her room as silently as possible. Her brother's notes were precise about how to walk with stealth, much more than her papa's. Start with placing weight on the tip of your toe and slowly roll to the ball, transferring your full weight as your heel touches the floor. Use slow, fluid motions, lifting and leading with your knee to begin the next step. Practice slowly and increase speed.

Smiling, Theo recalled the challenge Baldwin had given himself, fence without sound. Could she accomplish such a goal?

"You are making me dizzy, my lady."

Theo stopped her pacing and looked down at the valise that contained her mask, jacket, gloves, and plastron. The only thing she needed was a foil.

"Tell me, Wallace. Exactly how did you come about the fencing gear?" Theo was still amazed her maid had been able to obtain everything she needed on such short notice and in a size that fit perfectly.

"My lady, it is my job to ensure you have everything

you need. I'll be honest. I'm still procuring items for you; some are rather hard to obtain, but Emma is also helping."

Theo ran over Wallace's reply again.

"Would you care to explain how it is you knew I would need fencing gear?"

Wringing her hands, Wallace avoided looking directly at Theo as she quietly replied, "Your mark, my lady."

Theo realized that she had not bothered to cover the mark in Emma's or Wallace's presence. Now that she thought of it, her former maid who had served her family for generations had never made mention of her mark.

"What do you know of the mark?"

"It is the mark of the Crown, my lady. Anyone who bears the mark is to be protected and assisted as declared by the royal family. My family swore an oath of fidelity for generations to assist those who bore the mark. Emma's store sign bears the symbol that shows our commitment. Although you are the first woman my papa knows of that has ever… I had to seek out help from my cousin Mills, a valet to one who bears the mark. He is the one who provided me with a list of items needed. My lady, it is a great honor for me to serve you. Please, I promise to serve you loyally."

"Calm yourself. I asked because I was under the belief that only those with the mark knew of it. I still do not fully understand how the system works or whom to really trust."

Wallace's face turned from worry to seriousness. "My lady, you must always use caution. My papa warned me that I too must use extreme care now that I am in your employ."

What had Theo's maid said about a symbol? How many shop owners and those in service were aware of the league of men—and now a woman—whose duty it was to protect the royal family and the Crown's activities?

"Wallace, what does the symbol indicating fidelity look like?"

"They are all slightly different. The one on Emma's sign is an angel, and from her wings is a harp. Only families who serve PORFs are permitted to display the angel. It is always a harp, my lady. The fancier the harp is, the more knowledge they have."

"PORFs?" Good gracious, what an atrocious name. She was a PORF?

"Protector of Royal Family."

Theo jumped as the window casing rattled. Wallace scurried over to the window to release the latch. Graham climbed through with such ease that both ladies stood staring at him wide-eyed.

Graham chuckled. "I see you have settled in quite nicely, Wallace."

Wallace grinned and dipped her head. "I have, Lord Archbroke."

Theo cleared her throat to gain her maid's attention. Wallace's eyes were glued to Graham as if he were Adonis. "Thank you, Wallace. If anyone inquires, I'm resting. I promise to be back in sufficient time to prepare for this evening's outing."

"Yes, my lady." Wallace curtsied and left the room, quiet as a mouse.

"I see you are prepared," Graham said, nodding at her packed valise.

"Are you aware that we are referred to as PORFs?"

"Yes. A rather unfortunate name, wouldn't you agree?"

"I certainly don't care for the reference."

Graham picked up her valise. "Let's be off." He headed back to the window and with a swoosh of his hand indicated for her to climb out.

Looking down at her gown, she shook her head.

"Is there a problem, Theo?"

Without replying, she walked up to Graham and turned. "Archbroke, please assist me with my laces."

Graham grazed his hands up her arms. Each time his warm hands touched her, her skin prickled and was left wanting more. Once the material about her was loose, she stepped away and moved to the chamber that held her clothing. In the dark, she dropped her dress and kicked off her slippers. Theo reemerged dressed like a young man about to complete errands around town.

Graham's eyes raked over her. "Do you have a long coat?"

"Yes, but it is not cool enough to require it."

With a smirk, Graham said, "You require it."

Walking back, Theo retrieved a greatcoat and donned it. Trying to exude more confidence than she felt, she went directly to the window and stuck her head out and promptly stepped back to face Graham.

Graham placed her hand in his as he slipped out the window to balance on the ledge just below. "Trust me." As Theo swung a leg over the windowsill, he instructed, "Keep your hips close to the wall and evenly distribute your weight on both feet."

Graham dropped the valise, which landed with a rather loud thud.

"Slide your foot down and place it on the trellis."

"There isn't a trellis," Theo squeaked, but as she slid her foot down, her toe hit what felt like a piece of wood.

"I convinced your aunt and Landon that the garden would look marvelous with the addition of some climbing roses. Since they were recently planted, we won't have to worry about our posteriors being poked just yet."

Graham started to descend first. Theo couldn't help but laugh as she carefully made her way down the trellis.

Graham jumped the last few feet over the plants. Calculating the remaining distance to the ground, she caught Graham peering up at her. His gaze was affixed to her. Could he see under her coat? Her breeches left nothing to the imagination.

She hastened her descent, and as she reached the top of the plants, Graham said, "Jump. I'll catch you."

Theo didn't waver; she simply jumped into his waiting arms. She wiggled to be released, but he gave her a light squeeze before commenting, "You weigh nothing but a feather." He let her slide down the front of his frame. Her entire body came alive. She didn't want Graham to see the effect he had on her as her cheeks warmed. Head bowed, she followed him to the waiting coach.

"Home," Graham ordered.

"Archbroke, you promised to take me fencing."

"I did, and I am." And that was all he said for the remainder of the short journey to his town house. She shouldn't be alone with him at his house. Society would deem her irrevocably ruined if the *ton* found out about the activities she was engaging in.

As THEY APPROACHED Graham's door, Hinley opened it only to come face-to-face with Theo. Graham snorted at his butler's flummoxed expression and stepped around to enter the house. "Lady Theo, this is Hinley, my butler. Hinley, Lady Theo is welcome here no matter the time and from all entrances."

Hinley uncharacteristically did a double take at the implication of Graham's words. "My lady."

Graham took Theo's hand in his as he led her to the

ballroom. He knew he should not behave with such informality, but he liked the feel of her small hand in his.

He gave Theo her valise as they entered the ballroom, which meant relinquishing her touch as she grasped the handle. At the loss of her touch, Graham was struck by a feeling of being set adrift.

As Theo took in her surroundings, he couldn't tear his gaze away from her. What would she think of the makeshift practice area? When her features revealed nothing, his heart began to thump harder. Why did he care what Theo thought of his efforts to provide her a safe environment in which to train? He pulled his gaze away. All the furniture had been strategically rearranged, allowing ample room for them to fence, exactly as he had ordered.

Theo moved to the far wall and bent to gather her equipment. Spellbound, his gaze roamed over her delightful form. She moved with effortless efficiency, sliding the plastron up her sword arm and slipping on her jacket. He had thought he'd be required to instruct her on the process. No, he had hoped to have had the opportunity to have her close, with a reasonable excuse to touch her.

Why had she distanced herself? He missed the heat of her body and the silky feel of her skin on his. Graham ran a hand over his face as he briskly walked over to don his own gear. Making short work of the task, he turned to select a foil only to be faced by a beguiling Theo. She tested the weight and balance of a few before making a selection.

"You look very comfortable holding a foil," Graham said as he moved to get into position.

"I'm also comfortable with an épée or saber, but I see you favor foils," Theo replied.

"Who was it who indulged your interest in fencing, my dear?"

She stiffened as soon as he had uttered the endearment. "My brother, Baldwin. We often practiced together. While he was always taller and stronger, he taught me to focus on my strengths of quickness and strategy." She lowered her mask and said, "*Prêt?*"

Fixing his stance, Graham replied, "*Allez!*" and lunged to the low outside.

Theo easily parried and followed it with a riposte.

After only a few minutes of sparring with Theo, Graham was forced to change tactics from simple to compound attacks. Each of Theo's movements was deliberate and sought out Graham's weaknesses. The woman was extremely well versed and utilized intelligence and quickness versus strength to defeat her opponent. However, Graham was a master chess player, anticipating her every move until fatigue set in. He could use more exercise.

In order to stall another advance, he said, "Make sure your arm remains at a forty-five-degree angle when you attack low on the inside."

Theo lunged with greater force, throwing her off balance. Graham parried, but Theo recovered and released a low growl. His body responded to the primal sound, the instinct to plunder and conquer his opponent eradicating all rational thought.

She was probably aware that her form was perfect. Could she sense his strength draining? Theo launched an assault that had him parrying without an opportunity to riposte. She had Graham moving backward so fast that he ended up landing on his arse.

Throwing the foil to the side and removing his mask, Graham conceded defeat. After removing her own mask, Theo bent down to assist him up. Her cheeks were flooded with color, and her bottom lip was full and reddened. It was too much to resist. He pulled her to his lap. Face-to-face, the sparkle in her eyes prompted him to boldly angle her head for a kiss that would leave her senseless.

Theo softened in his arms and allowed his tongue to tease and ravish her. Savoring the taste, he mused that each time he took liberties the woman grew bolder. Had she enjoyed his previous kisses? Her eagerness told him yes.

She began to mimic the play of his tongue on hers. When she tugged at his lower lip, he let out a low growl. He started to nibble down her neck and back up to her ear. Her fingers ran through his hair, and when he nipped her lightly on the neck, she pulled on his locks. It made him groan yet again. Her salty taste utterly intoxicated Graham. His hands wandered like they had a mind of their own. He was cursing the fencing jacket when Theo gently guided his hand to cup her breast. Her boldness excited him, and as he kissed her, he removed her jacket and plastron, leaving her in a fine lawn shirt.

A force pulled at Graham, tempting him to sink deeper into Theo. Breathlessly she brought his head down to whisper. "Kiss me."

Unable to deny her, he granted her request, devouring her lips until Theo became restless. Graham lowered his head until he was able to take her hardened nipple into his mouth. Her back arched and he slipped a hand under her shirt. Her muscles jumped as he trailed only his fingertips down her back from her shoulder to her hip. Every movement and small sigh that escaped Theo made Graham's breeches tighter.

Theo leaned back and freed her shirt in its entirety. He knew it was too risky to remove her shirt as the door was unlocked, and while he had left instructions not to be disturbed, there were still two unruly children under his roof.

The thought of the children was like a splash of cold water.

His voice came out deep and husky. "Theo, we must cease."

The vein pulsating along her neck begged for attention. Graham peppered kisses there but inhaled deeply, working to steady his breathing. "Clare… I fear… she may burst in…"

At the mention of his niece, Theo straightened, and her eyes cleared. She placed a hand on his cheek and ran her thumb over his swollen bottom lip. "I'm looking forward to receiving further instruction from you." Theo gave him a quick kiss.

She popped up to her feet. After donning her plastron and jacket, she tied her loose tendrils with a ribbon. Slipping her mask back on, she resumed her position, ready to fence. Graham rolled to his feet, but his thoughts remained steadfast on how Theo felt in his arms.

"You need to focus. You have not won a point in over a minute," Theo scolded as she lowered her foil.

"My apologies. You will have to bear with me as I build up my endurance once again. I admit that I have been sitting behind a desk too long these past years."

With mischief in her eyes, Theo replied, "It would be to both our advantage for you to regain your stamina."

Graham muttered, "You are a little minx. Where is the aloof Theo that everyone is concerned about?"

He certainly seemed to bring out a very different side of her personality.

With honesty shining in her eyes, she replied, "I feel like a different person when I'm with you. A woman who could accomplish anything."

Graham approached Theo and leisurely removed her fencing gear, piece by piece. He could see her pulse quicken. He carefully placed the items in her empty valise and covered her luscious curves with her greatcoat. Turning Theo toward the door, Graham whispered into her ear, "I'll have my footman escort you home safely, and I'll see you at Hereford's later tonight."

Theo's back stiffened under his hand. He turned her to face him, cupping her face, his thumb caressing her luscious skin. He succumbed to desire once more and gave her a heated kiss. "You are too tempting, Theo." There was a bewildered look in her eyes. She was too innocent to understand.

He steered her into the hall. Seeing Hinley nearby, Graham instructed him to oversee Theo's safe return to Hadfield's town house. Then he sought out his own chambers, where he desperately needed to relieve himself of the ache that had him in agony.

CHAPTER FIFTEEN

Christopher escorted Theo into Hereford Manor. Her cousin slid a finger between his cravat and neck and tugged as if it was choking him to death.

"I'm sorry you had to escort me this evening." She laid a hand on his arm to keep him from thoroughly ruining the folds in his cravat.

"Don't be silly. I'd do anything for you. After all, you are family. I'd prefer not to have to interact with the *ton* if at all possible."

Taking mercy on him, Theo offered, "We won't have to stay long, I promise. As soon as Arabelle is done with her recital, we can leave. But first we must find Blake and Lucy."

Theo scanned the crowd, trying to spot Blake since he was head and shoulders taller than most of the other gentlemen. Her gaze settled on a gentleman with his back to her. He had honey-blond hair, the same shade as Graham's, but cut much shorter. She rubbed her fingertips, remembering the feeling of running them through Graham's wavy locks. The gentleman laughed like a hyena and turned. Her eyes widened as Graham made his way to her side. It wasn't his heavily patterned lavender waistcoat that caused her shock.

Smiling, Graham said, "Good evening, Lady Theo." He took her hand and placed a kiss upon her knuckles.

She was staring. What had happened to Graham's golden locks? His hair was now shorn close to his scalp. "Lord Archbroke?"

"After a round of rather vigorous fencing practice, I retreated to the library for a brief moment of peace and quiet. Clare found me resting upon the settee and decided that my hair needed a trim."

Theo couldn't help but giggle.

Graham smiled. "To tell the truth, it was a terrifying experience to wake up to a four-year-old wielding shears, which was only matched by the sight of Mills trying to rectify the situation. In the end, we decided it best to make it all even, which required quite a few inches to be removed."

Christopher made a sound that was half cough, half laugh. Theo turned to make the introductions. "Christopher, this is the Earl of Archbroke. Lord Archbroke, my cousin, Mr. Christopher Neale."

"Always a pleasure to meet members of your family," Graham replied.

Christopher raised an eyebrow and pointedly looked at their joined hands. Graham had not released her. Why had she not noticed? She didn't want him to release her, but she couldn't have him hold her hand all night.

Only after Graham released her did Christopher address him. "Lord Archbroke, your niece's actions remind me of someone who decided their cousin's eyebrows would benefit from…"

Theo spoke before her cousin could finish the mortifying tale. "Christopher, I can't believe you even remember that far back."

Graham's belly laugh caught them both off guard and drew the attention of the other guests around them. "I can only imagine how Theo must have terrorized Hadfield and yourself."

Lucy joined their little group and came to her defense. "Theo was never a terror."

Wrapping Theo up in a hug, Lucy gave her a squeeze. She stepped back, and Lucy assessed Theo from head to toe. "I must say, Emma truly outdid herself. You look beautiful tonight."

Theo turned to look for an ally in Blake, but he was nowhere in sight. He rarely left Lucy's side.

"Where is Blake?"

"Oh, he is off to get refreshments. It's rather warm in here, don't you think?"

Theo thought the room was well ventilated and not at all stuffy or warm; she deduced Lucy's body temperature was a result of her condition.

Lucy reached out and placed a hand on Theo's elbow before saying, "Gentlemen, we are off to seek out our hostess. Archbroke, if Blake returns, I hope you will keep him entertained."

Irritation flashed in Graham's eyes. Obviously, he didn't care to take orders from one of his agents.

In a blink of an eye, Graham donned a mask of ease and carelessness. "Why, Lady Devonton, I'd love to entertain the man insane enough to marry you."

Lucy ushered Theo around the room, all the while muttering under her breath, complaining of Graham and his humor. To date, Graham was the only individual Theo was aware of who could work Lucy into such a state, which in a wayward fashion made Theo admire Graham even more.

Lucy stopped in front of a fresh-faced debutante. "Theo, please let me introduce you to our lovely hostess, Lady Arabelle Risley. Arabelle, Lady Theodora Neale is my dearest and closest friend."

Arabelle curtsied and said, "Lady Theodora, it is a pleasure. I hope you will enjoy this evening's entertainment."

"I'm looking forward to your performance, Lady Arabelle. But please call me Theo."

"Only if you will address me as Arabelle like everyone else does. Lady is so presumptuous."

Arabelle was unique in her attitude. The skin on the back of Theo's neck began to prickle. Graham was near. Despite sensing he was behind her, she jumped slightly as he placed a hand on her lower back.

It was Blake's low baritone voice that broke into the ladies' conversation. "Lucy, my love." He handed his wife a glass of lemonade.

Blake turned and addressed their hostess. "Arabelle, you look enchanting this evening." Theo saw the blush rise in the young girl's cheeks and espied Blake's gaze on her. "Lady Theo, beautiful as always." Theo had never considered Blake other than as her best friend's husband, but now that she was the subject of his full attention, she understood the warmth and intensity Lucy must feel all the time. Graham's hand moved to Theo's waist in a possessive manner that drew her gaze away from Blake.

Bending, Graham growled into her ear. "Don't forget it is I who am courting you, my lady."

Perplexed by his comment and at the suggestion he might be jealous, Theo shook off the thought that Graham might actually care for her and reminded herself he had concocted the sham courtship to allow them to further her training—and for no other purpose.

Christopher cleared his throat before bowing. "My lady, may I introduce myself? I am Lady Theo's cousin, Christopher Neale. At your service."

Arabelle's blush deepened, and she held out her hand, "Mr. Neale, I'm delighted to make your acquaintance. I must go prepare. Will you be staying, Mr. Neale?"

"I wouldn't miss your performance for anything."

Theo didn't think the girl's cheeks could be any more inflamed. Arabelle curtsied and made to leave the group but paused briefly next to Lucy. Theo caught Lucy's slight nod. What had Arabelle shared that could not be disclosed to the entire group?

Christopher's gaze followed Arabelle. He was undoubtedly taken with her beauty.

"Lady Arabelle has been labeled the *Incomparable* for the Season." Lucy directed her comment to Christopher.

Was Lucy pointing out their incompatibility in rank? Theo bristled at the thought.

"Arabelle is the sweetest girl I know and does not put on airs." Lucy gave Christopher a saucy wink.

No, Theo's friend was encouraging her cousin.

Graham had removed his hand from her back, and it now rested at her elbow. "My lady, would you care to take a turn before Arabelle's recital? I'm sure Mr. Neale will reserve us some seats with an unobstructed view."

Graham didn't wait for the man's acknowledgment before guiding Theo away from the group.

"Archbroke, what makes you believe you are able to command everyone around you? I must inform you it is a very arrogant trait."

"Our families have been linked for generations. My family, in particular, has been granted knowledge and positions that no family has ever held." What was he speaking of? She glanced at their surroundings. He had escorted her to a semiprivate area.

Capturing Theo's gaze, Graham said, "This is not the place for me to give you a complete answer. It would be best if I explained everything tomorrow. I would come to you tonight, but I have matters I need to attend to later this evening."

Although Landon had informed Theo that Graham no longer kept a mistress, she suspected his evening meetings were in fact with another woman, which to Theo's distress put her out of sorts. She shouldn't care if Graham sought out another woman at night, yet the thought of him kissing another made her stomach revolt.

GRAHAM NOTICED the change in Theo's demeanor and silently cursed himself for agreeing to meet with his agents later in the evening at the Home Office. Since he had failed to appear at the office that day, his agents had cornered him upon his arrival with requests for his counsel on various matters. Issues Graham did not want discussed at a social engagement.

Graham led them to their seats and assessed his surroundings and the members of the *ton*. His undivided attention to Theo had not gone unnoticed. Perfect. Debutantes and their mamas cast narrowed looks Theo's way, which confirmed his assumption they believed Graham was courting Theo and it would only be a matter of time before a betrothal was announced.

Oddly, the idea was not abhorrent to him. What would life with Theo be like? He hardly knew the woman, but she stirred his blood and evoked thoughts and feelings he had never encountered before.

Theo sat with her back slightly to him. She had erected a wall he needed to break down. Theo watched Arabelle perform, and he watched Theo.

Arabelle stood and curtsied before leaving the stage. Theo elbowed Christopher as she caught him winking at Arabelle. "Christopher, that was not well done. Behave yourself!"

"I think I'll try to track her down to offer her my compliments on her performance," Christopher said in a rush and left.

Graham had found Theo and Christopher's byplay entertaining. Out of the corner of his eye, he caught sight of Lucy and Blake leaving the music room rather suspiciously. Were they on their way to meet Arabelle in private again? He needed to find out more about this mysterious investigation Lucy still had not apprised him of.

He turned to face Theo. "I need to locate Lucy and Blake. Would you care to join me?" He had intended it to be a question; however, it came out more like a command. He knew what Theo thought of his commands.

"I believe I will go find Christopher."

He had expected her to decline and replied, "Until tomorrow."

As Theo walked away to find Christopher, she had an odd sensation that something was amiss. Graham's acquiescence was too quick and easy. The hall was crowded, and without an escort, she found it hard to maneuver through the throng. Slowly, she made her way along the wall, squeezing past groups that appeared to be standing in semicircles with either bored expressions or engaged in laughter. Theo finally spotted Christopher standing near an alcove that was somewhat hidden from the main area.

Lightly tapping Christopher on his back, she ducked out of the way as his fist came swinging past her head.

"Theo! You should cease sneaking up on people." Looking down at her crouched form, he continued, "How do you to move about without making a sound?"

Straightening, Theo ignored his questions. "What has you on edge?"

"I think Arabelle is meeting with a gentleman behind the curtain. I hesitate to tell you… but I suspect it is Lord Devonton, Lucy's husband."

"I know who Lord Devonton is, Christopher. But why would you suspect him to be…," Theo replied.

In the next heartbeat, Blake's voice floated through the curtain. "Are you certain? No one can know, Arabelle. You do understand?"

Theo had to strain to hear Arabelle's response. "I do, my lord." Shocked at what she had overheard, Theo knew there had to be an explanation. Glancing at Christopher, he looked like he was about to do something rash and cause a scene, then from the corner of her eye she spotted Lucy and Graham in a heated discussion on the other side of the alcove.

Graham wore the same expression that Lucy's brother had when he was trying to refrain from strangling his sister while Lucy had a determined, righteous look on her face that Theo had seen many times when she was at odds with her brother. She knew the look meant that Lucy was up to something from which she would not be derailed by anyone.

Theo needed to find out what exactly they were discussing. Edging closer to where Graham and Lucy were standing, she pulled Christopher with her. Theo interrupted them. "Would one of you care to tell me what it is you two are discussing?"

Both of them turned to face Theo and replied, "No!"

Blake magically appeared, and came to stand next to Lucy. He placed a protective arm around her stiff shoulders, and blandly looked over at Christopher before inquiring, "Mr. Neale, what did you think of Arabelle's performance tonight?"

"What were you discussing with her?" Christopher replied, raising his eyebrow. His gaze shifted to Lucy.

Without blinking, Lucy replied, "I'm sure Blake was expressing how much we enjoyed her recital. She has a beautiful voice. Wouldn't you agree?"

Theo knew Lucy too well to not notice the brief glance she gave her husband that instructed him to let her handle the situation. Theo found it all very intriguing but was saddened by the knowledge that she and Lucy were keeping secrets from each other.

Christopher ignored the byplay and stated, "I believe it is time for us to leave."

Neither Graham nor Lucy would tell Theo any information in such a social setting. She turned to leave but lingered long enough to overhear the trio's brief conversation.

"Well?" Lucy questioned.

"Archbroke, I think it is time my wife and I also retire for the evening," Blake quietly replied.

Decisively, Graham said, "You two will report in an hour."

As Graham turned to leave, Theo overheard Blake say, "We need his resources."

~

GRAHAM ENTERED HIS DARKENED OFFICE. A footman swiftly appeared to light the fire. Rubbing the back of his neck, he could see in the dim light emitted by his lantern that his desk was littered with piles of correspondence. This was the consequence of neglecting his duties. But it was worth every moment. He had enjoyed the day away from the office, having spent the morning with the children and the afternoon and evening with Theo.

Releasing a heavy sigh, he shrugged out of his coat and removed his waistcoat. Seated, Graham stretched out his arms and methodically rolled up his sleeves. Initially, the mass of papers appeared to be mostly requests for agent expenses, but as he began reviewing the documents, some were detailed reports from his field agents. Dealing with the simplest items first, Graham signed requests for funds and approved leaves of absence.

He was pouring over a comprehensive account of the upsurge of opium dens when a small scratch at the windowsill caught his attention. *Must be a tree branch.* Frowning, he returned his attention to the document in his hand. Graham squinted as something sharp scraped against the window. *That was no tree.*

He rose and approached the window from the side; a niggling tension near his heart prompted him to unlatch the window and wait for the intruder to enter.

Graham wrapped one arm around the intruder's waist and the other around their neck before he let out, "What the devil!"

Smelling Theo's scent, Graham released her and spun her around to face him.

Bright bewildered green eyes stared back at him. How had Theo managed to follow and track him down? His brain and body were at war. He wanted to shake some sense into the woman, but the desire to hold on to her and reassure her that she was safe was overwhelming.

Theo looked around the room. "Where are we?"

"You are in my office."

"But what is this place?"

"It is the Home Office headquarters…"

"Home Office? You work…"

He glanced at the door and rashly maneuvered her behind his desk. He sat in his chair and pulled Theo down to her knees.

In a harsh whisper, Graham said, "We will have to continue this later; right now I need you to hide and remain quiet. Do not, for any reason, make your presence known."

He moved slightly forward in his chair and glanced down to ensure Theo would be completely hidden. She was crouching between his legs. It was an image he would not soon forget.

Moments later there was a scratch at his door, and gruffly Graham commanded, "Enter."

He focused upon the request in front of him in an attempt to banish the image of Theo between his thighs. Lucy waltzed into his office, trailed by a beleaguered Blake. They each sat in a chair that faced him while he took a moment to compose his features. After scrawling his name approving payment for lodgings for one of his agents, Graham slowly arranged his writing instruments and purposefully tented his fingers and placed them under his chin before raising his gaze to the pair before him.

"I'm certain the two of you are here to inform me of all your activities that have been occurring on domestic soil and will not leave out any details, no matter how insignificant you may deem them."

Blake replied, "Archbroke, the Foreign Office is willing—"

"Your investigations and activities are being conducted on domestic soil; therefore, they are in my purview, *not* that of the Foreign Office. Am I clear?"

Graham had never had cause to use such harsh, commanding language with the man before. Blake's smile indicated he was not unaccustomed to receiving orders, most likely from his own wife.

It was Lucy who responded. "Archbroke, Matthew believes he is close to tracking Addington down. He suspects Addington's sister, Cecilia, is assisting him in obtaining key information. Hereford instructed his sister to befriend her. Arabelle is sweet and extremely innocent, but she has managed to gain Cecilia's confidence, and tonight Arabelle informed us Cecilia is trying to track down a journal or book that contains a map that Addington is seeking. Addington hinted that the Hadfield family is holding it. Cecilia asked Arabelle to help make the appropriate introductions. Archbroke, I believe Theo and her family are in danger."

Theo grasped his thigh at the mention of her family name. Blood rushed to his loins. Repositioning himself, he focused on sorting through all the information Lucy had imparted. Blake's eyes had heated with anger at the mention of Addington. It was Lucy who had deduced that Addington was the traitor behind Blake's kidnapping.

Matthew had directly countered Graham's orders to remain in London and had set off for the Continent. Graham had reasoned that Matthew was intent on locating Addington and bringing him back to England to stand trial. Now, as he considered all the facts, he suspected that there was a large piece of the puzzle missing.

What was the reasoning behind Blake's abduction?

Why did Addington seek out a map?

Graham needed more time to reflect on all the facts available. However, he also knew if he did not take control of the situation, Lucy would soon formulate a plan of her own, especially since her own brother was involved.

Graham broke the silence. "Lucy, Theo is your best friend—"

Before he could continue, Lucy interjected, "Tell me, why are you courting Theo? Were you already aware of the danger and sought out a way to protect her when we made our agreement? What are you not telling me, Archbroke?"

Theo shifted as if she might reveal herself. He tightened the muscles in his thighs, preventing her from wriggling. It placed her head very close to his male member that was twitching as her warm breath continued to tease it to attention.

Graham coughed to cover the noise of Theo's movements. He carefully selected his words. "Do you doubt my attraction to Theo? She is a beautiful woman, and after seeing your marital bliss, I thought I might see if we suit." He paused, but as Lucy was about to reply, he cut her off and ordered, "You will do your best to accompany Theo when possible and continue to report back any information Arabelle is able to gain. I will take care of investigating the matter of the map. Devonton, if I'm able to obtain the map, I trust you will provide your assistance."

Blake did not hesitate in his response. "Of course. I too have a vested interest in this matter."

His response had effectively caught Lucy off guard. Her mouth hung wide open, but the rapid fire of questions Graham expected was apparently stuck in the lady's throat.

Blake rose and bent to assist his wife to her feet. Graham did not dare to move from behind the desk, for then Blake and Lucy would clearly see his uncomfortable state. Instead, he gave them a parting command. "You will inform me of developments as they occur and will not take action before alerting me."

Both Blake and Lucy nodded and quietly left the room. Success. He had finally made his notoriously mouthy agent speechless, with words that were honest and heartfelt.

CHAPTER SIXTEEN

Theo's legs were cramping. When the door clicked closed, she pushed Graham, causing him to grasp the desk and balance the chair on its two back legs. Her nerves were strung taut; she could not but notice the changes in Graham's body as the meeting continued. She needed air and space.

Theo crawled out and stood with as much dignity as she could muster. "Archbroke, how is it that another could even know of the book's existence, let alone its contents?"

She walked around the desk and leaned her hip against it. She stared at Graham, waiting for his reply. His eyes were glazed. Was he falling ill?

He muttered, "I have no logical explanation for you."

Unable to remain still, she began to pace but stopped when Graham continued, "To my knowledge, there are only three families that have each pledged their legacy to the Crown. It is my understanding each volume contains the same first four pages that outline the families' sworn oaths to protect and serve the Crown. Each family has a defined role; my family served to guard against attacks on the Crown and England. For the past three generations, we have headed the Home Office. Lord Burke's family for the past ten generations has served as personal advisors to the Crown, and your family has served in gathering and providing intelligence requested by both families for many generations. Have you had contact with Lord Burke?"

Theo was mulling over the fact that there were only three volumes. Absently, she replied to Graham's question. "I have yet to make his acquaintance, but he assured me via correspondence that there is no immediate need to seek him out. Since both my brother and papa noted they infrequently assisted Lord Burke, I never questioned his response."

"Lord Burke is aware that you hold the book."

"Not exactly. The correspondence arrived before Landon reached Hadfield Hall. I opened the letter by mistake." Actually, her old maid had insisted she open the correspondence. Still in grief and disbelief, her papa had entrusted the volume to her. Theo had not paid attention to the exact order of events. If it was her duty to share information, should she inform Graham of the odd notations Baldwin had made during his last assignment?

Tentatively she began, "Archbroke…" Did she sound as nervous as she felt? The memory of Baldwin brought a shiver that ran along her spine.

Graham immediately rounded the desk and pulled her into an embrace.

Barely louder than a whisper, Theo said, "I need you to come with me back to the town house. I must show you some of Baldwin's notes."

~

SWINGING her leg over the windowsill, her foot found purchase. Theo eased her way into her sparse bedchamber. With both feet firmly planted, she was thankful that Graham had convinced Landon to install the trellis as she was beginning to realize she was not fond of heights. Standing, Theo placed her hand in Graham's outreached one. With a slight tug, he gathered her into his arms. She had remained silent the entire journey to her residence. When Graham wrapped a comforting arm around her, she unashamedly snuggled into his warmth.

It was as if he had sensed her growing apprehension as they neared the Hadfield town house. Memories of Baldwin haunted Theo's thoughts, and she was unable to prevent the sudden shivers that attacked her. But in his arms, as she was now, she felt safe.

Theo pulled out of his arms to discard her greatcoat, throwing it over the back of a plush wingback chair she loved to read in. Striding to the adjoining room, she lifted the settee and moved it over a few inches, allowing her enough room to retrieve her family's volume from beneath the wood floor.

Glancing behind her, her brows furrowed as Graham finished lighting candles and leisurely sat upon her bed. He had removed his hat and coat, revealing an offensive lavender waistcoat. His short hair was in disarray, and there were dark smudges under his eyes. Perhaps she had been wrong in her assumption that he had been visiting a woman each evening. The burden of running the Home Office must be great.

Instead of sitting next to him, Theo removed her boots and crawled up onto her bed and rested her back against its headboard. She patted a spot next to her. "Archbroke, come closer."

Graham's eyes flickered and their blue hue deepened. After removing his boots, he inched nearer. She searched his features, wanting to read his thoughts, but she found no clues. Her skin prickled with awareness and she grew short of breath. She needed to focus on fulfilling her duty to provide information, not bask in his warmth.

As he settled in next to Theo, he rested his head and closed his eyes. The poor man was beyond exhaustion. She wanted to reach out and comfort him, just as he had done for her earlier. When she moved, he raised his arm, allowing her head to rest on his chest. His arm wound tightly around her waist as if it naturally belonged there.

She shouldn't allow such favors, but as she learned more about the complex man, she couldn't resist. While her family had been loving, physical affection was sparse. She basked in the feeling of being wanted, of Graham wanting her. He made her feel brave and free to be herself. Feelings she had not felt since Baldwin's death. She needed to show him Baldwin's notes.

Theo opened the book and turned to the pages she sought. Glancing up, her eyes locked with Graham's, for he was looking down at her and not the volume in her hands.

Seeing her brother's handwriting, Theo's throat began to close, and she wasn't sure if she could read the notes to Graham without crying.

As if he sensed her dilemma, he asked, "Would you like me to read it?"

Simply nodding, she handed Graham the book. Thinking he would read the notes in silence, Theo was startled when he began to read aloud.

June 10, 1812
Meeting with Prinny rather uneventful. Lord B has me running a fool's errand. He has requested I look into the matter of some missing crown jewels. Prinny overheard His Majesty rambling in one of his bouts of madness about having hidden some of the jewels on the Continent.

With Baldwin's words came the memories. Her beloved brother who teased her incessantly and brought her sweets in the middle of the night. She looked up at Graham, who had lowered the book. With tears streaming down her face, she wrapped her arms around him. Pulling him closer, she placed a kiss on his cheek. "Thank you." She released her hold and resituated herself against his chest and waited for him to continue.

Graham raised the book and began to read.

June 16, 1812
Goose chase continues... No documented list of crown jewels.
Accountings are inconsistent.
After examination no sight of 2 pairs of Armills or the Stuart sapphire.
Need to revisit history lessons.

June 18, 1812
Leaving for the Continent. Information has surfaced, there indeed is a goose.
Lord B, funding expedition.

July 3, 1812
Admittedly I'm coming to realize despite his madness, His Majesty is a rather clever fellow. Lord B hounding for reports, forwarded him a copy of the partial map found.

Theo shifted away from Graham as he moved to hold the book closer to the candle to view the rather rudimentary map. She missed his warmth and reached down to pull the coverlet up and over her. Graham tucked the blanket around her and settled back to continue reading.

July 15, 1812
Obtaining the remaining parts of the map is proving rather difficult.
Leads point to the south of Spain.

July 20, 1812
Obtained the second partial drawing required.
Only one remains.

Theo shuddered as tears wracked her body. It was the last entry Baldwin had made. Memories of the worst day of her life flooded her thoughts. She had been out riding and was racing through their estate when she was told to seek out her papa. Boldly she had entered her papa's study without warning. She had thrown her bonnet aside and fell into a chair facing him.

"Morris said you wanted to see me right away, Papa."

Her papa's eyes and voice were distant. "Theo, I received a letter from the War Office today. Baldwin was in Salamanca when a battle between French forces and an Anglo-Portuguese army led by the Duke of Wellington broke out. Despite Wellington prevailing, Baldwin perished during the battle."

Her papa had sounded as if he were speaking of another and not his own son. Theo's brain refused to process the news as she blurted out, "The War Office must be mistaken. Why would Baldwin be anywhere near the battles on the Continent? He's over there studying marbles. He has even sent me drawings he had done."

Her papa shook his head. "I received Baldwin's possessions along with the letter. There is no mistake. Baldwin is dead."

It was then that her papa's head bowed down, and his slumped shoulders shook. He was crying. Theo had left her papa to grieve. She had retired to her rooms where she remained for a fortnight before her papa left her to return to London.

~

Graham held her as she sat curled in his lap. Rhythmically, he ran his hand up and down her back and cradled her face to his chest as she sobbed.

"Baldwin, you crafty sod," Theo swiped a hand across her face and bolted from his lap, ducking into the adjoining room. She returned with what looked to be a stack of hatboxes.

"I remembered my brother sent me many drawings before he… died. We need to examine them."

Theo placed one of the boxes in front of Graham as she began to open another.

He sat watching her as she untied the ribbon and began retrieving bundles of correspondence that had also been tied with ribbon. As Theo organized the letters into chronological order, her entire demeanor changed. Graham had to admit to himself that even in her most vulnerable moments, she was a woman of great strength.

He forced his gaze from Theo and focused on the task she had given him, feeling uneasy as he pulled the letter from its envelope. "What are the drawings of?"

"At the time, Baldwin told me he was venturing to the Continent to find and study marbles. When I started receiving his drawings, I thought they were the worst renditions. I even teased Baldwin in my return correspondence, telling him Mr. Donaldson, his art instructor, had not been successful in his lessons on depth and form."

Theo paused and looked up at Graham. Remarkably, she wore a smile on her face. "Graham, my brother was a very accomplished artist."

Graham's heart skipped a beat at the sultry sound of his name upon her lips. Only his mama called him by his given name, and even she did so on rare occasions.

In complete silence, they worked together, opening what Graham came to realize was daily correspondence from Baldwin. It was evident that Theo and her brother had been extremely close. Feeling like he was intruding in a very personal part of Theo's life, he took on the task of only looking for the drawings and refrained from reading any of the correspondence.

After hours of sorting through the piles, it was approaching dawn. Graham had just finished going through another handful of letters contained in the hatbox that Theo had placed in front of him. Dozens of drawings were laid out in front of them both.

"It will be morning soon. I must return to my own lodging without issue."

Theo rubbed her eyes and arched her back. His eyes instantly fell upon her chest. He needed to leave before he could act on any of the sordid thoughts he had held in check during the night.

She leaned closer and gave him a chaste kiss on the cheek as she said, "Thank you for helping me." Theo looked at the stack of boxes they had yet to examine.

"It was my pleasure, and it appears there is still much more to do." Graham swung his legs over the edge of the bed and stood. His knees nearly buckled. He waited a moment before retrieving his boots and coat. Theo was about to untie another stack when Graham reached out and gently removed the letters from her hands.

"I'm going to help you place these in order, and then I want you to get some rest. I wish I could remain and assist you, but if we were caught together in your rooms, I'm sure I'd be meeting Landon on a field this time tomorrow."

Exhausted, Theo merely nodded and rose from the bed to join Graham. He outlined a system, and together they made short work of arranging the drawings, letters, and hatboxes. Amazed at how they had easily worked in unison, the task was completed swiftly.

Graham turned to leave through the window. Theo was close behind him. He couldn't resist holding her one more time. He pulled her into an embrace, neither passionate nor platonic. Theo slowly raised her face to meet his gaze. She shocked him by rising on her tiptoes and kissing his stubble-covered chin before moving up to place a direct kiss upon his lips. Theo melted into his embrace. After spending the entire night near her, yet not being able to touch her, Graham caved in to his desires and deepened the kiss. Coaxing her to open for him, he slipped his tongue in her mouth and ran it along her bottom teeth.

When her tongue sought out his, he remorsefully groaned and said, "I'll see you at Devonton's town house." He reluctantly released her and stepped toward the window.

Graham climbed down the trellis and strolled through the garden gate with a lightness in his step that had been missing, reflecting on the evening's events. Theo was a remarkable woman, and he was intrigued to learn everything about her. He was also curious as to what message Baldwin had hidden in his correspondence to her. Why had he not provided it directly to Lord Burke?

CHAPTER SEVENTEEN

"Archbroke!" Why was someone yelling Graham's name? He raised his head only to find a slip of parchment affixed to his forehead.

Ripping the paper away, he faced an amused Blake who released a hearty male guffaw.

Rubbing his eyes, Graham grumbled, "Who let you in?"

"Am I not welcome?"

"You are welcome to accompany your wife here anytime. Where is she?"

Blake's smirk promptly disappeared. "Lucy began to have stomach cramps early this morn. The midwife has ordered her to remain at home for the next few days and rest. She sent me here to deliver this to you."

Blake reached into his breast pocket and retrieved a missive. Reluctantly, Graham opened the letter he was sure contained some sort of directive from his most infuriating agent.

Archbroke,
Devonton and I have decided to retire to the country and hold a house party in a week. We will extend an invitation to you along with one to Theo's family and other interested parties. A few weeks in the country will be good for everyone's health. Given we are in the midst of the Season and good help is always hard to find, I seek your assistance in securing the additional footmen and outriders necessary to ensure a safe journey for all parties who accept our invitation.
Lady Devonton

Graham threw the letter down onto his desk and rose as he blustered, "Why on earth did you agree to a blasted house party?"

"The midwife suggested Lucy slow down a bit. It was the only solution I could come up with that would ensure she was not out and about every evening."

Graham stared at Blake. "This was your idea?" Blake had clearly lost his mind.

"Yes. It would ensure that we could keep a close eye on Theo and her family. If I'm correct, Addington's sister will believe this, and it will give her the best opportunity to obtain what she is looking for. We will make sure Arabelle is on the guest list."

Graham raised his hand to run it through his hair only to find that his hair was barely longer than the width of his fingers, which reminded him that he would have to check in on the children at some point in the day. Refocusing on matters at hand, he asked, "And who exactly is on this guest list?"

"Well, in addition to those already mentioned, we would invite Lord Roxbury and his sister."

"If you invite Roxbury's sister, Lady Mary, you will need to invite Waterford as well."

Blake lost his composure. "Like hell, I'll invite Waterford into my home. The man causes Lady Mary all sorts of distress. Lucy will not have him."

"He is one of my best agents. You will inform Lucy to ensure his name is on that guest list of yours."

"No. You advise Lucy yourself."

"Fine." Deftly he knotted his cravat and reached for his waistcoat and jacket. "Let's return to your residence. I believe Lucy is holding a lesson there that I'm most interested in observing."

"I have no idea what you are referring to, Archbroke. I'm off to the club for a bite to eat. Would you care to join me?" Blake inquired.

Graham saw the mischievous glimmer in Blake's eyes. Oh, the man knew exactly what activities his wife was up to. "My thanks for the invitation, but I'll catch up with you later."

From the corner of his eye, he caught Blake grinning like a cat who had just captured a canary. *The man must know what occurs in his own dwelling. Intriguing that he pretends to have no knowledge.* Brushing the absurd thought that he was about to attend a lesson he might find shocking, Graham left the Home Office and made his way to Devonton's town house on foot. He hoped the exercise would reinvigorate him as he was feeling the effects of having stayed up all night.

CHAPTER EIGHTEEN

Eager to see Theo again, Graham silently willed the butler to move faster through Devonton's town house. Voices of multiple women chattering with excitement filled the hall. The butler opened a door, allowing him entrance. The sight of two men naked to the waist brought Graham to a dead stop. The men were surrounded by women who formed a semicircle with Lucy and Theo in the center, none of whom noticed his entrance.

With a shake of his head, he silently communicated to the men not to alert the women of his presence.

The taller of the two continued, "Now… Evan and I will demonstrate how to execute a chokehold." The men started to circle each other. With quick, efficient moves, one of the men had the other in a chokehold and held him until the man tapped out.

As Graham considered the movements and strategy the men employed to combat each other, he realized that a female would need to use a varied technique in order to fend off an attacker. Graham concluded that the methods being demonstrated would be of no use to these women. The ridiculousness of the situation prompted Graham to finally speak up. "Gentlemen, that was a rather impressive demonstration."

Lucy turned to eye him as he approached. "Lord Archbroke, I don't believe I was expecting you to call today."

Graham saw the smirk on Theo's face, and he could not help but continue to goad Lucy. "While men are able to disarm one another with a chokehold, I would advise other techniques are taught to these lovely ladies. I wouldn't want any of them to come to harm. But I digress. I was, in fact, looking for Lady Theo, and was told I would find her here."

Lucy replied, "As you can see, Theo is rather busy right now."

Graham grumbled under his breath. "Busy ogling naked young men in their prime…"

He had seen the look of rapture on Theo's face when the men were exhibiting their fighting skills. An image of Theo looking at him with eyes ablaze with excitement, a little breathless, and hair spilling over his pillows flashed through his mind. His body ached with a need for her, but they were in a room filled with women and half-naked footmen.

Lucy's voice broke his imaginings as she quipped, "I'm sorry, Lord Archbroke. I did not hear you." The twinkle in Lucy's eyes indicated she had a fair idea of what he had uttered.

Before Lucy could see the jealousy raging within him, Graham spoke up. "Perhaps I might suggest the gentlemen show these young ladies where a man is most vulnerable to attack from one half their size."

Evan and John looked at each other before returning their gaze to Graham. Seeing their confused looks,

Graham moved to stand in front of the two sweaty men and addressed them, "With your permission, I'll have you volunteer to take strikes from these women after I have shown them the proper technique."

Without hesitation, the men nodded. Graham approached and waited for Theo to face him. The ladies had a clear view from the side.

Theo nervously wiped her palms on the front of her skirts. "What are you about, my lord?"

Ignoring her question, Graham turned to face the group and pointed to his throat. "This, my ladies, is one of the areas where you can hit a man and stall his attack." Graham proceeded to point to his eyes, the bridge of his nose, groin, and then knees. As he pointed to each part of his body, he briefly outlined how he believed a woman might effectively hit her attacker with the intent of breaking free and fleeing.

He turned and asked, "Lady Theo, perhaps you could be my assistant and help me demonstrate the moves I have just described."

"I'd be delighted to exhibit the moves." Theo took a step closer, then turned, placing her back to him and facing the women surrounding them. "Would you agree with me that it is more likely for a man to try to attack from behind than from the front?"

One of the maids replied, "Yes, from the back when you are not aware of their intent."

Caught off guard at the change of positions, Graham reached out to place both arms around her waist, pinning her hands and arms to her side. He wanted to have her willing in his arms. However, it was important for Theo to learn hand-to-hand combat. When she began to struggle, he tightened his hold and spoke clearly for all to hear. "Drop your chin to your chest. Since you are not tall enough to strike me in the nose or throat, you will need to rise on your toes to gain as much height as possible, throw your head back as hard as you can, and in quick succession stomp on my toes. Your goal is for your attacker to loosen his hold just enough for you to escape, or at the very least, release your arms."

Graham squeezed Theo to prompt her to try the maneuver. She hesitated.

He could keep her in his arms forever, but she needed to practice. Graham leaned in to whisper into her ear. "This is the best way to ensure you are ready for a mission if the occasion arises."

Without further urging, Theo attempted to execute the reverse headbutt but came up short, and the back of her head only thumped against Graham's chest. Acknowledging the technique had failed, Graham suggested, "Evan and John can practice on you, and those remaining will observe. Among us all, we should be able to devise a more effective move."

THEO STOOD and listened to Graham's instructions. The power and confidence he exuded reflected a natural leader. His commands brooked no arguments, but what surprised her was that he was willing to engage others and hear their opinions. Did he garner everyone's trust with such ease?

Theo remained on the sidelines, watching the ladies attempt to perfect the maneuver. Her thoughts were on Graham, who was circling the group and issuing instructions. As he repositioned one of the ladies, Theo's gaze fell to his hands. She recalled his slight lingering touches and longed for them to be alone.

Over the course of their brief acquaintance, there had

been moments where they seemed able to anticipate each other's thoughts and actions. Knowing he, too, shared a similar duty to the Crown created a bond stronger than she could have imagined with someone she had only met a few days ago. Were these strange feelings for Graham the result of that bond, or was there something else causing them?

Her gaze fell upon Lucy, who was frowning while absently rubbing her stomach. She could see her friend was itching to jump into the foray of activity and was frustrated at her inability to participate. Surprisingly, Lucy allowed Graham to take the lead. She looked closer at her friend, and it was evident that Lucy trusted and admired Graham as a leader. Few gained such unwavering loyalty from her best friend.

Theo wouldn't learn from watching. She joined a group of ladies working with Evan. Lucy was indeed lucky to have a man as fine as him in her employ. Theo's gaze wandered back to Graham. Their gazes locked for a moment, and all thoughts of Evan were immediately forgotten. Would he be as fine-looking as Evan without his shirt? No, the outline of his body showed signs of indulgence. But she was still curious to see what lay beneath his shirt.

Graham crossed the room. "Shall we practice?"

Theo let him guide her through various maneuvers. After several adjustments, she was able to execute each with finesse.

"Let's regroup next week," Lucy called out.

How long had they been training? Not once had Graham appeared frustrated, lost his patience, or rushed her.

Sweaty and tired, each maid and footman thanked Graham for his time, patience, and knowledge. He appeared as physically exhausted as Theo, but he praised each and every one as they left, giving each specific and individualized praise. They had all improved significantly. She could not help but admire his abilities. Not only did she respect him, but she was also beginning to care for him. She had to be careful not to actually fall in love with the man.

After everyone else had left, Theo approached Graham. "My lord, thank you for a most educational afternoon."

She caught a glimmer of mischief in his gaze. "It was an honor, my lady. You are a very quick study, and I look forward to being invited to next week's gathering."

Surely she would see him before next week. Would he be at Lady Essex's soirée later this evening?

Before she could inquire, Graham said, "My lady, I have invited your family to dine with mine tonight. I hope you don't mind dining with Max and Clare."

"Oh, I wouldn't miss the opportunity to see your nephew and niece. They are delightful, and I'll have an opportunity to compliment Clare on her hairdressing skills." Theo giggled.

Lucy stifled a laugh. Theo had forgotten all about her friend.

"Since I've strict instructions to remain at home," Lucy said, "I'll be busy planning and arranging for our house party a week henceforth. Theo, please advise Landon the invitation will arrive shortly, and while he may beg off, I fully expect you to attend."

"Why on earth are you hosting a house party at the height of the Season?"

Graham answered on Lucy's behalf. "She has been experiencing some birthing pains, and Blake decided they should retire to the country to ensure Lucy follows the midwife's advice for rest and relaxation. I, for one, would enjoy a few weeks away."

Theo turned to Graham. "*You* are attending?"

Lucy chimed in. "I thought it a grand idea. It will allow the two of you to get to know each other in a more intimate setting rather than under the ever-watchful eyes of the *ton*. Courting can be rather tricky business, I hear."

The smirk on Lucy's lips vanished. Lucy's shoulders slouched forward, making her look smaller, a feat given her present condition. Distracted by the change in Lucy's demeanor, Theo only noticed that Blake had entered the room when he passed her on his way to his wife. How had Lucy detected her husband before his appearance?

"How was your afternoon, sweetheart?" Blake questioned as he bent to kiss Lucy on the forehead. Theo smiled as Lucy surprised her husband by raising on her tiptoes and tilting her head to ensure his lips would land squarely on her own.

Graham slid Theo a knowing look. "My lady, please allow me to escort you to your carriage."

Graham winged his arm, and she gently placed her hand in the crook of his arm.

As Theo crossed the threshold, she heard Blake say, "To bed with you, wife."

Lucy never did well when given orders. What would her response be?

Lucy responded, "Only if you will join me."

Graham chuckled, which only made Theo frown.

"Don't worry. Blake will see to her care." Graham led Theo out to her awaiting carriage.

It was the middle of the day. Lucy was never tired. Were her birthing contractions more of a concern than what she was letting on? Perhaps a retreat to the countryside would be good for her.

Graham assisted Theo into her awaiting carriage. Why was it she blindly followed this man's lead? As she settled on the bench, Graham leaned in and gave her a chaste kiss.

He winked. "I can't wait until this evening."

This evening? Was he referring to dinner, Lady Essex's musical evening, or Theo's bedchamber? Images of him relaxed next to her on the bed flooded her mind. She hoped he meant to come and assist her with sorting through the remaining correspondence from Baldwin. Yes, she too was looking forward to an evening with Graham.

CHAPTER NINETEEN

"Uncle Gam! I can't hear what you are sayin'; you're too far away from me." Clare pouted. She had made it clear to Graham that she did not care for this evening's seating arrangement. She usually sat to the right of her uncle.

"Clare, we have guests tonight, and we need to adhere to the proper social etiquette."

Aunt Henri patted Graham on the arm. "I've never been a stickler for the rules. Let's let the little ones sit in the middle, shall we?"

"Oohhh. That is a wonderful idea, Lady 'adfield, then I get to be near Uncle Gam, *and* I get to sit next to you and Lady Tee-o." Clare was delighted and hopped up from her chair. The footmen seamlessly rearranged the seating. Max rolled his eyes but also stood, and he too switched seats, placing him in the middle between Landon and Christopher.

Graham looked at his niece directly and asked, "Are you happy now, Clare?"

"Yes, Uncle Gam, very 'appy!" The grin Clare gave her uncle melted all the hearts around the table.

"Why can't Lady Tee-o have dinner with us every eve?" Clare asked as she placed her tiny hand on Theo's arm. Not waiting for an answer, Clare declared, "Uncle Gam, you must marry Lady Tee-o then you can kiss 'er, and we can have all our meals with 'er!"

Landon's narrowed gaze fell upon him, prompting the smirk to emerge which Graham had been trying to prevent from appearing. His clever niece had read his mind. Theo would be a wonderful mother and a spectacular Lady Archbroke.

Max redirected the conversation. "Lord Hadfield, do you play cricket? I've been practicing my throws since I last saw you in the park."

Landon never removed his gaze from Graham but answered Max's question. "Have you? I haven't played cricket since I left Cambridge, but my brother, Mr. Neale here, is famous for his bowling skills."

Max turned to Christopher. "Mr. Neale, would you have the time to teach me how to bowl?"

Christopher looked at Graham over the boy's head. Graham gave his silent approval. Christopher replied, "I would indeed, Max. I'll come around tomorrow and take you to the park."

"Mr. Kissoper, can I go to the park too?" Clare asked. She rounded her eyes and tilted her head.

The girl knew exactly what she was doing. She was going to be a force to deal with when she became of age. Graham would have to help Beckham keep her out of trouble. Or she could... No, Flora would never allow her daughter to become involved with either the Home Office or their duties to the Crown.

His own children would have no choice. What if he

were to only sire daughters? Girls with dark pigtails and green eyes. He glanced at Theo. Yes, small replicas of the beautiful woman beside him. She would make him a fine wife. Intelligent. Brave. He wouldn't have to be fearful of her reaction to his family secret. Theo would be perfect. How to convince her that they should turn their faux courtship into a real one?

Christopher grinned at the child's attempt to manipulate him. "I can't deny a lady's request. Of course you may join us."

"Arghhh… but she can't throw the ball!" Max groaned.

"As her big brother, it is your responsibility to teach her," Graham interjected.

"Will you be joining us, Uncle Graham?" Max asked.

The excitement in the boy's eyes brought about a stabbing pain in his chest as he knew it would be extinguished as soon as he uttered his denial. "Unfortunately, I won't be able to Max. Perhaps next time."

The disappointment on the boy's face was exactly as Graham had anticipated. Immediately regretting his refusal to join them, Graham weighed the impact of delaying his meetings. Despite the urge to make Max happy, he knew he could not ignore the nature of his dealings. He had to address the matters without delay.

"Perhaps I will accompany you and Christopher after all," said Landon.

Max's demeanor brightened at Hadfield's words. Guilt crawled up Graham's spine as his shoulders slumped forward. His thoughts were at war. The constant duties of the Home Office and his obligations to the Crown made it challenging to satisfy his desires for a family.

For the rest of the meal, he remained relatively quiet; Theo and the other adults at the table took pity on him and maintained a steady level of chatter with the children.

Once the last dessert plate was removed, Max and Clare jumped down from their chairs and individually hugged each guest before saying good night to Graham.

After releasing Max from a hug, he held on to the boy's arm. "Max, I'm sorry—"

Max placed his small hand over Graham's mouth to prevent him from saying more. "Uncle Graham, you don't have to be sorry. You have many responsibilities. You have spent more time with Clare and me than our own papa has. You share your meals with us, and you truly listen to what we have to say. We love you, and I wish we did not have to leave with Grandmama in a few days." Max removed his hand from Graham's mouth and moved it to cup Graham's ear. Leaning in, Max whispered, "I thank you for offering an apology. It means much to me."

How was it Max was only six years of age? He had the soul and mind of a young man. Happy he had chosen to spend the time to become better acquainted with his nephew and niece, Graham made a mental note to speak to their papa, for Beckham was missing the opportunity to discover how truly extraordinary his children were.

Graham wrapped Max up in another hug and brought Clare into the mix.

Clare gave him a sloppy wet kiss on the cheek. She dashed to Theo's side. Clare pulled on Theo's sleeve, and Theo bent her head. What was his niece up to?

"Lady Tee-o, I know you can make Uncle Gam smile. 'Ee always does when 'ee looks at you. Maybe you can make 'im feel better."

He caught Theo's gaze. Her cheeks heated as she pressed a kiss to the girl's head and promised, "Clare, I will try my best."

All the woman had to do was look at him, and his

miseries were forgotten and replaced with rather indecent thoughts of her naked and under him.

"It's time we head to Lady Essex's," Landon declared.

Landon's entire family groaned in unison at his announcement.

"Hadfield," Graham asked, "will I see you at Gentleman Jackson's tomorrow?"

Landon frowned. "Are you not attending this eve?"

"Unfortunately, I won't be able to." Graham had uttered the exact same words earlier and received the same reaction of disappointment from Theo as he had from Max. Her disappointment had him experiencing a tightening in his chest.

Theo's gaze was focused on the tip of her shoes. He took her elbow to escort her to the foyer.

"Will I see you later?" Theo whispered as he draped her cloak over her shoulders.

"No, not tonight. I need to rest in my own bed tonight. But I promise tomorrow I will seek you out." He hadn't slept in over forty-eight hours. He needed to rest.

Theo's shoulders slumped, but when she turned, her eyes were clear, and there were no signs of tears. Thank goodness she was not one to bring about the waterworks when she didn't get her way, unlike his three older sisters. When he looked closer at her features, there was something akin to determination. What was going through that brilliant mind of hers? He was too tired to figure it out.

He only hoped whatever it was, she would be safe.

A LOUD COMMOTION coming from the kitchens woke Graham up. Rolling out of bed in his smalls, he grabbed his banyan and flew down the stairs.

"What do you think you are doing? Sneaking around the back…" Mills hauled a small vagabond through the servants' entrance door. He dragged the urchin by the arm closer to the kitchen fire.

When the urchin's hood slid back, Graham nearly snorted out loud as Mills released Theo and jumped back as if he might catch on fire. "Oh m'lady! I'm sorry… I didn't know…"

Mills's sudden release of her left Theo unbalanced. She fell backward, landing unceremoniously on her rear end before Graham could reach her.

He reached down and assisted her to her feet. Holding her tightly against his side, he addressed his valet. "Mills, thank you for seeing to Lady Theo's safety. That will be all."

In all the years Mills had been in service with his family, Graham had never seen the man rattled. He, too, was surprised by Theo's arrival, but happiness flooded his body, and her being close overrode any rational thoughts.

Theo buried her head into his side, but not before he caught the red flush upon her cheek. Theo trembled in his arms, and he began to rub her back to soothe her. But when she wrapped her arms around him, bodies flush against each other, he had to fight the urge to toss her over his shoulder and take her up to his room.

He made it a point to never bring lady birds to his residence, and for a lady to show up in the middle of the night was highly irregular. He trusted his servants not to gossip, but it wouldn't hurt to be overly cautious. He gently pried Theo away from him. "Love, we should retire to the library."

Theo stiffened at the endearment, but it had naturally rolled off his tongue, and he was not sorry for having uttered it. He wanted her to be his. His countess. While he had come to a decision, Theo might not have come to the same conclusion that they would be suited. He would have to be patient. It was not one of his stronger traits.

Theo remained quiet, but she allowed him to guide her. Her head bent and the hood pulled low, he couldn't see her face, nor could she see where she was going. She had entrusted him with her safety. He was making progress. He modified his stride to accommodate her slightly smaller steps. They moved effortlessly as one.

As he closed the library door, Graham turned her to face him. "If you are admonishing yourself for failing to enter undetected, you should have attempted a residence without highly trained staff."

Her cheeks were flushed, and she shrugged her shoulders. He let his hands fall but only to land firmly around her waist. He pulled her closer and bent his head.

Staring directly into his eyes, Theo lightly brushed her lips across his. "It would appear I require more practice." She turned and strode over to the fire.

Mills must have seen to it moments before, for the log was not fully ablaze. Theo stood, rubbing her arms. He approached her as he would a skittish cat. Slow and quiet. Standing behind her, he reached around and efficiently removed her cloak. Goose bumps appeared on her arms. He slowly turned her to face him and widened his stance. With his height lowered, he rested his chin gently on her shoulder. The natural fit of their bodies brought to mind the thought she had been made just for him. He gathered her up in his arms and tried to infuse his own warmth into her.

CHAPTER TWENTY

They stood not uttering a word, only the sound of their breathing breaking the silence. After a few moments, they both inhaled and exhaled in harmony. Theo's skin tingled from the simple act of breathing in unison. Warm and secure in Graham's embrace, she was loath to break the silence, but her legs began to buckle. "Graham, I... I need to—"

Before Theo could finish her request, Graham bent to pick her up, one arm under her knees and the other securely around her back. His warmth was inviting, and she wrapped her arms around his neck. Needing to be closer still, she shifted her weight until she was comfortably cradled in his arms. Effortlessly, he carried her to a nearby high wingback chair that faced the fire. The ease in which he held her made her feel as if she was as light as a feather.

Graham slowly lowered to sit with her in his lap, draping her legs over the arm of the chair. Theo peeked up at him, his blue gaze intense and mesmerizing. Her hands itched to move and explore his chest, but she kept one hand on his shoulder while the other rested in her lap.

"Are you comfortable, love?" he asked.

She was about to admonish him for using such an intimate endearment, for surely it wasn't sincere. But the depth of honesty and affection in Graham's eyes squelched her objections. Theo searched for the right word to describe how he made her feel. Cherished. Another feeling she was not accustomed to. It was as if he treasured every moment they spent together. She simply needed to allow him to care for her.

He moved his arm from under her knees and placed his large hand on the top of her thigh. She wiggled farther into his lap to prolong the moment. Held by Graham, it felt like home.

"Yes, thank you." And before she lost her courage, Theo admitted, "I adore being in your arms, and your kisses are divine."

She wanted him to kiss her again. Her gaze roamed over his features but landed on his lips that were forming a very seductive smile. Relaxed as he was, he was incredibly handsome. Distracted by the curve of his lips, Theo licked her own and began to wiggle. His fingers immediately dug into her thigh.

"Love, I caution you it is not wise to continue to move in such a fashion."

She was confused at first by his meaning, but then he moved. Something nudged at her hip, and she stilled for a moment. Deciding it best to be daring, she cupped his face with both hands and brought his lips to meet her own.

She peppered tentative kisses on his mouth willing him to respond but he remained still allowing her to take the lead. With each kiss she increased the heat and intensity until Graham rewarded her with a groan. The sound empowered her to continue. She raked her fingertips over his head with his short hair tickling her palms; the sensation caused her to giggle and break their kiss.

How was it Graham was able to bring out the bold, daring side of her? No one had ever made her feel this at ease or confident. She wanted to laugh and hear him laugh. Her blood heated when he touched her. Her skin's sensitivity heightened and was only soothed by his touch. When he was near, she felt daring and invincible. He stirred something in her heart.

Her focus was drawn to their hands as he reached out to take hers in his. He began to rub her wrists in a circular motion with his thumbs. When she raised her eyes to meet his, intense bright blue pools stared back at her. Theo's breathing hastened at the rawness of his gaze. Overwhelmed, she inhaled slowly through her nose and exhaled through slightly parted lips. Graham immediately inhaled, sharing her breath. Theo found herself mimicking his actions, and soon they were trading the air around them. Theo's body began to hum, and as she inhaled, it was as if Graham were infusing energy into her as he exhaled. The experience was electrifying. Shock and panic twisted at her as wetness pooled at her apex only to be replaced with a deep desire for Graham to touch her in the most private areas of her body.

When she tensed to prevent herself from wriggling, Graham asked, "Is there something bothering you, love?"

"No, all is well." Theo frowned and shook her head. She needed him to understand. "It is all very new and confusing. I feel connected to you in a way that I have not ever experienced with another." She paused again. Her mind raced, searching for the right words. "While your caress remains at my wrist, it is as if I can feel you throughout my entire body. As if you are inside me, yet I feel the need to get closer to you."

She had made a hash of explaining herself. Graham's features were strained. Was he not experiencing the same sensations? She was about to pull away.

"Theo, everything you are feeling and experiencing is natural and normal, nothing that should cause you alarm."

Shaking her head, she replied, "I don't think you fully understand."

"Oh, but I do, for I feel the energy between us also." He shifted his gaze to the top of her head and continued, "There is a tingling feeling that starts with your scalp. It feels as if I had wrapped your silky tresses in my hand and gently pulled on your hair. The slight feeling of pain is then swiftly replaced with lightness, as if I had massaged the hurt away." He lowered his eyes to her ears. "You can hear my heart beat as if it were in your own chest." His eyes continued to move down to her lips. "As you inhale the air I just exhaled, it brushes across your lips, and you can feel it enter your lungs as if I'm somehow filling you. In essence, a part of me continues to make its way to your heart, but then you feel the rush of blood throughout your body as it heats every muscle and fiber. It is the most euphoric feeling."

He lowered his gaze even farther to her breasts, and her nipples hardened visibly through the sheer white material of her shirt. He licked his lips as he ventured to express, "Your skin feels heated and extremely sensitive against your clothing. Any movement, no matter how slight, causes a tingling sensation that can be felt throughout, but most especially in the most intimate areas of your body."

Graham had slowly moved his hand farther up her thigh and now cupped her apex. "Theo, have you ever explored yourself?"

At the startling question, embarrassed, she shook her

head. Curious, she asked, "Do women touch themselves for pleasure?"

Unequivocally Graham replied, "Certainly."

Theo's mind whirled with questions and possibilities. Without further hesitation, she looked directly at Graham and began to ask, "Will you… could you…"

What was she asking? His eyes widened as if he knew exactly what she was requesting. Clearing his throat, he gruffly spoke. "My love, it would be an honor but not this evening. I must ensure your safe return, and then I really need sleep."

The dark shadows under his eyes were evidence of how tired he was. She should leave him to rest but was loath to leave his company. "I'd rather not depart right now."

As she rose, Graham did the same. She reached for his hand and interwove their fingers. Graham looked down at her and grinned, "You may remain for a while longer, but you will return before dawn. I won't have you compromised."

She couldn't contain her smile. Graham was going to let her stay. Eager to be in his company, she tugged him closer only to find herself falling, and he lifted her up to carry her out of the library.

He was muttering under his breath. Theo rested her head upon his shoulder as he carried her up the stairs. Would he tutor her in the ways to pleasure herself tonight? He had not denied her request, but had delayed it.

She deciphered some of his mutterings. *Honorable. Courtship. Relief. Sleep.* She couldn't piece his thoughts together. Content to be held, she closed her eyes. Odd, she had always been happy to be on her own and to an extent favored her solitude. Having been raised by extremely independent men, Theo was adept at seeking out her own amusements and interests. She prided herself on her own self-reliance, but Graham had in a short period become essential to her.

She opened her eyes as he gently set her down on an enormous bed. With her bottom perched on the edge, she bent to remove her boots. Not daring to look in Graham's direction, she calmly crawled to the head of the bed and slipped under the sheets. Graham began to remove his banyan but then hesitated. With a groan, he let the garment fall. Wide-eyed, Theo stared. Graham wore only his smalls. How was it that he was not cold? Her hands itched to reach out and roam his body. It was not as defined as Evan's, but she was still eager to explore him. She gripped the edge of the coverlet to prevent from reaching out. He slipped under the sheets and lay next to her. She didn't hesitate. She snuggled into his side, but her head rested at an odd angle. Graham shifted. She had no choice but to lift her head and scuttle back. But Graham's arm snaked about her waist and rolled her until her back was to his chest. He pulled her closer and stretched out his other arm in the space under her neck to pillow her head.

He kissed the back of her head and said, "Rest, my love."

Frustrated he had not changed his mind about tutoring her, she closed her eyes. Moments later, contentment seeped into her bones. What would it be like to share a bed with him every eve?

Theo awoke to someone pacing beyond the door. She began to grin as her eyes adjusted to the dim light. Next to her Graham was sprawled on his stomach, one arm hanging over the side of the bed and the other bent, lying above his head. Sliding quietly out of bed, she tiptoed to the end of the bed and picked up her boots and made her way to the door. She turned to glimpse at Graham one more time before she left. He was handsome when at rest. Her knees weakened at the sight of him. She needed to go before she sought out his warmth once again.

She opened the door quietly and exited. She was not surprised at the sight of Mills, mumbling and walking up and down the hall.

Smiling, Theo greeted him. "Good morn, Mills." She saw the uncertainty on his face and continued, "I want to thank you for assisting Wallace. It has made both her and my own transition into our new roles much easier."

Mills's shoulders relaxed. "It is our family's duty and honor to serve. Emma was wise to choose Bessie, for while she is young, she is smart and discreet. We are proud of her."

"Mills, perhaps you could assist me in allowing one of your footmen to accompany me home. I wouldn't want Lord Archbroke to worry, and I don't wish to disturb him at this moment."

"Lady Theodora, I am your loyal servant and will always assist you in any manner you request," Mills solemnly replied, but then to her surprise he winked at her.

CHAPTER TWENTY-ONE

Lucy's library walls were lined with volumes that Theo had found edifying. The books covered a wide variety of subjects—scientific matter, geography, astronomy—but there was one in particular that had caught Theo's attention. She had flipped through the book as Lucy lay dozing on the settee. The challenge was that the volume was written in Russian.

Possessing a rudimentary knowledge of the language, she was able to deduce that the novel made references to scantily dressed ladies of the night. It was the descriptions of their activities and references to the Bible that had Theo questioning her translation. When Lucy began to stir, Theo jumped up and exchanged the novel for another.

Theo lifted the book to nose level. The words were a blur. Her thoughts were miles away and on one particular person.

"Theo, come quick!" Lucy shouted.

Toppling the chair, Theo jumped up and in a panic ran to Lucy, who was lying on a couch. Standing over her friend, she urgently asked, "What is the matter? Should I fetch the midwife?"

"Look!" Lucy pointed to her stomach where the tight material of her dress began to move. Lucy grabbed Theo's hand and placed it where the baby had shifted.

"Lucy, that has to be the most incredibly odd sensation!" Theo remarked as she pulled her hand away and took a step back. What had she felt? The baby's elbow? Foot? Head?

"I know this sounds crazy, but I find his movements extremely reassuring."

Theo looked down at Lucy before asking, "How do you know it is a boy?"

"I can't be certain. But my mama told me from the looks of how I'm carrying the babe she believes it will be a boy. I have not shared that bit of information with Blake, for he has told me repeatedly that he hopes it will be a little girl. One who can keep the future heir out of trouble."

Theo laughed at Lucy's imitation of Blake. The truth was that she was a tad jealous of Lucy. Her best friend had found the one man who could match her intelligence and wit and utterly adored her eccentricity. As Theo spent more time in Blake's company, she found him to be an extraordinarily kind and considerate husband. Lucy had always been a strong, confident woman, but now she was also happy and more at ease. The couple complemented each other's temperament. Theo began to contemplate her own disposition and how it had changed since meeting Graham.

"Are you even listening to me?" Lucy placed her palms flat behind her and pushed, managing to straighten her elbows before she gasped and her frown deepened.

Before Lucy's pinched expression was gone, Theo was

beside her. She was perched on the edge of the couch and reached over to rub Lucy's back. "The midwife instructed you to remain on your side or back. What are you doing?"

Lucy rolled back to lay on her side. "Happy? Now tell me why you were woolgathering."

"I was thinking about Archbroke."

"The man can be extremely overbearing at times, but I do admire and respect him. He has run the Home Office with a maturity beyond his years. Many have commented that he oversees its operations with unparalleled efficiency and authority."

"I was considering him as a suitor, not as the man in charge of the Home Office," Theo quietly replied.

When Lucy's gaze narrowed on her, Theo knew she had made a misstep.

"I've never told you who my superior was until now." Lucy rose up on an elbow. "Suitor! Have you fallen in love with Archbroke?"

Theo stopped rubbing Lucy's back. She nearly thumped Lucy when she had uttered the word love. "No! I've enjoyed spending time and getting better acquainted with Archbroke. But love? No. He is... fascinating."

"Fascinating? Well, I guess that is one way of describing the man," Lucy snorted.

"Why do you suppose Archbroke assumes the obnoxious dandy role at events?"

"At first, I thought it merely an act to dissuade the marriage-minded members of the *ton*. But an eligible earl is still considered a prime catch regardless of how he acts or dresses." The crease on Lucy's forehead deepened. "Over the years, I've noticed his behavior mirrors the demands of the Home Office. The greater his duties become, the more outlandish he is in his deportment. He's not known for engaging in other vices; whoring, gambling, or drinking. I believe it is an outlet for him. A way to free himself of the responsibilities he inherited."

What Lucy didn't know was that not only had Graham inherited the duty of running the Home Office, but he was also bound to serve the Crown directly. A heaviness in Theo's chest had her struggling for air. How had Graham managed on his own all these years? The overwhelming burden of her duties had barely begun to weigh upon her when Graham had come along and offered to assist her. Theo would forever be grateful for his sound advice as to how to navigate the complexities of keeping their roles a secret when she had needed it most.

"If that is the case, he must have some rather hefty duties of late."

Lucy let out a chuckle. "Are you serious? Archbroke hasn't been in full character since…" The ripple in Lucy's gown indicated the child had moved again. Eyes squeezed shut, Lucy said, "You."

"Are you well? Should I go fetch the midwife?"

"No. Don't. Do. That." Lucy inhaled deeply. "Blake will insist we leave for Shalford immediately, and I do so enjoy spending time with you."

The pull on Theo's heartstrings reminded her that Lucy was a master puppeteer and would use any tactic available to get her way.

Eyes closed, Lucy appeared relaxed. There was no sign of discomfort on her features. Theo stared at her protruding stomach. *Children.*

A passage from the Russian novel flashed through Theo's mind. "I'm curious as to what exactly occurs between a husband and wife that results in…" Theo moved her hand forward and rubbed Lucy's protruding stomach and continued, "the wife becoming enceinte."

Eyes flying open, Lucy grasped Theo's arm. "Why do you ask? Has Archbroke tried to—"

"Oh no! Archbroke has been most honorable," Theo defended him. "We have kissed, but I'm certain there is more. And when he kisses me, it makes me feel…"

Lucy finished her thoughts by saying, "Alive… like you can walk on air… like you want to crawl into his skin… you need more kisses… shall I go on?"

"No need. That is exactly what I feel and more!" Theo was elated that Lucy understood.

"I'm certain that Archbroke knows exactly what to do and how to best guide you if and when the appropriate time comes. Are you considering marriage? Is the courtship progressing?"

Marriage. The idea hadn't even crossed Theo's mind, but a dalliance had. The similarities between the sensations described in the novel and those that Graham created within her were confusing. Her translation led her to believe if she acted on those wildly invigorating feelings, she too would somehow end up in Lucy's condition. However, she couldn't decipher from the book's flowery descriptions what exactly transpired between a couple to conceive a child.

"Theo?"

"Yes?"

"Archbroke. Marriage?"

Theo wished she could confide in her best friend. Confess the courtship was a sham. Marriage was out of the question. She had no idea how to respond without being dishonest. "Why don't I read to you?"

Masking her emotions was a skill Theo believed she had mastered. This would be the ultimate test as Lucy's narrowed gaze roamed over her features.

Releasing a sigh, Lucy leaned back and closed her eyes

once more. “That would be nice. But if you are going to read, please hold the book right side up this time.”

CHAPTER TWENTY-TWO

Theo was impatient for the midnight hour. She had spent the past few days assisting Lucy in preparing for the house party. However, Lucy and Blake had left early that morn for Shalford Castle to ready rooms and finalize menus with the cook. Theo had sent a note over to Graham's town house inquiring if the children would like to go on a picnic but was informed that Graham's mama had already left town and taken them to his country estate for the week before their parents' return. Graham was buried in paperwork at the Home Office, and she dared not disturb him in case he fell behind and would not visit her in the evening.

His evening visits were the highlight of her days. Each evening, he would sneak through her window, and they would work side by side, puzzling over how the drawings were interrelated. To date they had not succeeded in piecing it together. When they tired, they would crawl into her bed, and he would hold her until she fell asleep. He had not fulfilled his promise to teach her more about intimacy. To her frustration, each morn he would kiss her until she was unable to think and then leave her bed before the early streaks of dawn filtered into her room.

With no plans, Theo wandered the halls of the town house until she came across her aunt sitting in the drawing room by herself.

"Aunt Henri, I thought you had left to visit Lady Barstow for tea." Theo bent to give her aunt a kiss on the cheek.

"No, my dear. I've been meaning to talk to you about something rather important."

Guilt and panic began to raise Theo's heart rate. Her mind raced with all the various topics her aunt may want to address with her. She knew that Aunt Henri was extremely intelligent, but she had counted on her aunt's good nature not to bring up difficult topics. Trying to stall for more time, Theo asked, "Shall I ring for tea?"

"Tea would not be strong enough for this conversation. Why don't you come have a seat, and we can get on with it." Aunt Henrietta eyed Theo as she calmly sat facing her and arranged her skirts as a last effort to delay.

Finally, when Theo met Aunt Henrietta's gaze, she continued, "You are the daughter of my heart. Unknowingly, I married into a family that has held many secrets for generations. For selfish reasons, I listened to your papa, wanting not to burden my own children with the risks tied to the duties to the Crown. I do not know the reasons why your papa was so adamant you inherit the volume, but both your papa and I agreed that you had the strength and wisdom to honor the family's duty to the Crown. Initially, you seemed lost and uncertain of your own abilities, and I confess that in the beginning I worried for you. But you have far exceeded my own expectations and I'm certain your papa would be so proud of you." Aunt Henrietta reached out to place Theo's hand in hers as her eyes began to mist.

Theo was at a loss for words. She never knew her mama, who had died shortly after giving birth to her. Aunt Henrietta had been a stable influence and a source of strength for Theo during her year of mourning for her papa. Her aunt always sensed when she needed support or an encouraging word while she was muddling through learning the information contained in the volume. Now Theo squeezed her aunt's hand, finally knowing that she could discuss the matter with her as she had desperately wanted over the past few months.

"I'm aware that you are working with Archbroke on some matter, for he visits you each evening."

Theo responded by raising one eyebrow in her aunt's direction.

Aunt Henrietta continued, "I believe he told Landon some Banbury tale to gain permission to court you. I hope that Archbroke was completely honest with you and that your courtship was a plan devised to allow the two of you to spend more time in each other's presence without raising questions. Over the past week, I have seen a change in the way the two of you interact. I have faith that Archbroke is a gentleman and will not dare take advantage of you or the circumstances. However, Theo, you must know nothing more than friendship can occur between you both."

Theo's shoulders slumped. Agreeing to the sham courtship had been a mistake. Graham had brought down walls she had carefully erected to protect herself. Aunt Henrietta was right. They were honor bound. Theo's heart cracked. Graham had no intention of pursuing her to be Lady Archbroke. It must be why he did not pursue any further intimacy between them. He didn't want to be honor bound to marry her. While Graham had developed the habit of using the word love when referring to her, it was merely a word and not a sentiment. But his eyes had lied to her. There had been a flare in them. Could his bodily reaction to her in his arms be mere pretense?

As the truth of her aunt's words hit her, Theo's heart began to shatter. Straightening her spine, Theo blinked away tears she refused to shed.

Aunt Henrietta placed a finger under Theo's chin, forcing Theo to meet her serious eyes. "Any male child born to you would be expected to carry the burden you currently bear, and the same goes for Archbroke. It would be unreasonable to expect anyone to bear both burdens, and each role is critical to the Crown. I see now that in agreeing to your papa's wishes I have denied you the opportunity to have a family with the man you love."

Love? No matter how many times Theo told herself that her attraction to Graham was of a purely physical nature, she knew her aunt was correct. Graham had wheedled his way into her heart. Raised by the servants, without a mama, and with an often-absent papa, Theo had been well cared for, but love was an entirely foreign notion. Theo's tendency to distance herself from others was born out of necessity to guard herself from disappointment and heartache. Yet, it also meant she had denied herself from developing stronger bonds with others. And the relationship she had begun to form with Aunt Henrietta and her cousins made her whole.

Theo drew her hand out of her aunt's grip. "Why ever do you believe I am in love with Archbroke?" She could not admit to her aunt the truth. "He was indeed honest with me from the beginning of our association. He has assisted me in understanding a volume written by men intended for male descendants for decades and provided opportunities for me to train here in town. You are correct that we are currently working together on a matter. I appreciate you not mentioning the issue to Landon."

Theo took a deep breath. With all the bravado she could muster, she said, "Aunt Henri, you must not regret any of your decisions, for I understand my courtship with Archbroke is a farce. I have come to respect and admire the man. Who wouldn't? I think you have mistaken my regard for Archbroke, for I am not in love." But even as the words left her mouth, the pain in Theo's chest took away her breath.

Aunt Henrietta blinked twice before giving her head a slight shake. Theo stood up and moved to sit directly next to her aunt, wrapping her arms around her aunt's waist, inadvertently seeking out the comfort and reassurance all would be well.

When Aunt Henrietta instantly returned her embrace, Theo was infused with energy and warmth. She would have to be content with the love she received from her relatives.

Aunt Henri mumbled into her hair, "I'll always be here for you, child."

A GLOSSY, spit-shined Hessian slipped through her window. The rest of Graham appeared, and Theo released a pent-up breath. Standing, Graham stopped immediately. His eyes fell to the scattered papers and journals covering her bedroom floor. She usually waited for his arrival to begin, but she had been so much at a loss after the discussion with Aunt Henri that she had started hours before.

"Theo, my love?"

Hearing his endearment and the quickening of her

heart brought about the resolve to resurrect walls. She had replayed her discussion with Aunt Henri repeatedly throughout the afternoon and evening. Her aunt was right. Their courtship was a sham, and nothing could come from it. She spied him from the adjoining chamber, and after taking several deep, fortifying breaths, she poked her head around the door casing. "I'll be out in a minute. Stay where you are and try not to disturb anything."

Did he want to wrap her up in his arms and kiss her as he had every evening prior?

"What are you about, Theo?"

Was that irritation in his voice? She had to retain space and her resolve. "I have been re-reading Baldwin's notes, letters, and entries in the journal. His annotations become brief and rather obscure just before his death." Her voice wavered at the mention of Baldwin. She regained her composure and continued, "I was reading his letters and the markings alongside his entries, and I found something of interest."

She entered the bedroom but dared not get too close to Graham.

Graham's features darkened as he ordered, "Come." His hand reached out.

Ignoring his command, Theo tiptoed to place the most distance between them before saying, "Baldwin was suspicious of the information and resources sent to him on his last mission. He alluded that there were times he believed he was being trailed and that at other times he was one step behind another in his search for the maps."

Graham was now stalking her as they tiptoed around the strewn papers. She stopped to pick up one note in particular and immediately found herself wrapped in his embrace from behind.

He whispered in her ear. "Why are you avoiding me, love?"

She stiffened. "I… Archbroke, you should not use such endearments. It is just you and me. There is no need to pretend."

He turned her to face him directly. "What is the matter? Who said anything of pretending?"

Theo's eyes focused on his intricately tied cravat. Unable to find the string of words that would mirror her aunt's eloquent explanation as to why their courtship should remain a farce, Theo shrugged her shoulders. "We have work to do. Important work that affects many. Our courtship is a ruse. You do not love me and should refrain from using such endearments when speaking with me."

He released her as if she had slapped him. She slowly raised her gaze to meet his.

"I do not lie, Theo. I do not mistake my feelings for you. I apologize if I misunderstood your regard. I believed your kisses and embraces to mean that you cared for me. Now I realize how foolish I have been since you have yet to say the words in return."

Graham's tension and pain seeped into her pores and affixed themselves to her heart. She wished she could take back her cruel words. She wanted him to hold her once more. Instead, he moved toward the window.

With one leg swung over the windowsill, he said, "Your discoveries are most intriguing, and I do wish to know more. Perhaps you will send a summary of your findings; have Landon deliver them to me directly."

He looked out into the night before returning his gaze to her. "Please send word if you need my assistance."

And then he was gone. Graham's words were like a red hot poker being driven into her chest. He had always been truthful with her. Had he truly meant the endearments?

She stood frozen. A tear slid down her cheeks. His words sunk in, and her heart began to shatter. Graham had meant every word he had spoken. It was her own thoughts and feelings that she questioned.

Theo's vision was clouded as she looked at the array of papers. What a mess. Her eyes narrowed. A pattern among the letters and drawings appeared. Brushing away her tears, she began working on rearranging the items.

Streaks of daylight were beginning to streak through the window. Theo had eliminated most of the drawings and had whittled down the pile to ten. Standing, she stretched her back muscles after hours and hours of standing, kneeling, and bending over the renderings; her muscles were sore and tired. Her exhaustion was countered by exhilaration. She was sure the map was somehow contained within these ten drawings.

Fitfully tossing in her sleep, Theo was tangled up in her bedsheets instead of Graham's arms. Slowly, she emerged from her sleepy state only to find that a deep ache resided in the middle of her chest. Graham's parting words flooded her mind, and immediately she turned her head into her pillow and allowed the tears to flow.

Someone had entered her chamber, but not having time to compose herself, Theo did not move or address whoever had decided to enter without permission. She breathed in the fresh scent of violets, which was unique to her aunt, and simultaneously felt Aunt Henrietta rubbing her aching back with warm, gentle strokes.

Gently wiping the tears from her face, Aunt Henrietta asked, "Theo, what has you upset, dear?"

Throat raw from all the sobbing, Theo couldn't formulate words. She crumpled into her aunt's arms and began to weep again. Aunt Henri pried Theo's limp form gently away before looking directly into her eyes and pushed for an answer. "I cannot help if you do not confide in me, dear."

"I fear I made a monumental mistake," she croaked out between sobs. "I tried to explain to Archbroke as you had to me that nothing could come about between us, but…"

The haunting image of Graham and the hurt she had seen deep in his eyes flashed in her mind's eye. She began to cry as if her soul was being torn to pieces once more. She struggled to sit upright to finish her thought.

Aunt Henri cupped her cheeks. Eye to eye, she said, "But you are indeed in love with Archbroke."

Miserably, she nodded. "I am. However, I said things I did not mean, and… I'm not sure he will ever forgive me or trust me with his regard again." Water welled in her eyes as she added, "He left me with the impression he no longer wanted to see me… for any reason."

Her aunt pulled her gaze back up to hers. What did Aunt Henrietta see? Her aunt stared at her until a glimmer of hope appeared in the woman's eyes.

Clasping her by the cheeks, Aunt Henrietta proceeded to make a solemn promise. "I will figure out a way to make everything right."

How could her aunt make such a promise? Theo would refuse to relinquish the volume. She had made a promise to her papa on his deathbed, and she intended to honor it.

CHAPTER TWENTY-THREE

Footsteps fell outside his office door. Graham's heart pounded at the possibility that Theo would seek him out. He shook his head as if he could dispel the thoughts and images of her by the mere action.

Instead, Landon strode into his domain and planted his hands wide and flat on the desk. "What the devil did you do to upset Theo?"

Taking a deep breath, Graham steepled his fingers and placed them under his chin to prevent his mouth from falling open.

Landon fell back into the chair facing him and cracked his knuckles slowly, one at a time, one lip curled up in a sneer as he growled, "She has been crying for two days straight and has refused to emerge from her rooms."

Why was *she* crying? She had accused him of not loving her. She had coolly reminded him that their courtship was… what had she called it? A farce! It was nothing close to it in his mind. She had shattered his heart. Crushed. Pulverized. The one time he let himself feel something more than pure physical attraction, and this was his reward. Sleepless nights. Unable to eat. Unable to think of anything but her. Overwhelmed with concern for her well-being, he had even used Home Office resources to ensure she remained safe. Why hadn't his agents assigned to trail and protect her not reported Theo's distress?

With a sigh, Landon reached into his breast pocket. "She asked that I deliver this to you."

Graham eyed the parchment, debating whether he wanted to read its contents or not. Deciding to be done with it, he placed his hand out palm up. He neatly tucked it away in his own breast pocket.

"Aren't you going to read it?" Landon inquired.

"Later."

Brows creased and eyes narrowed, Landon placed his hands on his hips. "I've decided that we will adjourn to Devonton's early. Theo has always preferred the countryside to town. Are you still planning to attend?"

Graham motioned to the piles of correspondence on his desk. "Yes. However, I will only be on my way once I have addressed all the pressing matters here."

Landon eyed the stacks, his features fluid, reflecting a range of emotions from anxiety to confusion and back again.

"Did you end your courtship with Theo?"

Meeting Landon's glare, he remained steadfastly silent.

"Theo claims you are not to blame for her constant weeping, although I cannot fathom what else or who else could..."

"I can assure you, Theo made her feelings for me quite clear the last time we spoke. I am quite certain she has not been in agony over my lack of attendance on her these past days."

He had buried himself in work, ensuring that he was occupied from early morning to late at night in an attempt to ignore the deep hurt and anguish that lingered in his chest. Theo's blunt statement that she did not return his sentiments of love tortured his mind. He had wanted to return to Theo's chambers only hours after he had left her but wasn't confident he would be able to convince her of his love for her. Josie's words of advice haunted him—grant her freedom of choice and, most importantly, *be true to your heart*.

Landon rose to leave. Graham stood and met Landon's gaze. Anger blazed in the man's eyes.

Landon was the first to look away. "It has not gone unnoticed by me that Theo has accumulated a number of peculiar items that a daughter of an earl would not normally have in their possession. I *will* determine who has been assisting her in obtaining these items and discerning their purpose."

Should he share his predicament with Landon? Should he know that what was rightfully his was in Theo's possession? Never having acted impulsively before, he wasn't about to start now, even if it might mean a future with Theo.

"As the Hadfield patriarch, you should do as you see fit. That is until she is under the protection of a husband."

"I've informed you before there is no need for Theo to find a husband." Landon turned to leave and halted after a few strides. "Archbroke, ensure it will not be overly long before I see you at Shalford Castle."

As the door clicked closed, Graham slowly pulled Theo's missive out from his pocket and read:

Archbroke
All the drawings and letters have been evaluated.
I'm going to seek Lucy and Blake's assistance in reviewing a selection of drawings and letters.
Yours,
Theo

Clever girl. She figured it out on her own. She didn't need him. She sought out help from others and not him. The pains in his chest intensified. Theo's letter revealed no indication her feelings for him might have changed since their last meeting, each word more businesslike than the last. His only glimmer of hope was her closing. Carefully refolding the missive, he returned it to his breast pocket and refocused his attention back to the stack of requests awaiting his authorization.

CHAPTER TWENTY-FOUR

Theo attempted to ignore the banter between husband and wife as she arranged and rearranged the series of drawings to solve the conundrum of how they fit together to form a map.

Lucy held up one of Baldwin's sketches for Blake to assess. "This one looks… well, I guess I shouldn't say it in front of an unmarried woman." With a cheeky grin, she winked at her husband. "Well, my dear, what do you think of it?"

Blake glanced at the drawing purported to be a marble; its rendering was of certain aspects of the male anatomy. Coughing at the rather engorged rendition, Blake replied, "I'm shocked that Theo's brother believed it to be appropriate for her viewing."

With a loud sigh, Theo bemoaned, "We have been at this for days! I was certain that with the three of us trying to puzzle out the drawing, we would have the map in hand by now."

"Perhaps that is the problem; there are too many of us working on it concurrently," Lucy stated.

Was Lucy right? She was the most experienced and the one most likely to solve the rather complicated puzzle. Blake hovered over Lucy, rushing to her side every time she frowned. Meanwhile, Lucy was continually giving her husband devilish glances whenever he rubbed her back. Having him here might not be the most effective environment to encourage Lucy to focus. Combined with the couple's constant heated gazes and their sudden and often long absences, they were not making much progress at all.

"Theo, I believe my wife suggests we leave her to her own devices. Let's find Landon and see how he is faring with the lovely ladies in attendance."

Theo looked up at Blake from where she sat on the floor among the scattered sketches. "He might need a bit of a reprieve; Lady Cecilia has been rather determined. I imagine it is due to her suspicion that the map is in Landon's possession."

With an outreached hand, Blake offered to assist her to her feet. "That and I'm sure she doesn't find him hard on the eyes either."

"He does have fine features, but he's not nearly as handsome as you, my dear," Lucy said as she raised an eyebrow.

Theo tried not to roll her eyes but was unsuccessful. She liked the playful banter between the couple, but at times they were too much.

Lucy waved her hands at them. "Now off with you both! Blake, please have Carrington come attend to me and bring a fresh pot of tea."

Once Theo was on her feet, Blake approached Lucy who was lounging on the settee. He bent to place a kiss on her cheek, and as usual, Lucy caught him off guard at the last minute by turning and kissing him fully on the lips.

Theo envied the loving manner in which Blake treated

Lucy. Wistfully, she wished Graham was present and that they were back in accord with one another. But Graham had remained in London. It had been nearly two weeks since she last saw him. He had sent correspondence to Lucy about some matters he needed her assistance with at the Home Office. However, Theo had not received a single missive from him to date. She had spent many an hour dissecting the thoughts and emotions the man aroused in her. After confessing her love for him to Aunt Henri, she couldn't deny how essential he was to her. She only hoped she would have an opportunity to express to him her true feelings during the house party. If he ever arrived.

Blake guided her from the room. They found Carrington hovering in the hallway, laden with a tray piled with cucumber and raisin sandwiches—Lucy's most recent favorite items to eat. Holding the door open, Blake said, "Carrington, my thanks. Please make sure if she tires that you get her to return to our chambers."

With a semicurtsy, Carrington replied, "Yes, my lord. I will try my best."

Before Blake closed the door, he addressed Lucy, "I know you will resolve the issue. I will make excuses if you fail to appear for dinner, my love." Blake softly closed the door and saw Theo looking up at him. "Is something amiss?"

She blinked twice to prevent a tear from falling. "No. I'm glad Lucy found you."

"You mean rescued me?" Blake returned.

"Semantics. Now let's go find Landon."

"To Landon's rescue." Blake chuckled and winged his arm for her.

~

Walking into the garden, Theo saw that Lucy had arranged for her guests to partake in an archery competition. Three targets were assembled, and the guests had been paired into teams of two. Landon had been paired with Cecilia, Christopher with Arabelle, and Waterford with Mary. Footmen retrieved arrows as the male participants lined up, awaiting their turn.

Blake was scowling, his gaze on Waterford, who had apparently said something to make Mary frown. The man was not well liked by at least half the attendees. Why, Theo wondered, had he been invited?

"Archbroke ordered him to attend." Blake answered her unspoken question.

"I've never known Archbroke to act or instruct others without a purpose."

Blake's features transformed from a scowl to confusion. "I am in agreement. However, Waterford despises me, and I have no clue as to the reason why."

As they approached the archery contestants, Theo was greeted with wide smiles from the circle of ladies awaiting their turn. Smiles from all but one.

Cecilia's expression was closer to a smirk. "Lady Theo, I see you have finally decided to join us."

"Why, Lady Cecilia, I wouldn't miss the opportunity to cheer my cousins on." Theo's response dripped with sweetness. There was no better way to annoy someone who was filled with spite than to laden them with an abundance of kindness.

Both Landon and Christopher waved and gave her warm, loving smiles. She had begun to lower her guard with her cousins these past weeks as they had fawned over her, clearly sensing her sadness at Graham's absence. They threatened to pummel Graham once he made his appearance at the house party. Landon had expected him to have already arrived.

"Theo, if you would partner with me, I'll have another target set up," Blake said, jarring her back to the present.

"I would love to!"

At once, the footmen went to work arranging for another target to be added. Blake joined the men who were now placing wagers among themselves.

From the corner of Theo's eye, she caught a glimpse of a man at one of the upper windows of the house. Had Graham arrived? Theo's skin began to prickle, and she sensed someone was indeed watching her; but when she turned to face the windows, there was no one in sight.

"Are you regretting agreeing to stay out here and not hide away in the library or your chambers?" Cecilia taunted.

"I'm sure Lady Theo will prove to be a fierce competitor," Lady Mary replied in Theo's defense.

Theo wasn't intimately acquainted with Lady Mary. However, Lucy had informed her that the woman had a brilliant mind and a witty—and at times razor-sharp—tongue.

Theo smiled at the group. "I prefer knife throwing to archery."

Hearing a collective gasp at her pronouncement, she added, "Perhaps we should have a wager of our own, ladies."

With her youthful exuberance, Arabelle said, "Yes, that is a grand idea, Theo." With a slight frown, Arabelle tapped her finger over her lips. "The winner shall be granted a boon of her choice!"

An evil look crossed Cecilia's features before she said, "That is a marvelous prize. I am in agreement."

Wearily, Theo agreed. With Mary by her side, they

meandered over to the men who were ready to begin the round.

~

"ARCHBROKE! Please cease pacing. It is extremely distracting, especially when you make sounds similar to that of an angered animal," Lucy admonished.

Spying from the window, he watched as Blake escorted Theo outside to join the other house party guests. He didn't care for the hand Blake had placed on her elbow. He was aware of how in love Blake was with his wife, but no matter how platonic the touch, he did not care to see another man's hands on Theo.

He looked over at Lucy now madly scribbling notes. He had brought with him the key to the code that only the marked families used. When Lucy notified him that she had identified the code to be archaic in nature, Graham figured that Baldwin had used the secret code, figuring Theo would have access to it as well.

While he had extracted Lucy's promise never to reveal its existence, he still remained nervous about disclosing the generations-old code. "You are not to share the key with your husband, for once he sets his eyes upon it, it will be forever burned into his memory. I cannot risk his having such knowledge. Am I clear, Lucy?"

"Archbroke, I already gave you my word and swore on my dear child here," Lucy rubbed her protruding stomach.

"How much longer?"

"The midwife cannot confirm…"

"The code, Lucy. The map."

Lucy snapped. "It would be sooner if you were to be quiet."

He let out a growl and returned to the window. Why were both Blake and Waterford fawning over Theo?

Lucy paused to ask, "You are certain that you and Theo are in accord?"

Dragging himself away from the vexing scene, Graham sat in a chair near the fireplace and out of Lucy's direct line of sight. The woman was far too perceptive, and he wasn't in full control of his reactions when it came to the topic of Theo. "Lucy, you are fully aware as to how our courtship originated. It was a result of *you* begging me to ascertain the source of her mysterious change in behavior. We now both know it was related to the missives that lie before you. Time is of the essence, Lucy. The quicker we can determine where Baldwin hid the map or where he last believed it to be the better. Please, can we focus on the important matters here?"

"Theo is extremely important to me, more so than a stupid map. I want the truth…"

More to himself and barely above a whisper Graham uttered, "She is important to me too." It was apparently loud enough for Lucy to hear. She stopped mid rant.

"Archbroke, I believe you are important to her as well. Why don't you go freshen up and join them on the lawn? I will send you a note once I have completed my task of decoding the messages."

He wasn't assisting matters, and now that Theo was close by, he couldn't deny the ache to be near her. Graham left Lucy to find his chambers. Now if only he could get the damn butterflies in his stomach to cease fluttering. He didn't know what he would do if Theo continued to remain aloof.

~

WATCHING FROM HIS BEDROOM WINDOW, Graham saw Theo release her first arrow. Without hesitation, she pulled a second arrow from her quiver and placed it in the bow ready for release as the first hit the target. Impressed with her accuracy and quickness, Graham found himself grinning, and the warmth of pride spread through his chest. He loved the woman he saw below—beautiful, calm, and full of self-confidence. Quite the opposite of the cagey, withdrawn woman Lucy had feared Theo had turned into. Theo appeared much more at ease in the country.

It had been pure torture knowing she was miles away from him. Should she need him, he was too far. It wasn't only the physical distance that tore at him. He had to admit that he had uncharacteristically let something he treasured go without issue. Something or someone had caused Theo to withdraw. He had wrestled with the notion that she may never return his sentiments, but he was determined to assuage her concerns. Graham resolved to make it clear to Theo that he intended to have her as a wife and life partner.

It was time to stop hiding and go join Theo on the lawn.

GLANCING AT THE TARGET, Graham's mouth fell open, then closed, his lips forming a tight line. Lady Cecilia's three arrows had hit dead center, while Theo's third had missed. Theo and the other ladies gathered around. Lady Cecilia grinned like a Cheshire cat. Oddly, both Lady Mary and Theo shared a glance. What scheme had the two concocted? Had Theo intentionally allowed Cecilia to win?

Careful not to draw attention to his arrival, he listened intently to the women's conversation.

"So what is it to be?" Theo asked Cecilia.

Cecilia slowly glanced at each of the ladies in the circle, her gaze landing on Theo as she stated, "I want this evening's entertainment to be cards."

"Cards!" exclaimed Arabelle.

Smugly Cecilia replied, "Yes. We are among family and close friends. It shouldn't be hard for Theo to convince Lucy to hold a small card party, one where everyone may wager." Cecilia stared at Theo as if daring her to deny the boon.

"Even if I were to convince Lucy, I doubt the men will consent," Theo answered.

As if she had already anticipated the argument, Cecilia said, "Then Arabelle and Mary will have to use their wiles and convince Christopher and Waterford to agree."

"I don't even know how to play cards," Arabelle confessed.

Cecilia snorted. "That will make it all the more convenient. You can ask Christopher to teach you this evening."

Cecilia turned, nose in the air, and left the ladies in silence. Theo's gaze followed the woman until her gaze locked onto Graham. With her eyes boring into him, his chest constricted, and he attempted to heave in a deep breath but failed.

Theo darted her gaze away and announced, "Well, I'm off to find Lucy."

Why was she running? What was it that had her believing he didn't care for her? His hope that she would be eager to see and speak to him was dashed as she left for the house.

Landon appeared next to him. "You need to resolve whatever it is between the two of you tonight."

Graham raised an eyebrow in Landon's direction. "What outcome do you wish for?"

"Theo's happiness."

Landon's answer surprised him. He wanted the same for Theo. However, he was not sure how exactly to go about ensuring it.

~

GRAHAM WAS eager to check on Lucy's progress. He was stopped at the door by Lucy's ever faithful footman Evan. "Is Lady Theo with your mistress?"

"No, my lord. Lady Devonton remains alone with Carrington." The man's features softened the moment he mentioned the devoted maid. Did his own morph likewise when he spoke of Theo? Should he seek Theo out or check on Lucy?

His decision was made for him when Theo appeared in the hall with her head down and muttering to herself. She was nearly upon him before Theo lifted her gaze to meet his. Her hesitant, shy smile caused his own smile to broaden. He was about to greet her with an embrace, but Blake was only a few steps behind her. Blake's longer strides allowed him to shorten the distance between them, and they both reached Graham at the same time.

"Wonderful. It appears we are all intent on seeing how Lucy has progressed," Blake said as he brushed past him to enter the study.

Blake entered first, followed by Theo and Graham.

"What the devil?" Lucy muttered. Scowling directly at them, Lucy complained, "How do you think I'm to finish this confounded task when I'm constantly interrupted?"

Theo was the first to reply, "Lucy, I'm sorry to interrupt, but I must speak to you about this evening's entertainment."

"We are to play charades."

Theo shuffled her feet before saying, "Well, you see, I made a wager with Cecilia, and I lost. Whoever came closest to hitting the bull's-eye with all three arrows won. The winner was to receive a boon."

"*You* lost at archery? Impossible!"

"I thought it wise to allow Cecilia to win in order to determine if, indeed, she was up to no good."

Lucy asked, "Well, what did she request?"

"Cards." Theo, Blake, and Graham said in unison.

At the sound of angry male voices, Graham instinctively moved to Theo's side and turned as Landon barged through the door.

"Why are you behind a closed door with him?" Landon directed his question to Theo.

"Landon, it is not as if we were alone. Lucy and Blake are here to chaperone," Theo replied defensively.

"Then explain what the lot of you are up to," Landon demanded.

Graham smirked. "It will be *my* pleasure."

He breathed easier when out the corner of his eye he caught Lucy carefully maneuvering sheets of paper over the code she had sworn on her firstborn's life to conceal.

As he crafted an explanation for Landon, Graham's heart filled with joy as Theo stood by his side. Selecting his words carefully, he was able to keep his and Theo's association with the Crown a secret while he shared all the pertinent details of the situation, including the need to gain Cecilia's cooperation. Occasionally, he would deliberately brush up against Theo's arm and was happy when she did not flinch or shy away from him. He liked her close. It was precisely where she should remain. With him.

Partially satisfied with Graham's account, Landon groaned, "So, we are to play cards with the ladies then."

"Yes. Let's see what the witch has planned. Make sure

you do not find yourself alone with her," Graham answered.

"Once Lucy and Blake have the map, what is to be done?" Landon inquired.

"Waterford will leave as soon as it can be arranged along with a copy. He will be instructed to meet up with an agent currently on the Continent."

Landon appeared satisfied with the answer. He winged his arm out and spoke directly to Theo. "We should go and freshen up before dinner."

Theo hesitated before moving forward and away from Graham's side to accompany Landon. He overheard Landon say in Theo's ear, "Cousin, I believe there is still much more for us to discuss. Let's adjourn and find Mama."

Apparently, the man wasn't wholly satisfied with the explanation. Graham would have to trust Theo to reinforce only the facts he had shared.

THEO and her aunt sat demurely on the settee. She looked over at Christopher, who was slouched in an oversized armchair. Aunt Henri smiled as if she hadn't a care that her son had summarily summoned her. Theo, on the other hand, twisted her hands in her lap. Aunt Henrietta covered Theo's hands with her own, warmth seeped through Theo calming her nerves.

Standing legs wide apart and with hands on his hips, Landon switched his gaze between his mama and Theo, "I will no longer wait for either of you to disclose the secrets you are both withholding from me. Mama, as you have often reminded me this Season, I am the patriarch of this family. Thus, I demand to know why the two of you have been behaving as if I have no clue about all the late night visits from Archbroke or the packed valise that Theo keeps in her wardrobe."

Christopher bolted upright. "Archbroke has been sneaking into the town house?"

Landon paced back and forth in front of the settee as if he hadn't been interrupted. "Mama, please explain your lack of diligence in protecting Theo's reputation."

"Landon, Theo is a very responsible and wise girl. Lord Archbroke is a well-respected member of the *ton*, and I have no reason to believe he would take advantage of our dear Theo."

Frowning and not releasing her gaze, Landon sternly said, "I learned the art of deflection from you; however, you will provide me with the necessary answers even if I have to—"

Theo couldn't listen to another word. "There is no need to threaten your own mama."

She paused. How to convey the complexities of their family's link to the Crown? Her gaze flickered to her aunt, who smiled.

"My papa left instructions for me to inherit a family volume that, by tradition, should have been given to you. It outlines the family's responsibilities to the Crown. I admit that I've struggled to fully understand why he would insist on breaking such a long-standing tradition, but nonetheless, that is how it is. It is I who bear the mark of our family's oath to assist the Crown. It is my duty to seek and obtain the information requested by either of the two other trusted families."

Christopher interjected, "Crown? Mark? Who are these other families?"

Aunt Henri answered, "The Neale family has served the Crown for generations. Since Baldwin was set to inherit, your papa and I didn't think it necessary to have the mark placed upon you and Landon. As for the identity of the two other families, they are Burke and Archbroke."

Landon's gaze bore into Theo. "Are you telling me that you have put yourself in harm's way—that, in fact, I should have inherited some mark that you now bear in my stead?"

Theo nodded. Tears began to form in her eyes as betrayal and disappointment crossed Landon's features.

She blinked. "Well to be clear, I don't recall receiving the symbol. It's always been hidden from sight. I didn't pay much mind to it until my papa explained that the volume could only be viewed or inherited by someone who bore the mark."

Aunt Henri confessed to Landon, "I should have informed you upon Baldwin's death. You should have received the mark then." Shoulders sagging, eyes distant, she continued. "Your papa had passed, and when Theo's papa insisted she be the one to inherit the volume, I relented. George had wanted to protect you boys for the responsibilities to the Crown often placed those marked in danger. I gave my word to support and assist Theo when it came time for her to inherit and bear the duties of our family. I realize now that perhaps there are far bigger reasons why we should hold true to tradition."

Landon waited until Theo's eyes meet his. "Do you want to continue to carry on as you have?"

Confused, Theo's mind and heart were at war. Her heart told her to say no. Yet, her mind reminded her that their family's commitment to the Crown was imperative. Her papa had bequeathed to her an inheritance that had allowed her to be involved in something bigger than the social routes of the *ton*. The volume had given her life purpose.

Looking to Aunt Henrietta for strength and reassurance, Theo took a deep breath and replied, "Yes."

"Very well. Then that is how we shall proceed."

Why had Landon agreed without argument or further questioning? It was unlike Landon to agree upon any matter of import in such short order. Something was amiss with her cousin's behavior.

Christopher looked at Landon. "You cannot let this continue."

Landon sternly replied, "It is Theo's choice, not ours. We will support her decision."

CHAPTER TWENTY-FIVE

Theo took in her surroundings. The drawing room had been converted into a card room, the kind she imagined existed at a gentleman's club.

"I told the staff that Archbroke would instruct them as to how this evening's activities were to be arranged. I didn't think he would redecorate my drawing room," Lucy groaned.

It came as no surprise to Theo that the transformation was Graham's doing. The room was strategically organized. Tables arranged to accommodate two players were deliberately placed to allow one to easily converse or, alternatively, overhear the conversation of the other players. Decks of cards were fanned out on each table.

With a tinge of pride in her voice, Theo replied, "I think he did a marvelous job."

Lucy's pointy elbow caught Theo in the ribs. "Of course you would."

Theo rubbed her side and avoided Lucy's cheeky grin. "I wonder what the rules of play will be for the evening."

She could not afford to confess that she had given her heart to Graham.

"Archbroke and Blake are reviewing those as we speak. I'm certain it will be in the gentlemen's favor, for they naturally know we ladies could easily trounce them," Lucy taunted.

Unable to contain their mirth, the two giggled as her cousins entered the room.

Christopher nudged his brother in the ribs. "We are in for an interesting evening, brother."

"No doubt." Landon's dry reply undermined his words.

Cecilia and Arabelle appeared, heads together as if they were conspiring, and behind them Mary was escorted by Waterford, wearing his usual mask of disapproval.

Everyone gathered by the refreshments on the far wall, waiting for Blake and Graham to arrive.

"Cecilia, since this was your idea, what games are to be played?" Mary asked.

Waterford chuckled and responded, "I'm sure as host Devonton is taking care of the matter. Certainly, the stakes shall not be of consequence this evening."

Mary retorted. "Waterford, what are you implying?"

Theo had never seen two people irritate each other so much, yet there was a softness in their glances when the other wasn't looking. Mary and Waterford's relationship was a confusing and complex one that she wasn't sure she would want to emulate.

Glancing at the other men, Waterford arrogantly replied, "We all know that women have no way of honoring real debts. I'm of the mind that we will be playing for ha'pennies this evening."

Before she saw him, Theo sensed Graham's entrance. As Graham and Blake approached the group, Blake calmly corrected Waterford, "Actually, I discussed the matter with Lady Cecilia earlier, and we are to play for favors this eve. The names of the winners from each table at the end of each round will be placed in a hat, and at the conclusion of the evening, Lady Cecilia will draw a name who will claim a favor of their choosing."

Graham interjected, "We will be playing piquet. Each lady will pit her skill against every gentleman in attendance tonight. At the end of each round, the men will move to the seat to their right."

Noting Lucy's cringe as soon as piquet was declared the game of the evening, Theo inquired, "What is so troublesome about piquet? It is a game you love."

Lucy's gaze was solidly locked on Blake. "That was until I played with my husband. It was the one game I could naturally count on winning. However, his devilish skill to recall cards played and discarded makes it near impossible for me to win—unless, of course, I engage in devious antics to distract the man." At the mischievous smile and blush on Lucy's cheeks, Theo's own skin heated and she began to plan her own tactics to win against Graham.

Blake took command again, stating, "Let's begin by having the women each choose the name of a gentleman from the hat."

Lucy reached into the hat and pulled out a small parchment. "Lord Hadfield."

Next, it was Mary's turn. "Mr. Neale."

It was Theo's turn. "Lord Waterford."

Next Cecilia announced, "Lord Archbroke."

Blake declared, "Lady Arabelle, I shall have the pleasure of being seated with you."

Arabelle admitted, "My lord, it would be my pleasure.

I hope you won't mind instructing me since I've never played before."

It was brave of Arabelle to admit her ignorance. Theo wasn't sure she would have done the same.

Blake rewarded her bravery with a warm reply. "It would be my pleasure. And you know what they say about beginner's luck. It can triumph against the most skilled of players." Blake gave Arabelle a conspiratorial wink.

Waterford winged his arm for Theo, and he escorted her to her seat. The matrons and chaperones attending the house party entered the room. Each made their way over to the arrangement of cozy chairs and settees, content to gossip rather than partake in the evening's entertainment. Theo spied Aunt Henrietta and received a warm smile. She was genuinely grateful for her aunt's constant support. Then her aunt's gaze flickered over at Graham, bringing about a frown to the older woman's face.

Heat radiated off Graham. Why was he scowling? His gaze was on Theo's hand, rested on Waterford's arm. Graham didn't like her touching another man. Interesting. If he was jealous, it must mean that he still cared. The corners of her lips turned up as she began to plot her strategy to win her round against Graham. She should observe Lucy's round with Blake, she was always learning a thing or two from her best friend.

Graham took a detour to his seat. She hoped he would come close enough to speak, even if briefly. He didn't disappoint her. When he was close enough, she held out her hand for him. As he leaned down to kiss it, he whispered, "I've missed you."

She thought her heart might burst at his admission. She held his gaze and answered, "I've missed you too."

"Perhaps I could interest you in a private wager," Graham said as he made a show of pushing in her chair.

He leaned forward over her shoulder to stack the cards into a pile.

Looking into his eyes, Theo answered, "I'm listening."

A smirk formed on Graham's otherwise serious face. Breath held, she hoped he would suggest a wager that involved a kiss. Her eyes were trained on his lips. Images of him leaning toward her and holding her overtook her thoughts.

He raked his eyes over her face. Heat flooded her cheeks as Graham suggested, "The winner of our game shall be granted a favor that may be requested at their will."

Perfect. She couldn't prevent the grin from forming on her lips as she nodded. Theo reached out to take the cards from Graham. He inhaled at the touch of her hands, but as she began to shuffle with the skill of a card shark, he accepted her silent challenge with a bow and moved to take his own seat across from the devious Cecilia.

Ignoring the sounds of cards shuffling and the mummer of quiet conversations as the players began the first round of play, Theo glanced up at her opponent. "Lord Waterford, shall we cut the cards?"

"After you, my lady." He gestured for Theo to do the honors.

She held up the bottom card to reveal a king of diamonds.

Arrogantly, Waterford halved the cards again and revealed a nine of spades. Relinquishing the first deal to Theo, he puffed out his chest and relaxed an arm upon the table. Clearly, he believed he would win the *partie* in short order and without issue.

Knowing she would have a slight advantage being the nondealer on the critical sixth hand, she assessed the twelve cards before her. They each played with quick, decisive action, and the score was tied at the end of the fifth deal. She would have to win the sixth soundly to be declared the winner. He sat slightly hunched over the table with a scowl on his dark features, and she sensed he no longer believed the win to be a certainty.

Eyes averted to her left, Christopher was smiling and shamelessly flirting with Mary. Mary's laughter caused Waterford's play to become more erratic. To her right, Landon's fierce concentration on his cards lightened Theo's mood.

Waterford scowled at his cards. "Why, Lady Theo, you have such a sweet smile."

The man's lackluster attempt to distract her with a few flowery compliments had Theo smiling. "My thanks. What a lovely compliment. Perhaps you should save it for another who might appreciate it more."

After rearranging his hand for the third time, Waterford raised his gaze to Theo as her words finally sank in. Abruptly he asked, "And whom might that be?"

Responding with a slight shrug, she waited for him to declare his best combination, and once he was done, she merely stated, "Not good."

Waterford could not hide his surprise, and as they scored her hand, he finally gave her a genuine smile and gracefully conceded the *parties*.

After scrawling her name on a piece of paper and placing it in the hat, of which Aunt Henri was in charge, Theo and Waterford made their way to the refreshment table.

Waterford caught her staring at Graham and offered his insight, "He is probably prolonging the *parties* to gain insight into her thoughts."

Theo's posture stiffened. Graham's sultry looks and

suggestive body language prompted a snippy, "Is that what it looks like to you?"

"I've never known another better at masking his true intentions. However, if you pay close attention, the truth is always in plain sight."

How insightful. Theo turned to face Waterford. She rarely spoke more than two words to the man. His arrogance and prickly nature often pushed her away from his company. As she stared at him and followed his gaze, she was not surprised that it was again focused on Lady Mary, but this time, there was a tinge of regret in his eyes. What had occurred between the pair?

She gently placed a hand on Waterford's arm before saying, "You might win in the next round with Lady Mary if you were to employ a strategy similar to that of my dear cousin."

Waterford replied in horror, "Are you suggesting I flirt with Lady Mary?"

Wordlessly, she raised her shoulders and smiled before moving to stand next to Lucy.

Lucy was deep in thought and started as Theo asked, "Have you devised your plan to defeat your husband?"

"Unfortunately, I've yet to come up with an acceptable plan." Lucy paused momentarily as Blake rose to make his way to her. She added, "I'm certain your aunt and her cronies would strongly object to all the ideas that have crossed my mind for fear of corrupting the young and innocent."

Leaning down to greet Lucy with a kiss, Blake goaded her. "I'm looking forward to our match, wife."

In a voice loud enough to be heard across the room, Lucy replied, "If Archbroke would hurry up and lose, we could begin."

Turning in their direction, Graham gave them a

quelling look. Clearly, he was not about to be rushed, and to Theo's chagrin, he continued to charm Cecilia until the very last declaration. Her ire increased at Cecilia's high-pitched laughter. She wanted to go over there and beat a confession out of the lady. It was how her family had garnered admissions for generations. Why stop now?

Cecilia finally admitted defeat and announced to the group milling about, "Shall we continue? Thank you, Lord Archbroke, for the enjoyable round, but I'm interested to see if I will prevail in the next."

Without further preamble, the gentlemen presented themselves to their new opponents. Paying little attention to the cards played, Theo's focus was on Lucy's outrageous behavior. Landon efficiently trounced her, winning all six hands.

"While I take pleasure in claiming the win, it isn't half as entertaining as listening to Lucy's outlandish attempts to distract her poor husband."

Theo smirked. "I have to admit their banter did divert me somewhat, but you won fair and square. This time."

They rose together to stretch their legs.

As soon as they were out of everyone's hearing, Landon asked, "Theo, I want to know more of your relationship with Archbroke. Tell me, was the courtship an entire sham?"

His question drew her attention back to him. What should she say? Admit that her heart and body begged her to accept Graham's suit? There was no possibility of a future for them due to the mark she and Graham bore. With her gaze squarely focused on the tips of her toes, she answered, "No. But there can be no happy ending for us."

Landon gave her a look of pure confusion, and she tried to explain. "Our heirs will bear the responsibility to carry on our family's tradition to the Crown. A union between two families would place an extraordinary burden—"

Landon interjected, "Theo, allow me to—"

But she wasn't finished. "No. I told you earlier, it is a responsibility I wish to bear."

Landon had been a barrister before inheriting his title and a very respected one at that. He knew exactly how to twist words and arguments in his favor. Before he could sway her decision, Theo escaped to the safety of her aunt.

Theo placed the slip of paper that Landon had signed his name on as the winner in the hat that rested on Aunt Henrietta's lap.

"My dear, you are doing well this eve. Is it not two consecutive wins?"

"No, Aunt Henri, I conceded to Landon, but I chose to be the one to deliver the note."

Did Aunt Henrietta understand her intended message that she would not relinquish the family's responsibilities to Landon? It had been subtle, but when Aunt Henrietta gave her a knowing smile, she grasped that she would always have a cherished bond with her aunt.

"Perhaps the next round will prove more challenging," Aunt Henri said with a wink.

"It will certainly require all my wits."

Graham bent to place another sliver of paper in the hat. Had he overheard her conversation with her aunt? Had her aunt meant the wink for her or Graham?

GRAHAM LOOKED between the two ladies before him and arched an eyebrow in question.

Theo lowered her gaze to his lips, moistening her lower lip. The minx's actions had certain muscles tensing, which was particularly inconvenient considering they were not alone. He had much to discuss with her, but since his arrival, there hadn't been an opportunity to whisk her away. To be so close and not taste her luscious lips again was agony.

Reining in his thoughts, he winged out his arm for her. As soon as she placed her hand on him, his muscles jumped. Theo gave him a saucy smile. Loath to give Theo the upper hand before they sat to begin a round of piquet, he proposed they enjoy a glass of champagne first.

Taking a glass from Graham's hand, Theo teased, "Are you trying to ply me with alcohol, Lord Archbroke?"

"I will take any advantage I am offered, my lady."

Oh, how he had missed her easy banter. Could he whisk her away? Graham glanced about the room only to find Aunt Henri's knowing eyes glaring back at him. There would be no escaping with Theo without the woman's notice.

Aunt Henri's assessing stare spurred a desire within him to confess to Theo that his feelings had not altered. He wanted to admit that in her absence his heart and, rather disturbingly, other body parts, continued to ache for her. How would she respond if he confessed he would wait an eternity for her to return his affections? Would she want to hear his declaration? He was certain he would win her heart if only he could determine her reasoning for not wanting the courtship to become real.

If he were to win the round, his request would be for her to disclose her rationale for ignoring their undeniable attraction and suitability.

He glanced at Lucy and Blake. "They are well matched, wouldn't you say?"

Lucy rubbed two cards between her thumb and first two fingers as if contemplating whether to discard them.

The motion of the cards made Blake's eyes flare. Would Theo recognize the intense look of pure lust? Did his own eyes reflect his need for Theo?

Theo answered, "Certainly. It's as if they are two pieces of a pictorial jigsaw puzzle that would appear not to align, but if placed in just the right manner, they seamlessly form one piece."

"Like love. Not all the pieces link with each other, yet they come together to create something wonderful."

Theo said, "Exactly."

Graham nearly did not hear her reply as, at the same moment, Lucy jumped up and cried, "I won!"

After allowing Lucy time to bask in her success, Graham prompted the next round to begin.

He could sense Theo was eager to find out if she, too, would be victorious. What boon would she have in mind?

He assisted her to her seat. Once seated, he felt her skirts graze his leg. The minx had moved purposefully, ensuring he was fully aware she had placed her legs between his own. He cut the pile, revealing a king of hearts. She put her hand over the cards and deliberately picked up all but a few. He chuckled when she showed him the ace of diamonds. She was a card shark. Theo winked at him as she began dealing.

As each round progressed, Theo's attempts to divert his attention became more overt, ensuring his focus was on her movements. She raised her hand to push back a loose lock of hair behind her ear or tilted her head slightly to reveal the spot on her neck, the exact location that he had kissed, causing her to moan. Unwittingly, he himself groaned.

The pink tinge gracing Theo's skin revealed her own thoughts. It took every ounce of willpower to keep his hands in sight. Her fingers ran along the edge of a card, and instantly, he recalled her hand roaming his body in her sleep. He raised his hand to place a finger between his cravat and neck and tugged as Theo's leg rubbed against his.

Theo frowned at her hand. He suspected she had mistakenly discarded cards that would have ensured she would win the next trick.

She attempted the coy look that Lucy had employed with her husband. She didn't pull the look off, which made Graham cough.

On her second attempt, she glanced up and asked, "Is it my turn?"

It was his turn, but he was trying to decide if he wanted to throw the game to even the odds or to go for the win. "No, I'm still deciding if you purposefully threw your hand or if perhaps—"

Theo's gaze narrowed. "I'll tell you, Lord Archbroke. I'm playing to win."

She bit down on her lower lip. When she parted her lips and her tongue peeked out, a mirage of sordid images flooded his mind.

Attempting to focus, he looked down and slowly discarded the king of spades and a ten of diamonds. "I believe we are even now."

A flash of sadness crossed Theo's features. Had she wanted him to win? To take advantage of her mistake? She wanted something, and he had misread the situation. Theo remained focused and determined with each round.

During their last round, he asked, "Tell me, Theo, if you were to win, what favor would I be honor bound to provide?"

"I believe the terms are for the winner to disclose the favor at their will, are they not?"

"Certainly. Might you be willing to give me a clue?"

"Should I be the victor, my lord, make no mistake that I will be calling upon you later tonight to collect."

Had he heard her correctly? She would seek him out? Now his curiosity was seriously piqued.

Theo carefully placed her cards out for him to view.

"Why, Lady Theo, I believe you are the winner."

Theo's smile was rich and beautiful, causing his breath to hitch. He might not have won this round, but he considered himself a winner for having made her happy. Yes, he would make it his life's goal to ensure she was happy.

With pride, Theo scrawled her name across a slip of paper and rose to place it in Aunt Henri's possession. She couldn't remove the smile on her face even if she tried. She had won. Now to formulate her plan to corner Graham later in the evening.

As she joined Waterford, making the same trek to her aunt, she glanced at the sheet in his hand and stopped short. He had written Landon's name in place of his own. Theo whispered, "How is it possible you know the outcome of Landon's match?"

"It is all part of Archbroke's plan. I do not question; I just follow orders," Waterford replied.

Theo refrained from asking for further details as Lady Mary chimed in. "Ever the dutiful soldier."

Sensing that there was more to Mary's words, Theo attempted to lighten the conversation, "I had forgotten that you had served in the war, Lord Waterford. We are eternally grateful for your service. Aren't we, Lady Mary?"

From the corner of her eye, Theo saw Mary raise one brow as she said, "Eternally," and turned toward the refreshment table.

Waterford grumbled, "She will be the death of me, that is for certain," and he bent to present the note to Aunt Henri.

Aunt Henrietta quipped, "Are you saying Lady Mary might succeed where Napoleon failed?"

Waterford gave Aunt Henrietta a knowing look and conceded, "That is exactly what I am saying." Then he turned and proceeded to join the men near the brandy decanter.

Theo settled next to her aunt, "What do you know of Lord Archbroke's plans tonight?"

Lowering her voice, Aunt Henri replied, "Child, you need to learn how to be more discreet."

Theo moved to take the hat that held the names of the winners, wanting to confirm her suspicions.

"What do you think you are doing?" Aunt Henrietta questioned as she moved the hat out of Theo's reach.

"I want to inspect the entries."

"There is no need. Speak directly to Lord Archbroke."

Disheartened, Theo searched the room and spotted him next to Lucy by the refreshments. They appeared to be having a rather intense conversation. Was everyone else aware? Why would he exclude her? Feelings of anger, hurt, and betrayal raced through her. She should confront him and demand an explanation.

She had begun to walk over to join Lucy and Graham when Arabelle halted her progress, "Theo, a moment, please."

The girl was flushed. Most likely due to Christopher's flirting. Not wanting to be derailed from cornering Graham, Theo merely slowed her pace. Arabelle snuck an arm through hers, linking them, and Theo was forced to walk alongside the girl.

"Theo, I must speak with you in private."

"What is it?"

"I've been trying to gain Lady Lucy's attention, but Lord Archbroke has a nasty habit of getting to her first."

Arabelle's gaze narrowed upon the two individuals whom she was bemoaning.

"What is it that you need to tell Lucy?"

"Oh, yes. My maid informed me that Cecilia's maid was spotted trying to enter Lord Hadfield's rooms. Earlier, Cecilia shared with me that if she were to draw your cousin's name, she would request his escort back to town. I suspect she would like to gain access to his belongings."

"Well done, Arabelle. This is valuable information." Arabelle might be young and innocent, but she had her brother's knack for spying.

Arabelle whispered, "I'll be glad when this is all is over."

Cecilia approached them with a knowing smile plastered on her face. It would be dangerous for anyone to underestimate these young, intelligent females.

AFTER HIS GAME WITH THEO, Graham's thoughts were consumed by her resolution to seek him out later that evening. He was certain that the mischievous looks and overt touches were all part of her strategy to win, but there was an intensity that indicated there was more at stake than a piquet game. His resolve to act honorably and to respect whatever Theo decided was dwindling as his need to make her his overpowered all reason.

After all the rounds were completed, he gently woke Henrietta, who had dozed off on the settee.

"It's time to see who will be granted the honor of requesting a boon from any of the participants. Lady

Cecilia, will you be so kind as to draw a name from the hat?"

Cecilia jumped to do the honors, her smile broad and hinting at mischief as she chose a slip of paper and unfolded it. The she-devil had no idea.

"Lord Hadfield!" Cecilia declared in an astonished tone.

"Hadfield, will you inform the group from whom you will be collecting a boon?"

"My cousin, Lady Theo."

What the devil? Hadfield had been instructed to name Lady Cecilia. He was to ascertain her brother's whereabouts. What was he up to?

Their gazes locked as the man approached.

Landon said, "I'm not one of your agents whom you can order about, Archbroke. Don't worry, I will gain the information you seek."

Now Graham fully understood why Theo's papa had left the legacy to her and not to the dolt walking away from him—the man was remarkably obtuse and unbiddable.

CHAPTER TWENTY-SIX

Firelight peeked out from under the door of Lucy's study. Theo crept through the hallway in search of her friend; she needed to inform her of the conversation with Arabelle earlier. Slowly opening the door, she entered only to find that Lucy was not in the room. Another form caught her eye. A very familiar figure lay sprawled and asleep on the settee. Her heart began to pound as she neared Graham's prone form.

Muttering to herself, "I'll cover him with the wool throw and leave," she bent to lay the blanket over him.

"I see you have yet to master the art of stealth." He sat up to face her.

"Oh! You are awake."

"And you would be in a very precarious position if I had nefarious intentions." The glint in Graham's eyes hinted at the type of danger she might be in. There was an edginess to him ever since she had won their side bet.

Graham stood and walked over to the fire to stoke it back to life.

“What if I am curious as to what those intentions might be?” Theo asked.

She desperately wanted to throw herself into Graham’s arms and declare her love. But did he love her still? She remained rooted to the spot, standing alone.

Graham showed no intention of wrapping her up in his arms or kissing her senseless.

“Lucy was able to decipher the code this afternoon.”

Her mind on lips and tongue, it took Theo a moment to realize that he had switched topics.

Had he said something about Lucy and the code?

Graham leaned forward, arms outstretched against the mantle. Theo tried to mask her disappointment at his continued distance.

“Baldwin was very brave and a brilliant man.”

At the mention of her brother, tears welled up in her eyes. Would she ever be able to hear his name without despair?

Graham walked over to Lucy’s desk and retrieved the decoded message. Theo moved to join him. His hand grazed hers as he placed the parchment in Theo’s hands. The touch of his hand sent warmth radiating up her arm.

His gaze was intense but encouraging. “Read it.”

The words were a blur, and she repeatedly blinked. Desperate to sort through and focus on Baldwin’s words, she inadvertently leaned into Graham. He wrapped an arm around her waist and drew her closer. In his arms, hands slightly shaking, she began to read Lucy’s bold handwriting:

Caution Lord B
Pages marked δ will form the map you seek
Jewels are in three locations
Locations marked ψ

What had Baldwin meant when he mentioned Lord B? She struggled to concentrate. With Graham's chin resting on the top of her head, she closed her eyes and breathed deeply. The tension in her muscles began to melt as she sank deeper into his embrace.

Graham's lips lightly grazed her neck as he nuzzled the sensitive skin. Instinctively, she tilted her head to savor his attention. Was that she who had moaned or Graham? Her hands itched to reach out and touch him, but having her back to his chest made it difficult. She tucked her hands into the small of her back. Her palms rested against his stomach, which was now markedly different from the first time she had explored his body. Curious, she ran her hands up and down the plane of his stomach. She could feel the defined ridges of his muscles through his waistcoat and shirt. She longed to feel his skin directly on her palms.

Her hand drifted lower. Graham growled in her ear. His reaction encouraged her to continue her bold exploration. She skimmed her hands below his waistband, and Graham's body hardened in response to her light caresses.

"Theo, love," Graham murmured just below her ear.

He had called her "love." Joy rose within. Hearing the endearment reinforced her decision to be bold. Graham's hand shifted upward, his thumb grazing the underside of her breast. This was Theo's chance to show Graham that she returned his affection. Having spent time apart, Theo had feared he no longer loved her. The word no longer scaring her, she placed her hand over his and guided it higher, cupping her breast.

Graham squeezed and fondled her while the other breast ached and craved similar attention.

Theo squeaked, "Graham," as he pinched her hardening nipple. His fingers tended to the tender bud, gently soothing the sting away. Why had she enjoyed the slight pain combined with his gentle caresses? She should be appalled or offended that he would treat her so. But instead, it was a heady feeling, and she wanted more. Damp between her thighs, she shifted her weight.

He nipped at her earlobe, "If you are still able to think, I'm not doing a good enough job at seducing you."

Seeking out his lips, she turned her head. "I would disagree. I believe you are doing—"

Graham placed his lips over hers and demanded entrance. This kiss was not like any of the others. It was commanding and required her to respond with a level of passion that she herself was not aware had been bottled up inside.

Turning entirely, Theo reached up and placed her arms around Graham's neck, and when he moved to break their kiss, she pulled his head back down to crush her lips against his. Only when they needed to take in a breath did she allow him to speak. "Theo, there is much for us to discuss. I need—"

"I understand. Now that we have the map, I intend to—"

"No! You have fulfilled your family's obligation to gather the information. Now it is up to me to decide what action is to be taken next."

Theo lowered her arms and pushed hard against his chest. Instead of gaining space, she was crushed to his chest as he tightened his hold.

With ice in her voice, she managed, "Apparently, we have much more to discuss than I believed, for I fully intend to journey to the Continent and retrieve the jewels, just as Baldwin or my papa would have."

"I have already entrusted Waterford with the map to take care of the matter. There is no reason for you to attempt the journey. However, I do need your assistance in another matter."

"It was not for you to make that decision."

"Theo, even with the war over, it is still dangerous to venture across the channel."

"Lucy accomplished it with no issue last year!"

His eyes were hard but held a fraction of admiration. "Lucy has an established network which was cultivated over many, many years, and even so, she had to pull in every favor owed to her to accomplish her voyage. Theo, I think we need to discuss other matters that are far more important."

"More important? What could possibly be more important than finding the crown jewels and who might have been behind Devonton's abduction last year?"

"You are."

She searched his features. That was not the answer she was expecting. Was that uncertainty she detected? He was showing her a side of him, a vulnerable side, he had never before revealed. "Me? What about me?"

"Yes, you. We need to discuss our courtship and my feelings for you."

She didn't care about the faux courtship. Graham loved her, and despite her greatest wish to spend a lifetime with him, Aunt Henri was right. Marriage to Graham was out of the question. But a dalliance could provide her with memories to cherish forever.

Sliding her hands up over his chest and behind his neck, Theo gently him pulled his head closer. Rising onto her tiptoes, she softly placed her lips upon his.

With a half groan, half moan, Graham pulled back to nibble on her ear and whispered, "I will not take this further until you tell me the truth of your feelings for me."

Capturing his gaze, Theo admitted, "I love you."

As soon as the words left her mouth, Graham rewarded Theo with a soul-searing kiss. Parts of her body began to ache, and in some strange way, she knew Graham was the only one to alleviate the sensation.

Over the slight buzzing in her ear, Graham grumbled, "It's late, and it's unwise for us to remain here."

Without hesitation, Theo reached for Graham's hand and intertwined her fingers as she guided him to the door. Peering out into the hallway to ensure no one was about, she squeezed his hand to signal him to move. Leading Graham through the sprawling country estate, her heart rate quickened, not from the possibility of being caught but from what she hoped she would experience once alone in her bedchamber with the man she loved.

Tugging on Graham to hasten their pace, she turned to determine the problem. Graham's brows were furrowed, his lips set in a determined line. His features were not that of an eager lover. Assessing the risk of speaking, she held her questions until they finally reached her chamber.

Pushing open the door, Theo stepped inside only to have her arm nearly come out of its socket as Graham abruptly stopped at the entrance. As she turned, Graham released her hand and cupped her face with both hands and rested his forehead on hers before admitting, "My love, I cannot enter. My self-restraint has been tested for too many weeks…"

Grabbing him by both wrists, Theo pulled him into her room and twisted, placing her back to the closed door. She feared she had waited too long to admit her true feelings. Not knowing exactly how to convince Graham to stay, she tentatively placed his hands on her cheeks. As she peered up at him, his gaze was bright and intense.

"Theo, will you do me—"

Before he could finish a proposal she knew she could not accept, Theo linked her arms around his neck and brought his head down for a kiss that would leave no doubt as to how she felt about the enigmatic man standing before her.

The moment Graham's shoulders relaxed, she stepped closer, removing all space between them. Acting on pure instinct, she rose to her tiptoes, causing her balance to falter and her body to rub against Graham's solid form. He groaned as he pushed her up against the door. He placed a hand behind her head and the other on her derriere, lifting her slightly, aligning their bodies as he deepened his kiss.

Theo opened for him and boldly stuck her tongue in his mouth. She explored and tasted as he had done in the past only to be surprised when Graham gently suckled her tongue, sending a shudder of pleasure through her body. Pulling back, his mouth tilted upward at the corners. He had issued her a challenge.

Slowly unlinking her hands, she moved them down his chest, noticing the slight hitch in his breathing as she did so. Sliding her hands around to his back, Theo pulled his shirttails free and slipped her hands under, allowing her to feel his taut muscles. His skin was warm to her touch, and she wondered if his sharp intake of air was due to her cold hands or the result of her nipping at his chin.

Grabbing her wrists from behind his back, Graham placed her hands firmly on his chest before lifting her. Her legs naturally wrapped around his waist. With her legs tightening around him, he began to rock against her core. He leaned in farther, adjusting the friction as he rasped in her ear, "Theo, there are many sensations…"

A moan escaped her lips, and the next thing she knew,

he turned and was striding over to the bed. With each step, she bounced against him, garnering a deep growl from the back of his throat. As they neared the bed, she unwound her legs, and he gently set her down. Fearful lest he fully release her, Theo brought his head down for another kiss. His warm hands rested on her waist; unsatisfied with the placement, she placed a hand over one of his and guided it to her breast. Immediately, he began to rub his thumb over her hardening nipple. Heat rippled through her body. She needed to feel his hands everywhere. With a silent plea, she grabbed his hand and pulled him onto the bed.

Theo studied him as he lay on his back with hands folded behind his head. She was trying to determine how she might go about getting him to touch her when a flicker of uncertainty crossed Graham's features. Sensing now was the time to be bold, she moved and straddled him to prevent him from escaping. Graham sat up, and they were chest to chest. As she tilted her head to search his gaze for a clue as to what to do next, he leaned forward and began to nibble on her neck. The light graze of his teeth on her sensitive skin had her wiggling in his lap.

Warm hands gripped her hips, guiding her into a circular motion she quickly mastered. She looked into Graham's eyes; his irises had darkened. That was not his only physical reaction to her movements, but before she could increase her pace, his hands guided her to rise slightly onto her knees. He nuzzled her collarbone, and she began to feel overheated. She shifted off his lap and started to disrobe. His heated gaze warmed her insides as each article of clothing was discarded. Brazenly, she turned and reached for him. Goose bumps appeared on her skin.

"You are cold," Graham said gruffly as he rubbed her arms and shifted to allow him to maneuver her under the covers.

Would he leave? "Gra… Graham." Mentally debating whether she should vocalize her thoughts and wishes to see him naked, she lowered her gaze in embarrassment. There was a soft thud as clothes dropped to the floor. She raised her gaze and grinned as she pulled the covers back, inviting him to join her.

Standing next to the bed with not a stitch of clothing on, he asked, "My love, are you certain this is what you want?"

Seeing his arousal made her mouth dry and unable to speak. Eyes wide with interest, she nodded her head. Moments later, he lay beside her, running his hands over her body as she had hoped. It wasn't long before she became aware that she was not reciprocating his caresses, and she was eager to explore his glorious body. He immediately stiffened as she ran her hands over his waistline, which was at odds with his reaction to her movements over his arms or chest.

"I'm sorry," Theo whispered as she removed her hand from his stomach.

"Nothing for you to be sorry about," Graham replied as he rolled onto his back.

What should she say or do for him to resume his caresses? "Did… did I do something wrong?"

"Theo."

He hadn't uttered his usual endearment. Was he distancing himself from her? A jolt of unease made Theo surge into action. Darting her eyes to his lips, she considered. She needed to be daring. Leaning over him, she pressed her lips to his. Graham stilled, but when her tongue darted out and skimmed his lower lip, he opened for her. Perfect. She knew how to kiss, after all. He had taught her well. When he did not wrap his arms around her as he usually did, she deepened the kiss and lightly sucked on his tongue, finally earning an arm about her waist.

Theo snuggled closer, wanting to feel every inch of him against her. Her movements elicited a deep growl from Graham. Growing bolder, one hand stroked the back of his neck while the other roamed lower to his chest. The thump of his heart against her palm caused her to smile and pull back. Theo loomed over him. Her palms itched to touch him, but when she had dared to explore, he had retreated. How could she accomplish what she wanted?

"Minx. If you keep looking at me like that, I'll not last long."

Theo raised an eyebrow.

She blinked, and within seconds, Graham held her wrists tightly within one hand. She arched her back as he slowly raised her hands above her head. Watching him closely, his gaze strayed to her breasts momentarily, but when his eyes returned to meet hers, he ordered, "Leave them there."

Confused and hurt at his demand, Theo's eyes shuttered.

"I can't be distracted by your hands… please leave them where I've placed them no matter what happens."

Since he rarely used the word *please*, when giving an order, Theo nodded her assent. One moment she felt the breath he released, and in the next, his lips and tongue were on her neck, slightly below her earlobe—her most sensitive spot. Then the bed moved as he maneuvered himself over her. Wanting his lips on hers, she raised her head to get closer, but instead of a kiss, he slowly lowered his head to her chest and buried his face in her cleavage. The stubble on his cheeks rubbed along the underside of her breasts. Theo shifted and was about to lower her hand to run it through his hair.

Graham looked up with one eyebrow arched. "No hands, remember?"

Heat rose to her cheeks at being caught. Theo wiggled her fingers. "No hands. I promise." Returning her hands back where he had left them, she arched her back, forcing her chest to rise and the tip of her nipple to graze his chin.

Theo nearly bucked him off her as his tongue circled and flicked her nipple. She closed her eyes tight and let out a murmur of pleasure as he began to suckle her breast while his hand lightly circled and pinched her other nipple. Shock waves of pleasure began to roll throughout her entire body. She writhed under him as he continued to torture her with his expert caresses. He kissed and teased various spots—the inside of her arm, the underside of her breasts, the side of her stomach, and the inside of her thighs. When he found a particularly sensitive spot, he would linger and increase his attention. She inhaled deeply when he sucked the delicate skin of her inner thigh. Her muscles tensed at the slight stinging sensation as he sucked hard on her skin.

Before Theo could call out, Graham began to tease the same spot with gentle strokes of his tongue and light kisses. She wasn't sure which sensation she missed the most when he raised his head. She looked down; his head was between her legs, and she willed him to look up at her, but his concentration was on her entrance. She was fully aware of the moisture pooled in her apex. Theo couldn't tear her gaze away from him as he ran his tongue along her slit, then using his fingers opened her fully to him until he found her most sensitive spot. When he gently suckled her, she let out a loud moan, but he never looked up; he continued to lick and suck at her core.

She wasn't sure if she wanted to run her hands through his hair and hold his head in place or tug on his hair and pull him away. As she emitted more noises, he increased the pressure and quickness of his strokes. She was confident he knew what he was about as the escalating tension within her intensified. Theo thought she might burst. When his finger entered her, her muscles contracted around him, and a startling tingling sensation enveloped her.

She opened her eyes. Graham was right above her with a strained look on his face. She couldn't obey his order any longer. She pulled his head down and kissed him, tasting herself on his lips and tongue.

A tugging feeling shot down her center, and she broke the kiss. "Graham, I want… I want more."

She waited as he searched her features, his own contorted as if uncertain he should proceed. Desire radiated throughout her. She reached down and guided him to her entrance.

As he entered her, he whispered in her ear, "I love you. I'm sorry, my love."

Theo focused on Graham's words, the stinging pain a distant thought. He loved her as she did him. Gazes locked, he remained still as her body adjusted to accommodate him. She placed her hands on Graham's lower back. His muscles were stretched taut, and as she massaged him, he began to move slowly, the tension in his back mirroring the pull within her.

The sounds echoing in the room were foreign to her ears. She wasn't sure who was responsible for them, Graham or her. Graham rotated his hips as he guided himself in and out of her. Pure ecstasy filtered throughout her entire body. Theo sighed with rapture, and Graham quickened his thrusts. As her breathing became louder, Graham entered her faster, harder, and with urgency. She felt him increase, and when she doubted if she would be able to take any more, he shifted position and entered her deeply, causing every nerve within her to light on fire. A moan so guttural filtered through her dazed mind, then a warm sensation shot up her channel. Moments later Graham fell atop of her. His breath came in gasps. The weight of him upon her was heavenly. But he only remained for a few seconds before rolling onto his back.

Resting her chin on his chest, Theo mentally logged his features, which were relaxed and reflected his contentment. Graham was definitely handsome in his relaxed pose. Basking in delight that she was the cause of his mood, she ran her hand along his side, grazing her fingertips and drifting past his hip bone. She was surprised to see his member beginning to stir again. Her grin widening as he groaned and wiggled. Could she take him again?

Deciding she had a more pressing question, she asked, "Tell me, if I'm not to go to the Continent, what is it that you need my assistance with?"

With eyes half-closed, Graham replied, "I don't believe Landon nor Arabelle will be able to obtain the information I need from Cecilia to determine if or how her brother is involved. I need you to obtain evidence and a confession from the lady."

Theo shifted. Graham's eyes opened. He trusted her. He believed in her abilities. His clear gaze told her so. Theo's mind began to race with more questions.

GRAHAM CLOSED his eyes again as he waited for his pulse to return to its normal state. He mentally willed other parts of his body to also return to their relaxed state, but with Theo naked and wiggling next to him, it was impossible.

Theo drummed her fingers on his chest. "Do you

believe Cecilia's brother, Lord Addington, is the mastermind behind all this?"

"No, not the mastermind, but we need to determine his involvement." He suspected Lord Burke was the mastermind, but he needed to ascertain who all the players involved were and their roles. He still couldn't fathom why the holder of the third volume would act in such a treasonous manner.

"I'm not certain I'll be able to accomplish what you are asking of me."

The self-doubt in Theo's voice was heartbreaking.

"I have no doubt you will succeed." Had he instilled enough courage and confidence in his voice to convince her that she was more than capable of the assignment he had given her?

Theo smiled and leaned down to kiss him. The doorknob rattled, and Graham pushed Theo away. He rolled over the side of the bed out of sight. Seconds later, Graham spotted Henrietta's small feet at the threshold. He followed them as they made their way over to the bed. Had she paused to survey the room before entering? Was Henrietta looking for him?

"This is no time for modesty. I sleep in the room next door," Henrietta admonished. He heard her place a kiss upon Theo. Despite the caring gesture, she scolded, "I'm still in disbelief. We specifically discussed the matter of Lord Archbroke. There can be no future for the both of you."

Graham reached out and hastily donned his breeches and stood to address Henrietta's absurd statement that he and Theo had no future. He was going to marry Theo, and no one was going to stop him.

Henrietta gasped as she took in the sight of his bare muscled chest. In the weeks he had spent away from Theo, he had intensified his training, and his body reflected his efforts. A giggle escaped Theo, and he glanced over to see her looking in her aunt's direction. What had caused her laughter? His gaze returned to Henrietta, who was now a bright shade of pink.

"What nonsense have you been feeding your niece?" Graham demanded.

Henrietta straightened and glared at him. "Nonsense? I've been nothing but honest with Theo. It is not possible for the two of you to be… joined." Henrietta stumbled upon her last word, but then continued. "You have each pledged your loyalty and service to the Crown."

Theo slipped out of bed, wrapping the bedsheet around herself, and turned to face him.

Theo began, "My aunt is right…"

"Mama." Landon had slipped into Theo's room without the ladies noticing. What the devil was he doing here? "The reality is that Theo and Archbroke are in love."

Landon's voice caused Theo's arm to slip, nearly dropping the sheet that covered her lovely form as she spun around. Darting around the bed, Graham stood in front of Theo, providing a human shield.

Theo peeked around him. "Landon!"

The man's features appeared calm, but his gaze reflected pure determination. Why was he in Theo's chambers at this hour? Had all Shalford Castle heard them? Graham should be mortified, but the thought that everyone would be aware she was his brought about a sense of gratification.

"Cousin, I believe you are in debt to me, and I'm here to collect my boon."

Theo let out a squeak. What was Landon about? Surely he wasn't about to demand he take over their family's duties. The man wasn't even marked. It was an honor and a privilege to serve the Crown as a PORF. That duty had been bestowed upon Theo. It would crush Graham if another was to deny him that right, and he suspected it would have a similar impact on Theo.

Disbelieving, Landon indeed made the demand. "You will grant me the honor of handling the family volume."

Theo pushed Graham aside. "Landon, that is not possible. You do not even bear the symbol!"

Graham reached out to cup her face. He loved her fieriness. Looking directly into her eyes, he asked, "Theo, do you trust me?"

She nodded immediately, and he could feel her anger subsiding. He slowly bent, ignoring her aunt and cousin, and kissed her soundly.

"Uhmm." Landon cleared his throat.

Graham slowly released Theo and narrowed his gaze upon Landon. "Hadfield, I admire your desire to uphold the family tradition, and for obvious reasons, I'm in favor of you assuming the family responsibilities. However, now is not the time. It is imperative Theo complete her current mission. You are not prepared and ill-equipped to assist. Theo is our best chance of achieving success. I currently have two agents whose lives are depending upon it."

Theo's eyes darted between him and Landon. They finally landed on Landon who appeared to be processing all he had imparted, and from his features, he was not at all pleased.

Landon returned Theo's gaze. "It is my rightful inheritance. Theo, you will honor your debt as soon as this matter is resolved."

To Graham's delight, Theo burrowed into his side.

"Yes, cousin."

Graham rubbed her lower back to provided reassurance. He would always be her champion. She turned as he wrapped her in his arms and rested her head against his chest. Over her head, he watched as both her aunt and Landon left the room quietly.

When the door clicked closed, he began, "My love, would you like—"

Theo raised her head and simply stated, "Hold me."

He held her tight and she melted into his embrace. Her soft form had his body responding. He needed to leave, or he would take her again. It was too soon. As it was, she would be sore in the morning and he didn't want to cause her pain. He searched the room for the rest of his clothes. They were scattered about. He had no doubt Henrietta and Landon were fully aware that he had taken Theo's virtue, yet neither had demanded marriage from him.

Streaks of light were peeking from the window. Graham needed to return to his chambers. He looked around and found Theo's eyes roving over his body. He wanted to say to hell with society and its dictates and gather her up and take her back to bed.

Instead, he held her by the shoulders and said, "I wish I didn't have to leave. I'm looking forward to when there will be no reason for me to sneak out of your chamber."

Theo dropped the sheet covering her body and reached for one more kiss. With a groan, Graham slowly stepped back and darted out into the hallway. Leaving her naked and willing body was the hardest thing he had ever had to do. The only consolation was the knowledge that she would be his wife, and soon.

He hadn't proposed. She had distracted him. Tomorrow, he would seek her out and ask for her hand. No, it was already morning; he would do it after breaking their fast. His heartbeat raced at the thought of her response. Certainly, she would agree? Yet, a niggling doubt persisted. Theo had claimed she loved him. She had given herself to him. He didn't want to coerce her into marriage. He wanted her willing and excited to be Countess Archbroke, and he would utilize whatever tactic was necessary to achieve his objective. This was how he had operated for years. Why change now?

CHAPTER TWENTY-SEVEN

Pebbles covered in morning dew crunched under Theo's boots as she made her way to the stables. Unable to sleep, she needed to be outdoors to sort through her illogical thoughts. For most of the night, she had berated herself for stopping Graham's proposal.

Years of living with two males who had not been forthcoming about their activities, let alone their feelings, had conditioned her to question and doubt the words of others. With the knowledge of their familial responsibilities, she understood the need for her papa and brother to skirt the truth. But it still hurt to know they had not trusted her.

Theo's shoulders slumped as she peered into the stalls. She had behaved exactly like her male kin, not sharing her true feelings for Graham with anyone. No amount of logical reasoning would subdue the ache in her heart.

A young stable hand appeared. "Can I help you, my lady?"

"I'd like to go for a ride before breakfast. Do you have a mount ready?"

"Not yet, but I'll have one readied right away." The boy scurried away.

Hands clasped behind her back, Theo paced about. Coming to a halt, a smile formed on her lips. *Deal with Cecilia, then explain everything to Graham.*

A beautiful thoroughbred was brought around. The horse was bred to race, and Theo needed to feel the brisk air upon her face.

Taking the reins from the lad's hands, she cocked an eyebrow in his direction, and he cupped his hands at the ready to give her a boost.

Mounted in the saddle, Theo's stress melted away. Easing the horse to a trot, she left the stables and explored the immaculately groomed grounds surrounding Shalford Castle. She gave the horse its head, sensing its need for exercise. With her mount at nearly a full gallop, Theo's mind raced along, formulating a plan to ensnare Cecilia.

THEO HADN'T APPEARED for breakfast. Standing in Lucy's study, Graham mentally scripted the words for his proposal.

"Are you going to stare out the window all day?" Lucy asked.

Why had he ever agreed to work with the woman? Drawn back to the present, he looked out the window for signs of Theo but responded, "Lucy, what do you want?"

Relief flowed through Graham's body as he caught sight of Theo riding into the stables. He needed to talk to her. He turned to leave and was immediately faced with an irate Lucy.

"Need? Archbroke, I will have your word, Theo will…"

Why did the woman persistently challenge his authority?

"Lucy, do not forget, I am your superior." He made his way to walk past the pint-sized woman.

The differences between the two best friends made him smile. He appreciated Theo's quiet, calm reserve. It thrilled him that no other knew of or would be privy to the strong, passionate nature she had exhibited in her bedchamber.

Graham quickened his steps, leaving Lucy no choice but to follow if she wished to continue to speak with him. It would be uncharacteristic of her to give up. When her footfalls pattered behind him, he adjusted his stride to allow the woman to catch up and not require her to run in order to keep up.

"Your commanding ways will stifle her."

They walked through the kitchen, and he grabbed an apple off one of the prep tables, which earned him evil stares from the cook. Would Lucy stop to apologize on his behalf? He continued, repeatedly tossing the apple in the air and catching it as he made his way to the stables. What had Lucy meant: he would stifle her? No, he would empower her. Wouldn't he?

Leaves crunching behind him indicated that Lucy had not stopped and was on his heels. He decidedly disagreed with Lucy's assessment and said, "On the contrary, my position and resources will allow her the freedom that she would never gain with another."

Lucy's footsteps faltered and stopped altogether. Graham turned to ensure she hadn't tripped or fallen. Never had he seen the woman speechless. Intelligent eyes bore into him as if she were seeing him for the first time. What did she see to cause such a strange reaction? Had she seen through his authoritative shield? He had only displaced it for mere moments before shuttering his expression and raising his guard back up. Swiveling on his heel, he continued on to the stables, not caring if Lucy followed or not.

He muttered to himself, "These women would drive any sane man to question his own intelligence. Why Devonton decided to marry the chit I'll never know… To spend a lifetime with Theo would be…"

Theo's voice reached him through the stable walls. He peeked into the stables. She was brushing down a horse, bent and running her hand down the animal's flanks. Jealousy roared through his veins. This is what the woman had reduced him to. Jealous over an animal. He weighed the risks involved in taking her here as he closed the space between them.

Theo's movements slowed. He had lost the advantage of surprise. "How was your morning ride?"

"Invigorating. I needed to formulate a strategy to deal with Cecilia." Theo straightened and plucked the apple from his hand and gave it to her mount as a reward.

Theo ducked around the horse and headed back to the manor without a single word. What was her plan? Why was she not sharing it with him?

Graham lengthened his stride to catch up but then moderated it to keep pace with her. Simply walking next to Theo and having her within arm's reach distracted him from the pressing problems of Cecilia and how he was going to get Theo to agree to marry him.

Theo wordlessly slipped her hand into his, and he began to rub his thumb along the outside of her riding gloves, blast them. He would much rather feel her skin again.

They were halfway to the house when Theo tugged on Graham's hand and turned to face him. "Will you visit my chambers tonight?"

Her question ceased his woolgathering. Clearing his throat, he asked, "Are you not sore?"

A blush rose up her neck to her cheeks. "I'm well. However, I was hoping to discuss my strategy with you."

She wanted to discuss business. Graham's stomach began to ache, and his chest tightened. He shook his head, trying to clear the images of Theo lying naked under him as she came apart. Why was she not preoccupied with thoughts of him as he was with her? How could she ignore what had occurred in her chambers last night?

Graham needed time and space to think. Without uttering another word, he turned on his heel and walked away from the woman he wished to have as a wife. The woman he loved. A lady who placed duty first. Hadn't he been the same before Theo came into his life?

A HAND CLAPPED him on his shoulder, and he nearly jumped out of his skin.

"Archbroke, what has you walking in a daze?"

"What is it you want, Devonton?" His clipped tone would not deter Blake from prying; the man was as aggravating as his wife.

"Lucy sent me to deal with you since Theo has returned to the house in tears."

Stopping midstride to face Blake. "Tears? Is she hurt?"

"Not physically. Theo refused to disclose what had occurred. Since Lucy knew you were in her company, I have strict instructions to fix the matter. Now, what exactly did you do?"

"What did *I* do? The woman is acting as if nothing…" Graham caught himself before he confessed. "She is behaving as if this investigation is not fraught with danger. Theo needs to learn this is a matter of import, that—"

"And you are the man to teach her?" Blake interrupted Graham's rant.

The subtle comment led Graham to suspect that Blake knew more about the intimate nature of his relationship with Theo than he should.

"As I explained to your wife earlier, I'm the only man qualified and with the necessary resources to fulfill Theo's needs." He wanted to knock Blake to his knees when the man simply raised his brow and gave him a very smug grin.

"Well, you had best figure out how to deal with the woman and convince her that you are the only man worthy of her hand. I should also mention that I've ended the house party and am kicking everyone out. I want you all gone by tomorrow."

"Devonton, such changes to the plan need to be approved before they are implemented."

"Need I remind you that I do not work for the Home Office? Thus I am not under your direction. It is my home, and I say everyone goes."

Graham ran a hand over the short bristles at the back of his head. The motion had become a habit. Oddly, the rough texture against his palm helped calm and refocus his thoughts. Thoughts still a million miles away, he absently replied, "I shall have to return to the house and inform my valet then."

"No need for you to rush back. All the servants have been alerted and are on their way to ensuring my edict is followed. Why don't we go for a ride? I have a wonderful Arabian I'm sure you would enjoy exercising."

Blake's offer was an olive branch, and he gladly accepted, "My thanks."

He wasn't ready to face Theo. A hard ride would help him develop a strategy to deal with her.

POINTING HER TOE FIRST, rolling to the ball of her foot, and then softly lowering her heel, Theo practiced over and over. Where was Graham? He was a man of his word. He wouldn't renege on his promise to meet her.

She glanced out the window. The moon was in full sight, well past midnight. A tear threatened to appear. Why had he walked away from her this afternoon? It made no sense. She had shed enough tears this afternoon to fill a bucket. Sobbing hadn't helped solve anything. She swiped the back of her hand over her eyes, resolving not to cry.

Theo had spent the day avoiding Graham and subjecting herself to the company of Cecilia in the hopes of gaining more information. A shiver ran down Theo's spine. Only after hours of torture in the woman's presence was Theo able to convince Cecilia that it would be fun to travel back to London together. What Theo truly desired was Graham's company and preferably alone. They had matters to discuss.

She released a deep sigh and placed her hands on her hips. Being forthright with her thoughts and feelings was difficult. Theo had never experienced the need to share her concerns with her papa or brother, nor had they asked. Theo began to pace. Would she be able to find the words to explain to Graham?

"You will wear a hole in the carpet, my dear, if you continue."

He came! Not stopping to think, Theo threw herself at Graham. Absorbing the impact of her body against his, he wrapped his reassuring arms around her. She stretched up onto tiptoes, placing her lips on his.

Had he come because he wanted to hear her strategy or to make love to her again?

His warm hands glided down her back. All concerns left her mind as he deepened their kiss.

A soft moan escaped her lips.

Graham stiffened, but his lips brushed across her cheek as he placed a light kiss upon her temple. "We need to discuss matters first."

Determination radiated from the man. The sooner she advised him of her plan, the sooner she could kiss him again. She wanted to prove to him that she would be capable of carrying out her assignment. That her papa was right to bequeath the volume to her and not Landon.

Theo guided him to the sole wingback chair in her chamber and pushed him into it. She grinned as Graham fell into the chair with as much grace as a bull in a china shop.

A giggle escaped her lips. Standing in front of Graham, she cleared her throat and took a calming breath. "I've arranged to travel back to town with Cecilia, Landon, and Christopher. Lucy's footman Evan will be in charge of loading our carriage in the morning."

She shifted her weight from one foot to the other as she waited for him to react to her news.

Graham looked up at her with a heated stare. He patted his thigh. "Come."

Theo lowered herself to sit across his lap. It would be hard for her to concentrate with his lips mere inches away. She wiggled her bottom, sinking farther into him. His body's immediate reaction to her caused her to grin.

To her delight, Graham's voice deepened. "Theo."

Ignoring his warning, she continued to move in an

effort to make herself comfortable, wrapping an arm over his shoulder and resting her hand on the back of his neck.

Graham released a growl in warning.

Settled, Theo turned to face him. Where was she in sharing her plan?

His lips were pulled tight. Theo lifted her gaze up from his mouth to Graham's crystal clear blue eyes.

Blinking, Theo said, "Once we have returned to town, Landon has agreed to escort us to Vauxhall Gardens to see the tightrope walkers."

Theo bounced in his lap as she mentioned the tightrope walkers. She playfully rubbed the back of his head. Graham's muscles instantaneously began to relax. It was a heady feeling to have the power to affect such a disciplined man.

She continued, "While we are attending Vauxhall, I thought you might be able to arrange a visit to her lodgings."

She had to stop. Graham had placed his large hand on her thigh and was gently making circles with his thumb. His touch sent tingling sensations up her leg and straight to her core. Moisture was beginning to build at her apex.

Ignoring her body's response, she said, "Blake assisted in the preparation of the false maps that Landon will make accessible to Cecilia. If she successfully takes them and you find them in her rooms, we shall confront her and demand the information we need to locate Addington."

Finished regaling Graham with her strategy, she let her eyelids flutter closed. His hand crept higher and closer to her apex. Her breathing was shallow, and she shifted, with his hardened length snug between her legs.

Graham's lips grazed her ear as he confirmed, "I'll be waiting for you."

Perfect. He had agreed to her plans without argument.

Had she heard him correctly? He had decided to wait for her in Cecilia's room, hadn't he?

Graham unceremoniously lifted Theo from his lap. Why was he frowning? He turned her away by the shoulders and pushed her toward the bed. In quick succession, she was placed in the bed, tucked in like a child, and received a lingering kiss before he uttered, "I can't take you again so soon no matter how much I want to."

And with those parting words, Graham left her chamber. It was the second time that day he had walked away from her. He claimed he wanted to make love. No, he had said take her. Was it a dalliance he wanted? Had she misread his intentions? She buried her head in her pillow and wept, hoping her aunt next door wouldn't hear.

It would take time to iron out all the logistics of Theo's plan. He resolved to do everything in his power to ensure she succeeded, but that also would mean it could be days or even weeks before Graham would have an opportunity to be alone with her again. What was he thinking of, leaving her alone? Why had he not taken what she had willingly offered? Bloody idiot. He didn't just want her body. He wanted her heart and soul.

Theo had halted his earlier attempt at proposing. He understood her sense of duty required her to deal with the matter of Cecilia first, but he would have her for a wife. Graham would have to wait before he could enjoy her luscious body again. And before that, he would have Theo's declaration that she indeed wanted to be Lady Archbroke and share with him the rest of her living days.

But for his wishes to come to fruition, they would have to deal with the wily Cecilia. Graham considered once more Theo's strategy to trap Cecilia in her deception. The plan was riddled with weaknesses involving many parties. Coordination and overseeing the safety of all involved at a public venue would require him to employ more resources than preferred, but it would be worth it in the end. He needed to start right away. The first task would be to send out missives and instructions tonight. Graham headed to Lucy's office. He was surprised to see it already occupied by its owner.

Lucy looked up. "What are you doing here?"

"I could ask you the same question. I am certain Blake would not approve of you burning the midnight oil in your condition."

"Hmmph," Lucy said as she rubbed her enlarged stomach.

Images of Theo pregnant with his child flashed before Graham. She could already be with child. Sweat beaded at his temples. He added obtaining a special license to his long list of items to accomplish.

He leaned over Lucy's shoulder to read her notes. "What are you doing? Those are the same items and individuals I was about to send instructions to."

"I had thought perhaps you would be otherwise engaged this evening. I thought it might be wise for someone to work on Theo's flawed plan."

Lucy cringed as the words slipped out, and she corrected herself. "Not flawed, it's just—"

"One of an inexperienced agent. Similar to the one I remember a certain individual herself outlined to me years ago."

Lucy blushed, indicating she hadn't forgotten either. He recalled how inventive Lucy had been when creating a strategy to corner an elusive French informant. She was a quick study but extremely stubborn. Not in the mood to engage in an all-out verbal battle with Lucy, he began to calculate the viability of each aspect of Theo's plan.

Graham pulled a chair next to the desk. "I don't want her to know that we have meddled."

"Are you mad? She must never find out!"

Relieved that he would not have to engage in another argument with his most trying agent, he started in on helping to draft the critical missives. Lucy began humming a familiar tune.

"What is that sound you are making?"

Lucy glanced up at him with confusion. "Sound?"

"Yes. I've heard it before, but I can't quite place it."

"Oh, I must have been humming Matthew's favorite song. I do that sometimes."

The corners of Lucy's lips, which had been turned up in a smile, now turned downward. He was sorry he had inadvertently brought up the subject of her brother.

Unaccustomed to seeing this weaker side of his normally prickly companion, Graham gave Lucy an elusive rare smile. "This will all be sorted soon, and I shall summon him home."

"You were not the one who ordered him to leave. It was that miserable agency my husband works for."

Thrilled at the knowledge that Lucy's loyalty remained solidly with his agency and she had little affection for the Foreign Office, he reached for her hand and engulfed it with both of his.

"Get your bloody hands off my wife!"

Releasing Lucy, Graham stood to meet her overprotective husband. He raised his chin to meet the man's glare. "We are done for now."

"For heaven's sake, Archbroke, it is nearly dawn. What have you got Lucy working on that she must forgo sleep?"

He was pushed aside as Lucy slipped between them

and wrapped her arms around her husband. "My love, I'm ready for bed."

Graham snickered. Lucy had clearly manipulated her husband into escorting her back to their bedchamber. Blake looked over his shoulder one last time before exiting and winked. Who had manipulated whom?

CHAPTER TWENTY-EIGHT

Theo flew through her bedchamber door. She hastily cast off her evening wear and pulled the soft linen shirt over her head. She needed to settle her nerves.

"Slow down, my lady," Wallace pleaded.

Theo bent over and pulled on her breeches. Her poor maid was scrambling about her chamber. Magically, Wallace produced a pair of boots, which she placed at Theo's feet.

"I'm sorry, but I must leave at once. If I don't arrive before Landon delivers Cecilia home, all will be ruined."

"I understand, my lady, but it is important you be methodical and calm when you go about these things."

Theo squinted. "Have you been conferring with your cousin Mills again?"

"Yes and…"

Theo intensified her gaze.

"And Lord Archbroke," Wallace confessed.

"What?" Theo couldn't believe her ears. Why was Graham conferring with her staff? "Wallace, will you stop with the nonsensical tidying? What did Lord Archbroke say?"

"He wanted to ensure your safety, my lady. Honest, nothing more." Her maid was wringing her hands in her apron.

Theo released a sigh. "Very well, we shall discuss this later. I need to depart."

Wallace let out a puff of air, sending the tresses at Theo's neck swaying. Her cloak fell heavy on her shoulders. Theo didn't quite believe her maid. Her safety? She would have to ask Graham directly why he had taken it upon himself to instruct her staff. She didn't have time to ponder that now. She slipped out the window where she met her footman, who had been patiently waiting. They rode in silence across town, and as they neared Lord Addington's town house, Theo's nerves were shot.

Her footman gave her a boost up, and she swung a leg over a tree branch. She climbed up a few more branches before reaching Cecilia's second-level bedroom window. Theo had accompanied Graham the night before to determine the best way to enter the residence. The window was slightly ajar, indicating that Graham was already in position.

She raised the window to allow her to slip into the room. Taking a moment, she let her eyes adjust to the darkness. Graham's breath was on her neck. Seeking out his warmth, she leaned into him.

Footsteps in the hall indicated Cecilia had returned. Graham moved into position. She eyed the woman's maid, who was trussed up and lying on the bed.

Cecilia breezed into the room. "Tilly, tonight was…"

Graham wrapped an arm around Cecilia's waist and held a hand over her mouth. Theo instinctively clenched her fists at the sight of him touching another lady. *Control yourself, Theo.* She couldn't let irrational reactions rule her.

Graham's tone was soft and deadly. "Cecilia, we would appreciate your cooperation. We found the maps in your possession, and we would like to know what you had intended to do with them."

Cecilia struggled. He skillfully held the woman tight without hurting her. Theo wanted to rip Cecilia's eyes out as she maneuvered herself in such a manner as to rub her breasts against Graham's arm.

Theo had expected Cecilia to put up a fight. Instead, she nodded and sagged into his hold as if she was without strength. Graham slowly removed his hand.

Barely above a whisper, Cecilia asked, "What is it you want from me?"

Graham responded, "What were you going to do with the maps?"

"I received a message this morning, telling me to meet a gentleman by the name of Mr. Smyth at the Lone Dove tomorrow evening."

Graham's arm about her waist slightly twitched. What had made him react, the name of her contact or the location? Theo's gaze shifted to his other hand, which now rested in the valley of her breasts. So much for control!

She pulled Cecilia away from Graham, and the two women began to wrestle for the upper hand.

"Bloody Hell!"

Too busy trying to pin the hussy to the floor, Theo ignored the curse Graham uttered.

After what seemed an eternity but was probably mere moments, she sat astride Cecilia with the woman's face to the floor and her wrists held tightly in the small of her back.

Theo took over the interrogation. "How is your brother involved?"

Sobbing, Cecilia replied, "I'm not certain. I received a note from him stating if I did not succeed in retrieving the maps… it would be the end of his life. However, he also instructed me if I was caught not to fight. He s-s-said his end was already determined, and I should take whatever bargain was offered."

Theo loosened her hold on Cecilia but remained seated on the woman's back. Empathy combated with anger and jealousy. She would have acted as Cecilia had if Baldwin had asked it of her. She didn't want to like the woman.

"Do you know where your brother is now?"

"Somewhere on the Continent."

Cecilia's cooperation had her softening toward the woman. "If you assist us in capturing the messenger, this Mr. Smyth, I'm sure Lord Archbroke may be able to arrange a fair trial for you."

Cecilia rested her forehead on the floor before mumbling, "I'll do whatever you ask."

"I'll need to borrow some of your clothing, and we will need the use of the Addington coach."

Graham arched an eyebrow.

"I will deliver the maps to her correspondent."

Cecilia's body went limp, no longer combative. Theo stood and pulled Cecilia with her. Graham moved to take over, but Theo forced Cecilia forward. She was not letting the jezebel near Graham. Theo escorted Cecilia through the town house and outside via the servants' entrance where Home Office agents were awaiting them.

She looked over to find Lord Barstow, ready to haul Cecilia away.

Careful not to address him directly, Theo advised, "She is a tricky one. Don't fall for her wiles."

Theo transferred Cecilia over to Lord Barstow, who gave Theo a wink and a smile.

It was like a pat on the back or a silent "well done." Rocking to the balls of her feet, and with two small bounces, she smiled. Her papa would have been proud.

Graham's warm breath on the back of her neck only increased the heady feeling flowing throughout her body.

From behind, Graham said, "Allow me to escort you home."

Turning, Theo spied a glimmer of pride in Graham's eyes that set her heart soaring. For all his authoritative ways, the man had allowed her to take control of the situation, and she was grateful. Successful in proving herself capable, would he allow her to assist him once they were married? Regardless of what he may decide, she would be a fool to remain uninvolved.

As soon as Theo rested a hand upon his chest, Graham cursed the material that separated them. He wanted to remove all barriers between them. "Love, time for me to return you to your chambers."

Bouncing on her tiptoes, Theo reached up and wrapped her arms around his neck. "Will you…"

Leaning in, he kissed her. It was intended to be a chaste kiss, but her eager response had his tongue searching out its mate until he drew back at the clatter of hooves and an approaching coach. The coachman rolled to a stop right before them, and, pleased to see the flush of color in Theo's cheeks, Graham opened the door and assisted her up.

"Let us be off."

He couldn't wait to be alone with her. It would be a

perfect opportunity for him to propose. His mind slipped as his eyes locked on to Theo's deliciously formed bottom silhouetted in tight-fitted trousers as she entered the coach. He needed to focus. A tryst in the coach was not the way to gain Theo's heart and assent to marry.

He scanned the area one last time before bounding in. Theo's plan had been executed without a major hitch. A knot in his stomach replaced the stress of the evening as he thought about carrying out his own plans.

Theo sat squished in the corner, giving him plenty of room to be seated next to her. But she was too tempting, the exhilaration from the mission clearly reflected in her eyes. Graham sat on the rear-facing seat. He reached out for her hands, concerned, as a frown began to appear on her features.

Theo shifted forward, their noses only inches apart. Simultaneously they each uttered the other's name.

"Ladies first."

Blinking rapidly, Theo squeezed his hand. "Graham. I want to thank you for your assistance tonight. I realize that you and Lucy had to… well, you both made arrangements without discussing them with me." Theo's chin dipped to her chest.

Blast. How had Theo discovered Lucy's and his actions? It was the truth. He could not deny that he had kept his activities a secret.

She raised her head, and her clear emerald eyes stared directly into his. "I understand it was with good intentions, but… if we are to marry, I will not have you keeping secrets from me."

Tugging her forward, Graham reached for her waist and hauled her over to his lap. "Woman, what do you mean, *if*?"

He couldn't resist. Lowering his lips to hers, he kissed

Theo soundly. There was no doubt in his mind he was going to marry her—and the sooner, the better. Needing air, he released Theo. Her ruby lips were a beautiful sight.

The knot in his stomach disappeared as she rubbed the back of his head, soothing him.

Again they both spoke, but this time, as if they could read each other's thoughts, they each said, "Will you marry me?"

Theo was an amazing woman, and to think others saw her as shy and biddable. They were not privy to the bold, astute woman who was about to agree to make him the happiest man alive.

Graham raised an eyebrow. "Theo, are you going to make me wait all night for an answer?"

Pulling his head down to hers, forehead to forehead, Theo whispered, "I love you."

"And do you agree to be Lady Archbroke as soon as it can be arranged?"

Sliding her hand down the back of his neck and around to cup his face, Theo pierced his heart with a stare that he would never forget. He didn't need the words, but he wanted to hear them anyway. Her tongue peeked out, tempting him, but he remained resilient to her wiles. Graham pulled back slightly when she leaned in to kiss him.

Theo released a sigh. "Yes, Graham. I would be honored if you made me Countess Archbroke posthaste."

With his heart soaring, he crushed Theo to him, devouring her lips, her neck, and the luscious swell of her breasts.

Upon the release of a half moan, half sigh, Theo would not relent. "Promise. No more secrets."

Popping his head up to answer, Graham solemnly said, "Theo, you are marked, as am I. You have given me the great honor of agreeing to be my wife. I will give you my oath to love and cherish you. I am fortunate that you share and understand my views on duty and responsibility, for which I am grateful." He reached up to cup her face as she had earlier. "Theo, you will be my number one priority, always."

The clip-clop of the horse's hooves ceased, and they came to a halt. Breaking apart, Graham held the coach door closed a moment to give Theo time to straighten her appearance. Someone pulled at the handle from the outside. When she gave him a nod, he released his hold.

The coach door swung open, and a furious Landon stuck his head in. "Has the matter been dealt with?"

Taking her cousin's hand, Theo stepped down to the street. "All went well. No need to bark at us."

The coach door swung closed as Graham made to exit. Landon spoke through the window. "I shall meet you at your club on the morrow."

Chuckling, Graham nodded. He watched as Landon escorted Theo into the house. Once they were safely inside, Graham tapped on the roof and ordered to be taken home. He fell back against the seat only to be pricked by a hairpin. Theo's disheveled state had definitely soured her cousin's mood. Landon. Was the man worthy of the volume? Would he be capable of assuming the Hadfield duties and responsibilities? Graham broke into a smile. It would be interesting to find out.

CHAPTER TWENTY-NINE

Theo rested the back of her head against the plush material of the wingback chair she occupied. *Why had Landon sent a footman to summon her if all he was going to do was pace about?*

Theo's eyes followed Landon as he stomped past her.

Tap.

Tap.

Tap.

Theo stilled her forefinger in midair as Landon swung around to stare at her. Rather than tapping the box she held, Theo ran a finger along the edge and returned her cousin's glare.

When Landon turned to complete another lap around the drawing room, she began to count. One. Two. Three laps.

Unable to hold her silence, Theo straightened her spine and pulled back her shoulders. "Landon. Whatever is the matter?"

"Your fiancé refuses to provide me with answers. I need

information. I need to…" Landon stopped and faced Theo. "I had worked for your papa for years, serving as his legal counsel. Mind you there was a time or two… never mind about that. The point is I believed he trusted me." Shoulders slumped forward, he began his circuit once more.

"Papa, always spoke highly of you."

"Then why did he bequeath the volume to you and not me?"

"It wasn't possible. You don't bear the mark."

"To my thinking, when Baldwin died, your papa should have seen to it that I did receive the blasted mark."

Theo's eyes widened. "Well, perhaps Papa had…" What was she to say? She had no clue why her father had blatantly broken tradition. "I'm certain he trusted you, Landon."

"Your papa was no dunce. He must have had a specific reason to leave the volume in your hands, and that is why I didn't demand you relinquish it. But now that I'm to receive it, I need more information to determine why your papa acted as he did."

Theo rose and stood before her cousin. Reaching for Landon's hand, she gently placed a small box with an elaborate R engraved on its cover.

"Papa left instructions in the book for me to retrieve this from Rutherford's as soon as I returned to London. But he also stated I was to pass it along only when you were ready and agreed to take on the Hadfield family responsibilities. I'm not certain Papa predicted that the volume would remain in my possession for long. But thank you for understanding and agreeing to wait."

Landon took the box from her. "You are welcome. Tell me, is it your heart's desire to marry Archbroke?"

A blush rose to Theo's cheeks. "Yes. I love him."

Landon's eyebrow arched.

"It's true, and I believe he loves me."

Looking down at the gift she had given him, Landon opened it to reveal a very ordinary-looking pocket watch. Theo had inspected the piece as soon as she had picked it from Mr. Rutherford's store. Disappointed that her papa had chosen such a simple timepiece, she had examined it more closely, finding a series of numbers engraved on the inner rim of the cover.

"What do these digits mean?" Landon ran his finger along the ridge.

"I have no idea. I had hoped they might mean something to you."

Landon squinted, taking a closer look at the inscription and then the face of the watch before snapping it closed. "Thank you for passing this along to me."

"Well? Is it a lock combination? Map coordinates? Reference to a bank account? What?"

He bussed Theo on the cheek before quickly striding to the door. "I'm sorry, but I'm late. Archbroke will not be happy."

Theo wanted to stomp her foot. She had seen the flash of recognition in Landon's eyes.

GRAHAM LOOKED into his glass as the brandy swirled around and around. He had been waiting nearly an hour when Landon finally arrived at the club.

Eschewing a proper greeting, Landon stood next to Graham and growled, "Did you obtain the special license?"

"Of course, but we have a slight problem."

"Archbroke, what could possibly be the problem? You are the only one I know who has direct access to the archbishop."

"He demands the ceremony be conducted by him and that the royal family be present."

Landon remained standing and waved his hands as he asked, "Why, such extravagance? You are not even a royal duke."

"Our families have..." He paused and knew this was not the setting in which he should be sharing such sensitive matters. Unwilling to postpone the discussion any longer, Graham continued, "The prince regent has declared it, and we must adhere to his wishes."

Bracing himself for Landon's response, Graham imparted the next obstacle to his marriage to Theo. "Besides, there is the matter of you..." He lowered his voice even further, stating, "of you obtaining the mark."

Landon's eyes widened. Graham had insisted Theo and her aunt not share any details with Landon and had extracted promises from both that they would allow Graham to be the one to explain what was entailed in the Hadfield volume. He indicated a chair, and Landon obediently fell into it.

Grinning, Graham suggested, "Perhaps we should partake in a few drinks before we go to fulfill the necessary task."

Landon took the drink offered to him and consumed the strong liquid in one swallow. "How long do you expect we will be out tonight?"

"That all depends upon you, Hadfield."

"Theo has been acting strange this eve, and I would like to return as soon as possible."

At the mention of Theo, Graham's muscles tightened. He had not been able to find a moment of privacy with the woman, and he was near desperation to have her again.

After consuming three drinks in quick succession, Landon rose to leave. "Let's get this done."

GRAHAM MOVED to the rear-facing seat. He was tired of continually bumping shoulders with Landon, whose pallor had turned an ungodly shade of green. Having more room, Landon braced his feet apart, dug his elbows into his knees, and let his head fall into his palms.

"How much longer?"

Graham peeked out the window and replied, "Not much."

"Where exactly am I to receive this mark?"

"I've considered the matter carefully, and I'm against it being placed anywhere above the waist. However, it must be accessible swiftly if necessary, and it's imperative that it remains hidden from all who do not bear the mark."

There was much he needed to discuss with Landon, and there was no better time than the present. "Once you are married, your wife and children will also bear the mark. It will be expected that your heirs will inherit the volume and the duties and responsibilities that go along with the title. We will also have to discuss your brother."

Landon's posture changed when he mentioned Christopher's name. Over the past week, Graham had debated with himself over the issue of Christopher.

"Since he does not bear the mark, I'm of the mind he is not to be informed; however, if he is to remain unmarked, you will need to find a bride soon to produce an heir."

Landon's gaze narrowed. "And what if I produce this heir and I meet my demise while he is still a child?"

"Then he will be protected by all those who are marked, and we will assist until he can fully resume the responsibilities. Our network is well established and can handle every possibility." As the words left Graham's lips, he knew their irony. The possibility of a female had never presented itself before, but now the society was more aware, and everyone involved had performed their duties exceptionally well. Especially Theo.

"Christopher and I have never kept secrets."

"Obviously, you two are close since you have worked hard to provide sound legal services and are respected for it. However, you are now the Earl of Hadfield and are about to assume the familial duties to the Crown." Graham stared at Landon.

Was he ready? Being a lawyer, truth and honesty were cornerstones of his character.

Landon huffed, "I am more than ready to take on all the responsibilities linked to the title. There is much for me to learn and understand since I've not been provided the volume to date. I've been reliant on the pieces of information from you only. Even my own mama has denied me."

The coach rolled to a stop. Was Landon prepared? Once they left the coach, there would be no turning back. He made one final assessment of the man sitting across from him. "Ready?"

Landon jumped from the coach, and Graham followed. Landon took in his surroundings. After they stretched their legs, he led Landon to a nondescript shopfront. To the ordinary eye, most would assume it was just another snuff store, but those who knew looked for the symbol. A very intricate depiction of an angel graced its signage. He looked over at Landon and nearly let out a full belly laugh at his expression.

"Archbroke, I don't use that nasty stuff."

"Be quiet and follow me." Graham walked to the side entrance. As he approached, the door swung wide open, revealing a man with silvering hair and stooped shoulders.

"M'lord, welcome." Graham looked at the proprietor and smiled.

He motioned for Landon to precede him.

Graham took in the scowl upon the man that had assisted him all his life. "Cadby, I apologize for our tardiness; however, I'd like to proceed immediately."

Cadby turned and sized up Landon. "This is the one? Bit ol', ain't he?"

Graham couldn't contain his laughter, a rusty-sounding full-hearted laugh. "Cadby, let's get on with it."

Apparently, he had not issued the order with enough authority, for Cadby remained unconvinced. Not accustomed to his orders being challenged, Graham turned and frowned at Cadby. They didn't have time for a staring contest. Graham said, "He has recently inherited the title of Earl of Hadfield."

"I hea'd he only got the title."

Eyes narrowed, Graham bit out, "He is to inherit all that goes along with the title, and he will do so starting now."

He started to make his way down the hallway. When he didn't hear footsteps following him, he turned, Cadby's arms were crossed, and he remained stock-still.

"I don't like the looks of 'im."

Graham's patience worn thin, he grated, "You don't have to, Cadby. Your job is to place the mark on him, and I expect it done this eve."

Cadby moved to follow Graham only to grumble,

"Hea'd the chit was doin' just fine. Don't see why this nob needs the mark."

Ignoring Cadby's complaints, Graham led the way to the back office and made himself comfortable near the fire.

"Where you want 'e to put it?" Cadby asked.

Landon removed his waistcoat, pulled his shirt tails out, and lowered his breeches slightly to reveal the spot he had chosen for the mark.

Seeing the location Landon selected, Graham interjected, "That will not work."

"Why? You said below the waistline."

"And how do you intend to have relations without baring the mark?"

Smugly, Landon replied, "I suppose I'll have to marry before I engage in that activity."

Graham mulled over Landon's statement and grinned. "Fine. Cadby, you may proceed."

GRAHAM AVOIDED RETURNING Landon's heated glare and tried to hide the smirk on his face. Landon continued to readjust his position on the seat of the coach. He had spent the past two hours in agony as Cadby tattooed the mark on his hip. Graham suspected Cadby had drawn out the process to test Landon's mettle. Landon's skin had been red and inflamed, and he had uttered the occasional growl, refusing the brandy placed in front of him. Stubborn bugger.

"Hadfield, visit me at the Home Office tomorrow. I'll provide you with the volume and answer any immediate questions you may have."

"How very accommodating of you, Archbroke. How is it you have the volume and not my cousin?"

"Theo entrusted me with it." It hadn't been as easy as he made it sound. Theo had extracted numerous promises from him prior to handing over the volume.

The coach rolled to a stop. Landon reached for the latch on the door. "I'll meet you at your offices. Early, at nine."

Out the window, Graham saw it was nearing dawn. It wouldn't give him much time with Theo.

THEO WAS LURKING in the hall. Why was it taking Graham and Landon an eternity to return? Horse hooves beat impatiently as Landon exited the coach.

Landon walked through the front door. "Yes, Morris, you may assume I am now privy to all that goes on under this roof."

Morris replied, "Yes, my lord. I shall have Milton bring you a salve."

Nothing went unnoticed by the staff. Theo rushed up to her room. Landon's footsteps were right behind her. Jumping in bed, she was fighting with the coverlet when there was a scratch at her door.

Steadying her breath, she called, "Come in."

Landon walked straight to the window and looked to the floor where he was standing. He must be looking for evidence that someone had entered.

"Landon! What are you doing?"

Landon's gaze narrowed. "Why are you awake?"

"I was running over the plan for tomorrow's mission. Having spent more time with Cecilia, I realized she was acting out of concern for her brother."

"As you would have for Baldwin, correct?"

Graham, Landon, Blake, and Lucy had all cautioned

her about placing any faith or trust in Cecilia. They referred to her as the she-devil and suspected she was still withholding vital information.

"Of course. I would have done anything Baldwin asked of me."

"And me? Would you do anything I ask of you, Theo?"

Theo's gaze roamed over Landon's features. "Yes."

"Because I now bear the mark."

She flinched at the cutting remark.

"Yes and no." Theo sat up in the bed, bringing the coverlet over her. "If I could have, I would have shared everything from the beginning, but there are stringent rules and instructions as you will find out for yourself."

"Explain."

"I cannot, for I have given my oath to Graham that I would leave it to him to share the necessary information."

Landon's features scrunched in pain as he ran his hand through his hair. Where had the mark been placed? Was that what was causing him pain now? Landon turned to leave but then came closer and was nearly upon her when he stopped and kicked the underside of the bed.

"Owww…"

Landon growled, "Get out from under there, Archbroke."

Graham rolled out from under the bed. He must have entered when she was still downstairs. How had Landon detected his presence? He was going to be great at fulfilling their family's duties to the Crown.

Landon glared at Graham and barked, "Out!" Then Theo felt his gaze on her as he ordered, "You will not allow him to enter through that window again."

"What?" Graham and Theo shouted in unison.

"Fine. I'll have the window nailed shut."

Landon escorted Graham to the window. Before

Graham slipped from sight, he said, "She will be my wife soon. There is no need—"

"She is under my care until you are *properly* married."

Landon turned to leave. Theo sunk back into the bed and covered her head with the blankets and groaned.

CHAPTER THIRTY

The Lone Dove was not at all what Theo had envisioned. The rough wooden trestle tables in the center were well-worn, and the smell of stale ale lingered. Glad to be seated at one of the intimate square tables that lined the walls, Theo clasped her hands tightly in her lap and straightened her spine. Dressed in disguise, her hands itched to run up and down her thighs beneath the table. Squeezing her fingers, she resisted the urge to adjust the deep neckline of her gown. The tendrils of hair that had been artfully pulled from her coiffure tickled the back of her neck as she strained to see who was about.

There were but a few other patrons scattered throughout the room. Were they agents of the Home Office? The elaborate angel and harp on the inn's sign indicated its owners were PORFs. Theo cringed at the horrid reference.

How long would she have to wait for Cecilia's contact to arrive and approach? She glanced at the looking glass that hung by an exit. With the combination of Wallace's face-painting skill and the dim lighting, Theo was transformed into the spitting image of Cecilia.

From the corner of her eye, Theo spotted a young man enter the inn draped in a worn great cloak and with a hat pulled low over his face. Theo's leg began to bob up and down under the table. She placed a hand on her knee to still the quaking. The pounding of her heart increased with each step the man took, closing the gap between them.

"Miss, may I introduce myself? I am Mr. Smyth. I believe you have a package for me."

Mr. Smyth stiffened as she brought up a hand from under the table. Palm up, she indicated the empty chair opposite her. "Why don't you join me for a drink first?"

"I'd best be on my way, miss. If you would just…"

She attempted to peer under the man's hat in an effort to memorize his features, voice, and accent. Graham had described the Mr. Smyth he regularly employed, but the boy in front of her was no more than sixteen years of age, his arms and chest still not yet filled out, cheeks still smooth. He was an imposter.

"I would love the company. One drink won't delay you that long." Theo tried to push the chair opposite her out from under the table. Unfortunately, her legs only managed to make the chair move.

The young man scanned the immediate tables surrounding them. His gaze flicked to the exit and back to Theo. "Just one. I must be leaving with the package."

As soon as he agreed, Theo's neck and shoulders relaxed. Mr. Smyth seemed to respond to her softening, turning the chair and straddling it as he sat. Smart. The way he positioned his seat allowed him to easily move in the event he needed to leave in a hurry. He waved down the barmaid. His attention focused on the girl's hips as she made her way over.

Mr. Smyth's eyes were alert and drawn to the deep valley between the girl's breasts. "Bring us two ales."

The barmaid turned to leave but halted as Theo said, "Make mine a brandy." The girl gave Theo a cheeky wink and waltzed away, holding Mr. Smyth's attention as she left.

Taking a deep, slow breath, Theo waited for Mr. Smyth to return his attention to her. Her nerves were a tangled mess. How long would it take for the girl to bring back the tainted ale? Not wanting any risk of a mix-up, she had changed her order to a much stronger drink. Brandy would take the edge off. At least she hoped it would.

"Never known a lady who could drink brandy."

"Well, I've not met…" Theo wracked her brain for the right words. "…such a handsome young…" *Oh goodness, what was she saying?*

"Aye, he's a han'some one, all right." The barmaid leaned over and grazed Mr. Smyth's shoulder as she placed their drinks upon the table. "Drink up, and I can bring ye another."

What a clever girl to encourage him to drink fast. Theo smiled. Things were moving along rather well. She raised her glass to her lips and over the rim watched as Mr. Smyth gulped down his ale.

Lowering her drink, she patiently waited, but the man's eyes began to dart about the room. She needed to distract him long enough for the sleeping tonic to take effect.

Theo dropped her shoulder and let the sleeve of her dress fall. "The ale is reported to be the best in the area. Would you agree?"

"It's not bad." Mr. Smyth frowned into his empty tankard.

Theo wanted to smack her hand against her forehand. Why had she mentioned the ale? She should be flirting, not speaking of beverages. The sleeping potion had better start working soon. The light fluttery feelings that had her grinning earlier rapidly dissolved. Now her palms were sweating in her gloves, and her leg began to quiver and bounce under the table once again.

Her gaze searched the room. Where was the barmaid? When had the room emptied? The few patrons that had been at tables were gone. No one was about but the two of them. Mr. Smyth turned to look behind him, a frown appearing as he set his eyes upon Theo.

Theo released a sultry laugh. "It appears we are alone."

"Perfect. I'll have the package now."

She couldn't fail. It was too soon. The man displayed none of the signs that Graham informed her to look for. His eyes were clear, not cloudy. He spoke with clarity and not at all slurred.

She raised her glass. "But sir. I've not yet finished my drink."

Mr. Smyth's eyes followed Theo's tongue as it peeked out. She ran the tip slowly along her bottom lip.

"Unless you can summon the lovely wench to bring me another." Mr. Smyth blinked and gave his head a slight shake. "What… what did you…" Without warning, the man's head hit the table with a thud.

Releasing a deep sigh, Theo tentatively reached out a hand. Her fingers hovered over the back of Mr. Smyth's head. On an inhale, she tapped him on the back of the head, which rolled to the side, drool pooling on the table. Success.

Two agents appeared from the shadows and hauled the man up from his seat and dragged him away. Theo stood, ready to follow the men out back, where Mr. Smyth was to be interrogated. She stalled as Graham approached.

Searching his features, her heart beat faster at the sight of his all-too-confident smile.

Graham straddled the empty seat as the false Mr. Smyth had. Theo lowered herself back into her chair, her gaze locked on Graham.

Heat blazed from Graham's eyes. "Well done, my love."

"I was a bundle of nerves. It took an eternity for the sleeping potion to take effect."

"You did well. Everything went without a hitch thanks to you."

"I want to visit with Cecilia before she is transported."

Theo was thankful Graham had arranged for Cecilia to be transported to Australia instead of having to wait in Newgate prison for trial.

Graham frowned. "Her ship leaves tonight."

"I understand, but I want to thank her for cooperating. Please." She subtly placed a hand over his and continued, "We have her correspondent in custody, and hopefully he, too, will cooperate and provide us with the information we need to find and apprehend the traitors."

When Graham released a long sigh, she knew he would grant her wish. He finally muttered. "I'll have it arranged."

GRAHAM SURVEYED THEIR SURROUNDINGS. What had he been thinking in bringing Theo here? He needed to work on saying no to her. The clever woman had brought a lavender-scented handkerchief and held it up to her nose.

A flash of green silk caught his eye. Debating whether to investigate the odd sight or stay with Theo, he blew out the breath he had been holding through his nose, for the smell around him was rancid.

Landon appeared from behind one of the crates. "Hadfield, what are you doing here?"

"Ensuring my cousin's safety."

"Perfect," Graham pushed Theo gently toward Landon. "Take her."

He walked over to where he last saw the green silk disappear. He silently placed a curse upon Landon should anything happen to Theo. Turning the corner, Graham froze. A slight form wearing a dark hooded cloak struggled with the woman in green. His eyes adjusted to the dim lighting—*Cecilia.* Arching her back, Cecilia clawed at the arm that had snaked about her neck. The kidnapper skillfully positioned a hand on Cecilia's chin. A quick twist would mean immediate death. Cecilia's chest was still heaving, but she no longer fought with her attacker. A hood was placed over Cecilia's head, and the kidnapper whispered in her ear. Whatever was said had Cecilia moving along without a fight. Graham dashed forward, his feet slipping on the wet cobbles. *Damn it.* Trying to regain his balance, his boot hit a pile of boxes, and the kidnapper's head jerked up.

Gazes locked, Graham stopped in his tracks. It was Lady Grace Oldridge, the daughter of Marquess Flarinton and Lucy's close friend. Before he could recollect his wits, the two women disappeared into the night. Standing where he had last seen them, he heard the rattle of a carriage and instantly knew he would be unable to catch up to them.

Cursing like the sailors who were milling about, Graham made his way back to Theo and Landon.

Theo broke away from her cousin. "What is it?" she asked.

"Cecilia is gone."

"Gone? Her ship departed early?" Theo whisked her head around. The ship Cecilia was to board was still docked. Theo's features revealed her feelings of betrayal. Theo whispered, "She escaped?"

"Love, I will take care of the matter." He wrapped her up in his arms and rubbed her back.

Over Theo's head, Landon purposefully looked at Graham and stepped forward to remove Theo from his arms. "Archbroke, I will escort Theo home."

He reluctantly released Theo. Landon bent and said something in Theo's ear that Graham was not privy to. He glared at Landon, who merely said, "I will see you on the morrow."

Graham shook his head. "I will accompany you both."

Theo held her ground, "Graham, you have matters to attend to. Time is of the essence. Deal with the issue, and I'll see you soon."

CHAPTER THIRTY-ONE

Theo calculated it had been over a month since Cecilia's disappearance. Mr. Smyth's impersonator's refusal to provide further information led to his untimely demise, leaving questions unanswered. The details regarding Cecilia's escape plagued her. Had Lord Addington returned and taken his sister away? Each night various plausible scenarios rattled about her mind, but all of them left Theo uneasy, as if she was missing a vital piece of information.

While Theo had been buried neck deep in wedding preparations, Graham and Landon had been meeting daily, and she resented the fact they had not included her in their discussions. She had hoped her marriage to Graham would result in a partnership similar to the one Lucy and Blake shared. She still bore the mark, and she was determined to remain involved regardless that Landon was now in possession of the volume.

Theo stared down at the invitations she dutifully stuffed into envelopes. Everyone was referring to it as the wedding of the Season since the prince regent and other royal dignitaries had invited themselves.

Lucy was busy at Shalford Castle, preparing for the birth of her first child, and had sent her regrets at not being able to attend. Considering Theo had missed Lucy's wedding, it was only fair that her best friend missed hers.

As if her aunt could read her thoughts, "Lucy is near full term. She wrote, informing me of her hope that her brother will arrive in time for the birth."

Absently she replied, "Graham received word that Matthew should arrive in time."

"It is wonderful that Lord Archbroke informs you of such matters," Aunt Henri singsonged and added, "My papa never shared a thing with my mama. However, my mama was always informed one way or another."

Was Aunt Henri hinting at something? Theo had come to realize that she should pay closer attention to whatever her aunt said, for it always contained a deeper meaning than the words themselves.

Theo asked, "Did you ever learn of her secret as to how she obtained information?"

Aunt Henri laughed, "Of course, my dear."

Theo waited expectantly.

"She used her pin money to bribe the servants." Aunt Henri was having a good old chuckle, and tears began to form as she reflected upon her deceased parents. "She never approved that George worked as a barrister, and neither did Papa. But even so, she still sent me gifts on special occasions, and while I never had the opportunity to speak to her after my marriage, I knew she still cared."

Tears flowed from Theo's own eyes as she rushed over and wrapped her arms tightly around the woman who was like a mama to her. Pushing back and looking into her aunt's teary face, she declared, "Thank you, Aunt Henri. I shall use my pin money wisely in the future."

Glad she was able to place a smile back on her aunt's face, Theo rose and bussed her aunt before making her way to Landon's study.

THEY HAD BEEN DISCUSSING the same matter over and over for weeks, and Graham had lost all patience. He suspected Landon was withholding information regarding the maps and Cecilia's disappearance, but the stubborn man refused to come clean.

"It is your duty to gather the required information and provide it to me. It is *my* duty to see the information is utilized and do with it as I see fit."

Landon's bored expression nearly had him jumping over the table and hauling the obstinate man up by the lapels to pummel him. They had even gone rounds at Gentleman Jackson's earlier in the day, which had released none of the pent-up frustration Graham was continuing to accumulate.

"As I have informed you already, I am still in the process of gathering all the information, and I will report to you with my findings when I see fit."

Graham was going to murder his future in-law. More than once, he had schemed Landon's demise, but then images of Theo and the pain it would cause her always prevented him from carrying out his plans. Not that he wanted Landon to come to harm; the man did have certain qualities he admired and respected.

It was apparent that Landon was exceptionally clever. He had successfully engineered every situation to ensure that Graham and Theo never had a moment alone.

Perhaps his frustration was the result of his inability to outwit Landon and have Theo to himself. As if his thoughts had summoned her, Theo breezed into the room and stole Graham's breath.

"Archbroke." Theo rarely addressed him by his given name in company, which only made it all the sweeter when she did in private. He hadn't heard his name on her lips since their formal betrothal.

Knowing it would raise Landon's ire, he greeted her with "My love."

"Good Lord, man, have you no shame?" Landon scolded. "Cousin, what is it you want?"

"I've come to offer my assistance."

Graham stiffened. There was something in Theo's tone that caused the hairs on his arms to stand on end.

Landon rose and stepped in front of Theo. Looming over his cousin, he looked down at her through narrowed eyes. "What assistance are you offering, Theo? Did I ask for such a boon?"

Theo placed a hand on Landon's arm.

Graham's blood heated. He hungered for her body. In fact, he would settle for any type of physical contact after being deprived of her company for days. Images of Theo's hands upon him had Graham shifting his weight. He moved to occupy one of the wingback chairs, giving himself and the two cousins some privacy.

He reined in his wayward thoughts and listened to their conversation.

"I believe I know a method we can uncover the information you seek, *dear* cousin."

"Don't dear-cousin-me Theo. Out with it."

"I'd be happy to share if you are willing to share with me."

Graham smirked. His brilliant fiancée was about to

obtain the details that Landon had refused to share with him. He should have known to involve Theo. Would he ever learn?

Graham hoped they had forgotten about his presence, but he was sadly disappointed when Landon declared, "Perhaps we can have this discussion over supper?"

"Gladly. Archbroke, have you decided upon our plans for after the ceremony?"

Clearing his throat, he shared, "I've been rather busy, my dear. But I'm happy to take you anywhere you wish. Paris? The coast?"

"I don't wish to venture far. I would like to be close by and to visit Lucy as soon as possible."

He wanted to take her on a month-long journey. He had been busy getting all his affairs in order to allow him the time away. It appeared that all his efforts were for naught. It also reminded him that he should have consulted with her first.

"As you wish, my love."

Graham saw Landon roll his eyes as he uttered the endearment.

Theo clapped her hands and said, "Then we shall remain in town until we depart for Shalford Castle."

With a smile that could bring him to his knees, Theo waltzed out of the room. He vowed to do whatever was necessary to affix that smile to her face at every possible moment. He had definite ideas as to how to achieve his goal, but for the interim, he would have to vow to consult her more when making future plans.

CHAPTER THIRTY-TWO

Unable to stand still, Theo paced the small chamber she had been placed in to await the royal family's arrival.

"Theo, if you do not cease, you are going to make me ill," Aunt Henri grumbled.

For the past day and a half, Aunt Henri had been particularly prickly. Theo understood her discomfort at being scrutinized by the entire *ton*, but there was something else bothering her aunt, and Theo had been unable to wheedle it out of her.

"Perhaps you could share with me the matter that has had you at sixes and sevens all day long."

Aunt Henri lowered her gaze, "It's your wedding day, my dear. I will not burden you with such information on this day."

"What information!" Theo yelled. Realizing she had used an awful tone, she sat next to her aunt and wrapped an arm around the older woman's shoulders. "I'm sorry. Please share with me what has been burdening you so."

Slumped and defeated, Aunt Henrietta confessed,

"Landon will be leaving for the Continent as soon as the ceremony is over."

Theo grasped Aunt Henrietta by the shoulders and shook her, "Why? For how long?"

"I'm not privy to the reasons why, but it will be for as long as necessary until he produces the information he seeks."

Theo's mind raced as she tried to recall the numerous discussions she had held with Graham. Since the day she had stormed Landon's study, Graham had answered her multitude of questions regarding the mystery of Cecilia's disappearance and Devonton's kidnapping. He even shared information without her prying. Why had he not mentioned Landon's trip?

"Is Graham aware of Landon's plans?"

Aunt Henrietta slowly shook her head. "Lord Archbroke does not know. Landon made me promise not to share with anyone, but I have been extremely worried about his welfare."

If Graham was not informed of Landon's plan, he would be irate when he found out. What information could Landon be searching for on the Continent?

"Aunt Henri, Landon has spent countless hours with Graham learning all he can. They have gone over the family volume numerous times. Landon has it memorized. He has practiced daily with a wide variety of experts. Graham has ensured he received the very best training, and Landon excels at everything he attempts; even Graham praised his ability to rapidly learn and devise stratagems."

"I'm extremely proud of what he has accomplished in such a short amount of time, but as his mama, it is my job to worry about him."

Her aunt's guilt over not informing Landon sooner

surely factored into her current worries. Theo wanted to comfort her aunt, just as her aunt had provided comfort in those early days of mourning after the loss of her papa.

There was a scratch at the door. Moments later, Arabelle entered and announced, "It is time."

Both ladies rose, and Aunt Henri gave Theo a quick last-minute hug before dashing off into the church.

Theo wiped her damp palms down her sides and said, "Let's go."

Arabelle gave her an odd look before pressing a note into her hands, "Can I trust you to get this to Lord Hadfield before he leaves?"

Startled that Arabelle was aware of Landon's plans, Theo nodded and tucked the note into her sleeve as she moved to enter the church.

WHAT WAS THE DELAY? Graham's nerves were stretched taut. The thought that he might suffer an apoplexy had crossed his mind a time or two. Or three. He glanced down the aisle for the hundredth time. Clare was hopping from one foot to the other, which meant Theo was about to make her appearance. His gaze fell upon his stoic nephew. Max stood like a miniature soldier, hands clasped behind his back and spine ramrod straight. An urge to ruffle the boy's hair was quelled when Max gave him a glare that warned *don't even think it.* That ominous look would service Max well when it came time for him to inherit the dukedom. The boy broke into a broad smile, and Graham followed Max's gaze, landing on a most beautiful vision.

Theo was exquisitely dressed in a rose-pink silk dress with long sleeves and a modest neckline that only revealed the slightest hint of a perfectly rounded bosom. Graham sent up a quick prayer and thanked the Lord for blessing him with such an intelligent and resilient woman.

Theo took Clare's hand, and they started to walk up the aisle. Where was Landon; why was he not with Theo? Graham scanned the crowd, but Landon was not in sight.

He looked down at the slight tug on his waistcoat.

"Uncle Gam?"

"Yes, Clare?"

"In't she beautiful?"

"Yes, Clare, inside and out."

Clare tugged on Theo's hand and pulled her down to whisper in her ear. When Theo straightened, her cheeks were flush, and her eyes glittered with laughter. Graham caught Theo's gaze and slowly raised an eyebrow, "Care to share what my dear niece said?"

"That I will only have to wait a li'l while longer before you can kiss me."

The woman had the audacity to actually wink at him. Didn't she know the effect she had on him? He was standing in front of the royal family and half the *ton*. Graham strategically positioned Max in front of him before he winged his arm for Theo. Heat shot through him as she placed her hand on his arm. Graham turned to face the archbishop, who wore a deep scowl.

Averting his gaze, Graham focused on the beautiful woman standing next to him. Smiling at his soon-to-be wife, he was oblivious to the proceedings. When Theo dug her elbow into his side, the frown upon the archbishop's features indicated something was expected of him. His pledge. Graham dutifully repeated after the archbishop. As the rings were being blessed, his nerves began to get the best of him. His hands shook as he reached for the ring, and only when Theo's hand was in his did they become steady.

Staring into Theo's eyes, he slid the solid gold band onto her finger as he solemnly stated, "With this ring, I thee wed, with my body I thee worship, and with all my worldly goods I thee endow. In the Name of the Father and of the Son, and of the Holy Ghost. Amen."

Graham struggled to remain still as they took communion. Impatient for the archbishop to cease reciting scripture and prayer after prayer, his mind began to picture Theo, lying naked in bed, ready for him to join her. When the prince regent himself coughed and eyed him suspiciously, Graham shuffled his feet and readjusted his position so none of the other guests could hazard a guess at his wayward thoughts. As he scanned the crowd, he did a double take when he caught sight of Landon. For a brief second, he thought he had spotted Lady Grace standing next to him, but when he looked closer, he only saw Lady Arabelle. Theo nudged him again in the side, and he tried not to flinch. The woman had pointy elbows. Realizing the ceremony was over, he began to guide her over to the registry.

LANDON WAS STANDING at the edge of the crowd. Where had the man been during the ceremony? Theo paused and left Graham's side. He backed up half a step, but his eyes bored into the note Theo had discreetly passed on to her cousin. What were the pair up to now? Ready to reclaim Theo, Graham began to step forward, but midstep he paused as Theo rose onto her tiptoes and said, "Be safe and come home to us, Landon."

Landon bussed Theo on the cheek and left. Anger boiled as Graham realized his soon-to-be wife had kept yet another secret from him, but at the sight of her watery eyes, his anger disappeared into thin air. He would have to have faith that over time they would no longer hide secrets from each other.

As if she was capable of reading his mind, Theo said, "I have no knowledge of its contents, only that Arabelle asked I ensure Landon received it before he departed for the Continent."

In one sentence, the woman had not only answered his concerns, she had also managed to allay his fears. Eager once more to have her sign her name and lawfully become Lady Archbroke, Graham guided her to where the archbishop and the registry awaited.

A smile formed on Theo's lips as she scrawled her name along the parchment. As soon as she had completed the task, Graham felt a lightness in his heart that he had never experienced before.

He leaned down and said, "I love you, Lady Theodora Archbroke."

Theo wound her arms around his neck and honored him with a kiss that left no doubt in his mind that his wife loved him too.

ALSO BY RACHEL ANN SMITH

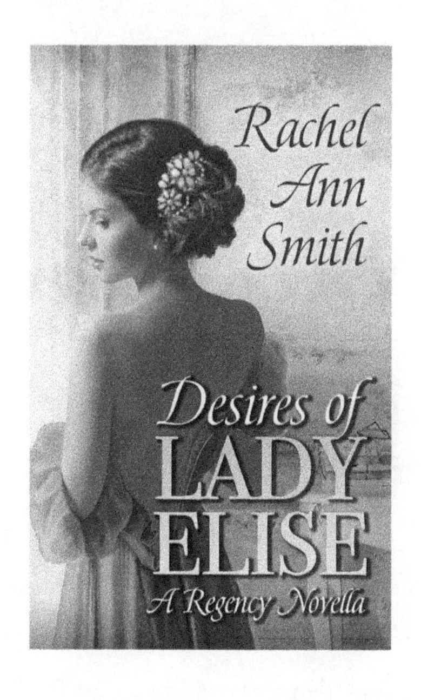

Desires of Lady Elise

He has the reputation of a rogue.

She is too busy with investigations to bother hunting for a husband.

But when the man who shattered her heart re-enters her world, will she be able to resist him?

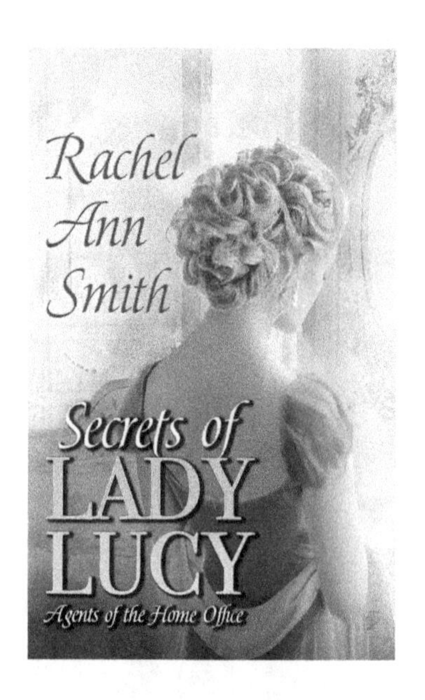

Secrets of Lady Lucy

She is determined to foil an attempted kidnapping.

He is set on discovering her secrets.

When the ransom demand comes due—will it be for Lady Lucy's heart?

Coming in 2020

Visions of Lady Mary

Confessions of Lady Grace

ABOUT THE AUTHOR

Rachel Ann Smith writes steamy historical romances with a twist. Her debut series, Agents of the Home Office, features female protagonists that defy convention.

When Rachel isn't writing she loves to read and spend time with the family. You will find her with her Kindle by the pool during the summer, or on the side-lines of a soccer field in the spring and fall or curled up on the couch during the winter months.

She currently lives in Colorado with her extremely understanding husband and their two very supportive children.

facebook.com/rachelannsmit11

twitter.com/rachelannsmit11

instagram.com/rachelannsmithauthor

CPSIA information can be obtained
at www.ICGtesting.com
Printed in the USA
BVHW070831310821
615687BV00011B/232